THE BENDS

Bart Hopkins

THE BENDS

Library of Congress Control Number: 2017903816
CreateSpace Independent Publishing Platform,
North Charleston, SC

ISBN: 1540805638
ISBN-13: 978-1540805638

DEDICATION

This is for those of you that live with me: three girls, one boy, and the furry one.

Also from Bart Hopkins

Like
Texas Jack
Fluke
Dead Ends
World Wide Gone

CHAPTER 1
Wednesday

Kane had played in worse places than Bob's Saloon.

A bar ran half the length of the main room—polished wood—scarred, but in good condition. There was a mirror behind it with cursive writing across the top.

On the eighth day, God had a beer.

Round tables dotted the floor, four or five chairs at each. Clean. Orderly.

The restroom had the standard piss trough along one wall; however, it boasted three sit-down stalls—and all of them had locking doors and toilet paper.

There was even a small room behind the stage where the musicians could stow their gear and get ready. Maybe change clothes, if they needed to.

Indeed, he'd seen a *lot* worse. This was practically paradise.

The waitresses weren't half bad either. There was one out there now named Lucy. She'd been giving him the eye since he came in to ask about a gig. *A guy could get used to looking at that Lucy*, he considered.

Nothing wrong with good scenery.

Kane eased his guitar case onto a table in the dressing room and popped open the latches. He lifted the lid gently, almost reverently, and traced his fingers along the headstock and down the neck. It was a beautiful guitar, a Fender Telecaster, worth twice as much as the horse he rode in on ... a seventeen-year-old F150.

He called her Honey—after Fender's official color for the guitar, which was Honey Burst. Well, that, and because she was so sweet in his hands.

Very creative, I know, he thought as he pulled Honey out of the plush lining.

Every guitar he had ever owned was given a woman's name: Evelyn, Sue Ann, Cheryl, Donna, Lacey, and half a dozen others. When Kane got his first guitar, he'd named it Betty Jean, because Jimi Hendrix had named *his* guitar Betty Jean ... after his high school girlfriend.

Jimi was the man—could play his ass off—and was the main reason Kane detoured into the music store one day. Of course, Kane figured it wouldn't hurt his chances with the ladies, either.

He slid into Honey's strap, and then looked at himself in the mirror on the wall. Blue eyes, enviably white teeth, the nose that had been broken. Hair was short, only slightly longer than when he was in the Army. Guys who got out sometimes went a little crazy with the hair, growing beards and ponytails, but Kane liked his trim. He smiled when he realized he probably hadn't combed it since before basic training. Never needed to after that—just rolled with it as it was, straight out of the shower.

"You almost ready, darling?"

Kane turned and found Lucy smiling at him, even as she chewed her gum. She had a bar tray tucked under one arm.

"Born ready," he told her. "Are you going to be ready to fight off the crowds when I start playing?"

She laughed, moved in closer, and put her hand on his forehead. "You feeling okay? This is Marathon ... we don't exactly get crowds here."

Pale blue-green eyes peered up at him, expectantly. They were almost turquoise—reminded him of the water in Destin, Florida. He'd done some training with the Air Force guys down there at Hurlburt a few times. Every now and then, he'd gone to Destin in the evenings to relax and get away from all the alpha-male bullshit that surrounded him for eighteen hours each day.

He'd pick a spot in the sand and just drop down to watch the Gulf of Mexico. There was an indescribable peace in those waters...

Not that he felt peaceful. Not now. The scent of her perfume invaded his senses, and it made him lightheaded. The air seemed to grow dense around them. Familiar stirrings awakened below his beltline.

Before he knew it was happening, the two- or three-inch gap between them vanished. Her chest pressed against him, and he couldn't help but appreciate the view down the front of her white cotton blouse. With a husky sigh, he leaned down and kissed her, and she returned the kiss, looping her arms around his neck.

A throat got cleared.

Then it got cleared again, louder.

"Oh hey, Bob," Kane said sheepishly, pulling back from Lucy, who snapped upright and began straightening her clothes while looking everywhere except at Bob's face.

"Make the customers happy," Bob said. "That'll make me happy. And then, after we close, then you can make Lucy happy. Right?" He looked stern, but Kane sensed humor beneath the stony façade. Or so he hoped.

"Roger, boss," he answered.

Lucy's cheeks turned some shade just shy of crimson before she dashed away, leaving the men by themselves. Bob laughed quietly.

"She's a hot number," he told Kane. His face didn't reveal much, but Kane didn't sense any anger. He did, however, feel like he was being evaluated.

"Yes, sir," he agreed.

Bob nodded and thoughtfully stroked his chin. "She's an adult and does what she wants," he said after a moment. "Sometimes she jumps without thinking. Knew her daddy … was a good friend of mine. So have your fun, but no rough stuff."

It wasn't a question, and Kane was mostly a good guy, so he just nodded quietly.

"We're starting to get some people at the tables, so whenever you're ready."

"Born ready," he said for the second time. He started to follow Bob, but then went back to his guitar case for his lucky hat. It was tan, with an American flag stuck to the Velcro on the front. He'd had it since his unit helped the Marines in Fallujah. Worn it in Afghanistan on raids he couldn't tell people about. It was his personal talisman—insurance against bad things.

A lot of the guys in his units had been superstitious like that; he was no different.

"Yep," he said, as he slid it on. It was like a coat of armor—chain mail—and he immediately felt better.

Out on the stage, the light seemed a little brighter than when he had played those impromptu songs for Bob that afternoon. He tilted his head down, and the glare disappeared. The sun was no longer burning its way through the two windows up front. Darkness had fallen at last on the humble town of Marathon.

Kane took a sip from the water bottle some mysterious employee of Bob's had deposited on stage for him. He wondered if it was Lucy as he plugged into the amp and stepped up to the microphone. About thirty people were sitting at the tables, or standing along the bar, most watching him with mild interest, but others engaged in quiet conversation.

"Hello everybody," he started. The microphone whined, and he adjusted it, then pulled back a few inches. "Name's Kane, and if I do okay tonight ... well, Bob might let me stay for a while."

There were a few nods, and a polite laugh or two. Not much, but enough, and the potential for more.

A few of the faces looked grim. Even though he came from a town like this—small, in the middle of nowhere— he wasn't from *their* town. Wasn't one of *them*. They were used to transients. People moved through their town daily: tourists, climbers, and hikers. Those were the normal ones. They also had the occasional unsavory type, on the run from something ... broken marriages or drug habits or maybe the law. Sort of like the Wild West, he imagined.

Cautious. It was a cautious group. They'd accept him or they wouldn't. As simple as that.

With a flick of his wrist, he brought his right thumb down and across the strings, and moved into "Turn the Page," a Bob Seger tune. It was one of his favorites, and he played it well. The chords rang through the speakers more quickly than the original, a hybrid of the original Seger and Metallica versions.

After that, Kane rolled straight into Willie Nelson's "Two With A Ten," then "Dinosaur," by Hank Williams, Jr. People were tapping their boots and smiling. Several had sung aloud with him. Two songs later when he took his first break, there was a solid round of applause.

He lifted his hat and rubbed an arm across his damp forehead with a smile. "Thank you. I appreciate that. Really do," he told the crowd, which was now more than forty strong. "I'll be back in five."

After gently setting Honey to the side, he jumped off the stage and started for the men's room. He shook a few hands that popped out at him along the way. Everyone seemed happy.

"Good tunes, son."

"Thanks." He turned and found himself face to face with a man he guessed was nearing sixty. A generous gut pushed the khaki shirt tight around his midsection, and a silver star twinkled over the left shirt pocket.

Yep, Wild West, he thought and smiled. "Sheriff?"

"That's right. Bigsby," he replied. They shook hands, and Kane found himself surprised by the firm grip. It was the handshake of someone who worked with his hands. "What's your poison?"

6

"Oh, well … what are you having?" Kane asked, pointing at the tall, brown drink in front of the sheriff, but Bigsby just laughed.

"Sweet tea."

"Really? They sell that here?" Kane laughed, too.

"Bob's girl Shirley keeps a batch around for me. Don't drink. Not for a long time, now."

"I don't know, sir. I guess a beer would be nice. I sure appreciate it. If you'll excuse me, I have to hit the head, and then get back on stage."

"Yep. They'll get rowdy if you don't."

"Right."

When Kane got back to the stage, there was a beer waiting for him. It was ice cold going down, and he nodded a thanks at Sheriff Bigsby, who nodded back.

He kept the songs coming and accepted a couple more beers that happy guests sent his way. Lucy winked and smiled at him as she laid out coasters and cold drinks. The people and sounds and emotions around the room coalesced into something mellifluous and inviting.

For the first time in a while, the call of the road, and the need to keep moving, subsided. Kane thought Marathon might be a place he could stay for a while.

Then he wondered about Lucy's impulsiveness—things had moved fast backstage—but he shrugged it off. Everyone had demons, and handled them differently. After all … he had a few of his own chasing him.

CHAPTER 2
Wednesday

Bird watched the woman intently.

He devoured her with his eyes, like a child licking an ice cream cone. She sat behind the wheel of her fancy, fire-engine-red sports car, applying lipstick to two of the lushest and sexiest lips Bird had ever seen, and that included real life and the Internet sites he cruised at night.

Slowly—so slowly—she pushed that applicator across those lips. Teased it on, really, in deliberate strokes. Eyes fixed on her face in the rearview mirror.

She pressed her lips together, moved them around, paused, and puckered at her reflection. The color was just a shade away from blood.

Red Lips. Red hair. Red everywhere. Hell ... Bird liked red. *I might even be in love*, he thought with a grunt that might have been laughter.

The car was an Audi. Bird recognized the TT model even though he preferred good old American muscle any day of the week, and twice as much on Wednesday. And, it just happened to be Wednesday ... all day long, as his old man would have said.

Long way from home, he thought, reflecting on the New York license plates.

Red was parked at pump number four—the *slow* one—the pump that drove customers to double-check the sluggishly rolling black-and-white numbers and repeatedly squeeze the trigger to get it flowing faster. Then, of course, they would get pissy with *him*.

"Excuse me—there's something wrong with this pump!"
He heard it at least twice a week, beads of sweat falling from the distraught brows of customers, dark spots flowering out from their underarms. South Texas heat could make anyone crazy. Bird knew that, all right. It about killed the tourists.

"Hmph ... hafta look into that," he'd reply.

But he never looked into anything; he didn't give a damn.

Little Miss Red Lips and Sassy Hips wasn't pumping gas, though. No, sir. He leaned back a little further in his chair, turned his head left, and let fly with some tobacco juice. It splattered on the pavement next to him. The result was both lumpy and runny at the same time and looked like one of those images the head doctors would flash at people—ask what they saw. The Horseradish test or something.

He'd seen it on television. Usually, he saw women's private parts in those black blobs.

A smattering of the brown stuff landed on his bare shoulder, too, so he shoved his chin out and rubbed it around. Rubbed in the juice.

But his eyes never left Red.

She was putting some blue stuff on her eyelids now. *Kinky thing, ain't she,* he thought. *Really taking her time. Rubbin' them fat lips around...*

He reached an oversized hand down to his crotch, adjusted himself through his overalls, and grunted unconsciously in appreciation. Not every day a man got to see something like that. It was like watching that late-night cable channel ... *Skin-a-max,* they called it as kids.

Maybe this was romance, he figured. They didn't offer up *romance* on the sex sites. Just the pump and dump.

After enjoying a leisurely episode of the woman painting herself up, Bird watched her get out of the car. She rose in slow motion, like a cake in the oven, until she was standing beside the car. Casually, she looked around, not a care in the world, defiant of the summer heat that threatened to cook the brains right inside Bird's skull. Tan hands pushed down from hips to thighs, smoothing her dress out. The fabric grew taut around her cleavage; Bird felt his underwear grow taut in response.

Glancing down, he noticed his recent spit was already drying up, leaving little lumps of Red Man on the ground. He leaned down and gave it another spit in the same spot. Rectified the situation.

"Excuse me…" It was almost as if she breathed it at him instead of having spoken out loud. He could swear he felt it on his face and ears and under the hair on his scalp. Without seeming to move, she was now on the side of the car closest to him.

"Yes'm?"

"Should I just pump my gas? Do you need to turn anything on?"

"Jus' pump it," he replied, amused. He shook his head. Just like a woman to ask something like that.

"Thanks," she replied. Smiled. Reached down and pulled her snug dress down a little lower. Pushed it down nice and flush against her legs. Red fingernails, too, he noticed. Cleavage everywhere. She went about the business of unhooking the gas pump and putting it into her vehicle.

Bird continued to ogle her, in no hurry to do much else. Grunted again. Adjusted himself again. Kept watching her.

He didn't so much as blink when a drop of sweat rolled slowly down the underside of his arm, tickling his side the whole way. He was too engrossed in *Little Red Riding Hood* and the firm grip she had on that gasoline nozzle. Watched while her hand twisted the handle, a little bit one way, and then the other. Her hand was, no doubt, moist from this summer heat...

"Excuse me—"

Her words sliced through his thoughts like a hot knife through butter. He brought his eyes up to meet her face.

"Yes'm?"

She smiled. As her lips moved, he caught the sweetest little peep of tongue in one corner of her mouth. It was only a second, but whew! Pink and pretty— delicious—he could almost taste her.

"Can you tell me where Rising Sun Lodge is?" Her voice was like honey, sticky and sweet, and his mind was sort of gummy from it. Like after he had half a dozen beers.

Bird stood up from his chair and lumbered over. He wanted to get a good look at his red treasure, and he enjoyed the way he made people feel—knew they were afraid—could see it in their eyes. He put himself right in front of her, almost up against her. The toes of his size-fourteen boots nearly touched the pointy tips of her red heels.

"You ha' business o'er there?" he croaked, his voice husky. He was enjoying himself, feeling good.

"Well…" She pursed her lips and looked him up and down. "I'm going to be staying there for a while." She didn't move back an inch or bat an eye. That he hadn't showered in several days didn't seem to faze her.

Bird felt his arousal grow, both mentally and physically. She didn't seem scared at all. No, not a bit. *Might be an interesting summer after all,* he mused.

"That sounds real nice," he said out loud and licked his lips. "Yeah … real nice." He eyed her up and down again, not a clean thought in his head, and smiled. "Well, it ain't too far from here."

"Oh, yeah?" She smiled at him.

Damn if she ain't flirtin' with me, he thought.

"Yeah … Just take 90 going west, and then jump on 385 going south. Can't miss it. Be on your right side, 'fore you get to The Bends."

"The Bends?"

"*Big Bend.* That little park in front of the Chisos over there," he said, pointing vaguely off to the mountains. He took a step closer to her—took a deep and obvious breath, inhaling her perfume.

"Right over there?" She pointed off to the mountains in an uncanny imitation of Bird.

The automatic shutoff on the gas pump clicked, but neither of them moved. Bird stood staring at her, but she didn't back down. It didn't happen often—almost never—but he was a little uncomfortable.

And that confused him.

Bird was big—six foot five and at least 250 pounds—and used to intimidating people. Even when he didn't try, he scared them. Kids gave him a wide berth.

That was when something flashed across her eyes. He was reminded of when the sunrise reflected off a rainbow trout, but with the texture of a snake. For a second it seemed like she was looking down at him, taller than him, towering over him.

Bird took an unconscious step backward, and then another. An unfamiliar feeling skittered across his neck.

Fear.

He squinted and focused on Red's eyes. Licked his lips to fight the cottony feeling that had taken over his mouth, and blinked. They looked normal again. Nothing unusual about her eyes.

"Mmph," he grunted. Must have been his imagination. She only looked at him curiously and smiled.

"Are you okay?" she asked.

"Yeah," he croaked, as if he were speaking through gravel.

"Okay then," she replied.

She watched him just a minute longer before walking back to her car. As she started the engine, she peered at him through the passenger window.

"It's not Horseradish, you idiot." She laughed then, an ugly gleam in her eyes. Rocks and dirt flew as she peeled out of the lot. She hit sixty miles per hour in about five seconds. An instant after that, she was gone. He was confused. Had he said that about the test out loud?

Dust floated around, capturing the afternoon sun, and things grew hazy. In the distance, a vulture landed next to a dark shape on the shoulder of the road, and Bird snapped back to reality. Shook his head ... wondered if he'd imagined the whole thing.

CHAPTER 3

"Sheriff, look at this," Deputy Tom Slidell called out. He reached down and checked the body for a pulse. It was purely force of habit—no life could possibly remain in the bloated corpse in front of him.

"Rattlers, Tom?"

"Yeah, Sheriff … looks like she stumbled on a whole nest of 'em."

"Hmm." Sheriff Bigsby eyed her body—puncture marks riddled the exposed flesh. He'd seen plenty of snakebites in his time—it was Southwest Texas after all—but this was the most vicious attack in his memory. "Sons-of-bitches were really ornery with her," he remarked, pushing his mustache down thoughtfully with his thumb and forefinger. Tom knew that meant he was deep in thought and stood patiently at his side.

The two of them wandered over to the truck in a comfortable silence. They'd been working with each other for a couple of decades, and Sheriff Bigsby had been friends with Tom's father. They were, in their way, like an old married couple. An old married couple with matching mustaches and uniforms.

"That's a mess," Tom said, looking inside the cab. Internal organs were splashed around the dashboard and seat like an abstract mural.

"Yep," Bigsby replied.

"Hmph," Tom grunted. "Don't smell too nice, either."

"Nope," Bigsby agreed.

15

They stood together, each man lost in thought. The sheriff stroked his mustache again.

"That's the third one this year," Tom remarked.

"Yep."

"Same area, too," Tom added. "Maybe there's a connection."

Sheriff Bigsby raised an eyebrow and looked sideways at Tom. He'd been thinking the same thing. "Two times could have been a coincidence..."

"But three—"

"Three doesn't smell right," the sheriff finished for him. He squatted down and pulled a telescoping rod from his shirt pocket. Extending it, he poked around the inside of the truck. A flicker caught his eye. He reached in further, leaning the edge of his hand against the doorframe for support. Pushing from side to side, he was able to wiggle the object over without touching it."

"GPS," Tom said.

"Yep."

"Hmph," Tom grunted.

While they watched, the screen flickered to life ... then turned off again.

"Never trusted them things," Tom said.

"Me either," Bigsby agreed. He brushed his fingers across his mustache again and thought about the three accidents they'd had along that part of Big Bend. He looked at the GPS. Then he looked at the truck again. For a second, he wondered if ... maybe...

"Oh, hell..." He shook the thought out of his head. "Let's get our guys out here and get this stuff collected up for the next of kin. After the forensics guys get done with it." He squinted and looked at the GPS—felt drawn to it—sort of wanted to touch it.

"You got it, boss." He radioed in the sheriff's request to the dispatcher, who arranged everything.

The sheriff shook his head yet again. "Let's get back to the SUV, Tom. We'll wait for the forensics boys there."

The pair hiked the half-mile back to their vehicle. They walked carefully, more wary of rattlesnakes than usual, after what they'd seen. Mountain lions, coyotes, and the occasional black bear were also threats.

Sheriff Bigsby reflected that the animals were a little more aggressive with people lately...

"That's six dead people this year," Tom said. He reached out his boot and batted a black scorpion out of his path. It scuttled backward away from Tom, leery, pincers raised.

"Six in six months," Bigsby replied. It was only June. He nodded at Tom to go on.

"All within about a mile of each other," Tom continued. He was thinking out loud—spitballing—a habit Bigsby nurtured. One day, Tom would replace him, and he needed him to think through situations logically. "Two washouts after thunderstorms. Mountain lion chewed up that one couple that was camping."

"But ... were they camping?"

"Good point, Sheriff. Maybe they didn't intend to camp there. Automobile was just off the road. Looked like they pushed it. Car trouble, maybe."

Bigsby nodded again, and Tom pushed on.

"Several loose connections," he started, but shook his head. "Damned frustrating, though, because I don't know how to bring it together. It's like Mother Nature is conspiring to kill these people. Kill their cars, and then send in the animals."

They mulled that over quietly.

A shadow moved by on the ground in front of them, and both men looked up just as a large bird went into a dive—fast—and they involuntarily ducked their heads in unison. Bigsby pulled his revolver as he squatted, just in case.

The peregrine falcon grabbed something—snapped it sharply and released it in the air—then caught it again before it touched the ground. They'd seen it before. The falcons often killed prey that way.

Tom thought about the animal factor in each accident and shivered. He glanced at the sheriff, who still had a bead on the bird, which was now moving away over a hill, and he figured he was thinking the same thing.

The relief was palpable when they made it to their vehicle and climbed inside. The sheriff's office had bought the truck new in 1996, the last year Ford made the Bronco. *A travesty*, Bigsby always thought, those feelings somewhat amplified this morning. He glanced down at the shotgun clipped in its holder between the front seats.

"Next time, Tom…"

Tom nodded. "Bring the shotgun."

Bigsby cranked on the AC, and was relieved when the air started blowing cold. Twenty years old, and the Bronco was still pushing out icy air, with only minimal maintenance through the years. Tom did more and more of the work as the county got stingier with funds, and Bigsby felt lucky to have him.

When the two forensics guys arrived, Tom briefed them about the rattlesnakes. It wasn't necessary—they were good old boys and knew how to handle themselves. Three guns between them, along with two hiking bags of equipment. They tipped their hats and started walking in.

Bigsby swung the Bronco around. Soon enough they were on Park Route 12, which became Main Park Road, which became 385. He caught a glance of Emory Peak in the side-view mirror. Normally, it felt like home; today, it was ominous.

The entry road to Rising Sun Lodge was coming up on their left. All types of people ended up there. It was quite a spread with a main lodge, clusters of cabins, and a pool, all nestled in the crescent of Lone Mountain, on the southwest side. It wasn't possible to see it from the road, but he'd been there before. Mostly as a kid. They had guides who led groups on horseback deep into parts of Big Bend, and his old man used to take him out there now and then on those rides.

The owners were a bit reclusive, but the staff always seemed friendly enough.

As they passed the turn for the lodge, he saw a red Audi parked off the road, and slowed down. A redhead was leaning on it—sort of hugging it, her body pressed up against the side.

That car has got to be too hot to touch, he thought. It was already in the nineties outside, and it wasn't even noon.

Bigsby stopped and rolled down his window. As he did, an errant breeze picked up, causing her red dress to billow. He might have caught a glimpse of matching red panties.

"Everything okay?" he asked.

She smiled broadly. "Perfect, Officers."

Bigsby nodded. He couldn't see the woman's eyes; they were covered by large, designer sunglasses. Women didn't wear that style around Marathon, but he'd noticed them when he visited Houston and Austin. Something they wore in the big city, or like Jackie Onassis wore. Despite the shades, he felt her eyes on him.

"No car trouble, I hope."

"No … just taking in the view," she replied.

Bigsby nodded before glancing at Tom. He could tell *Tom* was sure taking in the view. Not the same one she was talking about, but she didn't seem to mind.

"Well, be careful. We get some … nasty critters around here."

"Like rattlesnakes?" she asked, and though he wouldn't have thought it possible, it seemed her smile stretched even wider.

The sheriff eyed her sharply. Squinted. Licked his parched lips. Thought he felt a large crack in the flesh of his upper lip. He resisted the sudden urge to draw his weapon. The temptation was so strong that his right hand twitched for a second on the steering wheel.

He fought for control of his senses. Glanced over at Tom, who seemed frozen in place. Finally, he steeled himself and looked back out the window…

At a lady in a red dress. Perfectly normal. Just a woman out of her element.

A raggedy sigh escaped his lips, and he relaxed a little. Galloping heart slowed down. He tried to smile, but it probably looked more like a grimace. His heart was galloping.

"Well ... all sorts of animals," he said, watching her. "Snakes ... coyotes ... just be careful."

"Thank you so much, Officer. I'll watch out."

After waiting a second, he tipped his hat, and then drove away. He glanced in the rearview mirror...

Son-of-a-bitch, he thought, almost hitting the brakes. He could see her looking after them, and would have sworn she was laughing.

CHAPTER 4
Thursday

Bird was sleeping, eyelids dancing to the rhythm of overlapping dreams.

He'd started drinking when he closed the gas station at 8:00 p.m. the night before. The posted closing time was 9:00 p.m., but nobody had come in for nearly an hour, and he was itching to leave.

After knocking back most of a rack of Pabst Blue Ribbon at his trailer, Bird had taken his Ruger SR-762 into the backyard and blown through a couple of hundred rounds. He shot whatever caught his attention among the sundry junk items scattered around, and he didn't get bored until nearly 3:00 a.m., when he stumbled inside and passed out.

When his old man met his maker a few years earlier, he'd left him the gas station, and the little patch of desert his trailer was on. People wondered how the hell old Zeke Taylor had paid for the place. It was one of those small-town mysteries that came up now and then, to no avail.

Bird knew, though.

His old man came from nothing. None of the Taylors, as far back as anyone could remember, had ever amounted to much. An occasional good run at high school football until they dropped out. That was it. They scraped by as all their dads had before them, repairing tires, selling scrap metal ... nearly all of them working at that very gas station. Until Zeke.

Somehow or other, old Zeke got hooked up with a rancher's wife. Not just any of them, but the richest one around. Sometimes, Bird would come back to the trailer and the damn thing would be rocking so hard he thought it would fall off the cinder blocks. Then Blondie would emerge, looking flushed, and peel out in her Mercedes.

One night, however, Zeke had an idea that eclipsed all the other Taylor schemes combined, and that was saying plenty, because they'd always been a scheming lot.

Zeke poked his head into Bird's room and said, "Come with me."

Bird tossed aside his *Guns & Ammo* magazine and followed his old man down the hall, across the living room and kitchen, to Zeke's room at the other end of the trailer.

"What's up, Pop?"

"Take this," his dad said urgently. Bird looked down questioningly at the little digital camera that Zeke had thrust into his hands. "Get inside that closet. When me and Blondie start going at it, take pictures. Take a lot of fuckin' pictures."

"The fuck?" Bird asked. "I don't wanna see you and some..."

Zeke landed a quick jab to the side of Bird's head. He wasn't as big as Bird, but he was the meanest son-of-a-bitch around. Tough as a railroad spike. No one fucked with Zeke.

"Do what I tell you," he replied. "Go! Now, for crissakes!"

Bird shoved aside cardboard boxes and shirts and overalls, squeezed his huge frame into the closet, and slid the door shut. The camera came on easy enough with a soft beep. He tapped the big button on top and took a test shot just as he heard the door open.

Bird had cursed quietly to himself as Zeke started to work Blondie over, not that it stopped him from getting an erection. He could see she was a real blonde when his old man's hairy ass wasn't in the way. Zeke Taylor could have been mistaken for a black bear.

Ten minutes later, they collapsed laughing, and Bird felt relieved. His back was hurting from being hunched over, and he needed to take a leak.

Except it was only halftime. The laughter quickly turned into more screwing, and despite his pain, Bird put the camera into video mode and didn't finish until his dad did. Even the sorriest of sons wanted to impress his dad.

It wasn't long before the blackmail money came in and paid for the gas station. A few years later, they found Zeke dead from a gunshot wound. Apparent suicide. Another small-town mystery, one for which Bird had no answers, only suspicion. Of course, his life was better without Zeke around. He could waste money on beer and guns and do whatever the hell he wanted after that.

Bird snored loudly as he dozed, sprawled out on his ratty brown sofa, legs poking over the end. Saliva drained from the corner of his wide-open mouth and down his cheek.

In his dream, he was shooting his guns in his backyard, just as he had earlier that night. Brass casings littered the ground completely—he never policed it up when he finished—and his boots crunched on them with every step.

"Hey," someone called from the shadows behind his trailer.

"Who's there?" he replied, but dream Bird already thought he knew the answer to that question.

"Come on over, Bird. I need to tell you something."

As he got closer to the voice, he saw her eyes shining in the darkness. Her red dress was tighter than ever.

"Whadda you want?"

"Come closer so I can tell you," she prodded. Unable to stop himself, dream Bird crunched along until he was so close he could smell her. Taste her. Those velvety lips pulled him along as if she were the pied piper and he was the captivated rodent. Those eyes bored into him, and he felt things liven up down south. Except, he also felt just a little bit of *it* again.

Fear.

She began to whisper. The sound of her voice was so sweet. Wind chimes and dandelions and fresh baked bread. The promise of everything he'd never had was right there for him, if he could just do this thing for her.

"Don't fail me," she whispered at the end. Then she was gone.

Bird woke up and looked around, wiping the slime off the side of his face. He almost expected to see her. Could still smell her...

He sat bolt upright. The trailer smelled like her. Not like the remnants of a dream, but like she'd been right *there* with him.

Red's whispered words came back to him, and he nodded slowly. He knew what he had to do.

CHAPTER 5

Kane woke up with a start—alert—listening.

He reached for the Smith & Wesson tucked under his pillow, but it wasn't there. He furrowed his brows for a moment in the semi-darkness before he remembered he wasn't in his room, and this wasn't his bed. Didn't even have a place to stay in Marathon. At least, not yet.

The air conditioner cut off, replaced by the hum of the refrigerator across the room. Somewhere in the distance, a dog barked, and a human barked back, "Keep it down!" Or something like that. A truck with glass packs fired off, and then was gone.

Nothing out of the ordinary, especially for this part of Texas.

A large rectangle-shaped pinstripe of light dominated the far wall, like a glowing picture frame ... sunlight trying to sneak its way in, around a heavy set of drapes. Kane sat up and let his eyes adjust to the gray murkiness. His watch said 9:00 a.m.

Lucy rolled over next to him on the foldout sofa, murmuring something in her sleep, and he smiled. They'd left Bob's around two, but the extracurricular activities had lasted past four. No rough stuff, he thought to himself, remembering Bob's admonition to him before he took the stage.

Back when he'd gone through the Army's Ranger School, there were generally two types of guys: the Sleepy Ranger and the Hungry Ranger.

Sleepy Ranger was always tired. Long, brutal days followed by four hours of sleep—sometimes less—left him perpetually tired. Drained. Some people just needed more sleep, and exhaustion was their worst enemy.

Hungry Ranger, on the other hand, never got enough to eat—ever. Ranger School was two solid months of hunger pains. Their stomachs spoke to them—literally. Many times, especially at first, it woke dudes up. Despite shaking out every crumb from the MRE pouches, it was never enough.

If Sleepy Ranger was smart, or lucky, he paired up with a Hungry Ranger. Then they could trade food for sleep. Give Hungry Ranger some of his rations in exchange for a twenty-minute nap, or a shorter watch at night.

Kane's stomach growled—he was a Hungry Ranger.

He padded around Lucy's kitchen until he found a box of cereal bars. He felt guilty about it, but ate two of them while he sucked down a glass of tap water. He'd have to remember to buy her more of the breakfast bars later.

As quietly as he could, he slid on his jeans before stepping outside. The wooden porch responded to each step with a soft creak, but it wasn't rickety. When he grabbed the handrail, flakes of white paint bit into his palms. Dry and hard. Much like the land surrounding him.

The house was faded yellow, paint flaking and peeling like the porch, a product of the merciless sun. A large dog was sprawled out on the back porch of the blue house next door; it eyed Kane for a second, but then went to sleep. A cyclone fence ran around Lucy's property, and a broken pavement driveway lay between it and the house. His old F150 was almost at the rear of the dwelling. Barefoot and shirtless, Kane walked over and opened the camper of his truck.

Everything he owned was inside. It wasn't much to look at. Not that he minded. It had been liberating selling off most of his worldly possessions. Life took on a new sense of freedom, and he was so much happier, unburdened of all the worthless crap that people accumulate.

There was a black duffel bag near the hatch. It had extra clothes, running gear, and most importantly … his pistol. After reaching inside to make sure everything was where it should be, he hauled it out and went inside to change.

*****

Heat, and plenty of it, Kane thought, jogging down 6th Street.

Sometimes when he was cooking, grease and oil puddled at the bottom of the pan, innocent-looking, glistening, until it popped. Then scorching hot specks burned the arms. Or face.

The intensity of the sun in southwest Texas was a lot like that oil. He sighed, feeling his exposed skin heat up. Kane kicked himself—he'd forgotten to use sunblock.

He turned right on Avenue E.

His Asics punched into the ground, hard crunching impacts in the dirt, rocks, and pavement. *Crunch. Crunch. Crunch.* He was running on the left side of the road, against traffic flow … if there had been any. There wasn't.

Spoke too soon, he thought, looking up.

A single truck rolled by on his right, then turned right and disappeared. A drop of sweat gathered in his eyebrow, and he swiped a finger under his Oakleys to remove it.

An ACU pattern CamelBak was snugged tight on his back, loaded with water, an extra cereal bar, and his Smith & Wesson. It was the M&P 40 Shield model, with the extended magazine that held seven rounds. He always kept it loaded. Otherwise, *what was the point?*

He hit 1st Street and could see the post office as well as what appeared to be Marathon's main drag. Instead of sticking to the road, he cut across a lot, jumped a set of railroad tracks, and decided to check out the area.

Next to the post office there was a little shop with souvenirs and homemade wares, and next to that … a restaurant called The Famous Burro. He caught a whiff of something good and decided it would be worth checking out. He kept running.

Kane jogged past an art gallery, a bank, and another restaurant. He glanced down at his GPS watch, and it said he'd gone half a mile in three and a half minutes. Good pace, and he felt great.

When he looked back up, he lost his rhythm and slowed down for a beat. Up ahead was the Gage Hotel. He trotted by on the highway side, admiring the landscaping. There came the sound of splashing and laughing kids, and then a glimpse of what looked like a beautiful, cross-shaped pool. The parking spaces were all full, and he noticed a sign for a hotel restaurant.

For such a small place, Marathon seemed to have some things going for it. He wondered if the national park was magnetic enough to keep places like the Gage Hotel in business.

Just as he neared the far end, heading west, he happened to glance back to his left. There was a black Chevy Tahoe moving slowly along about a hundred yards back. Probably innocuous, but it almost felt like they were tailing him.

There were times in Iraq when guys thought something was innocent. Or safe. And then a soldier would find himself petting a cute little dog that happened to be strapped with enough explosives to take out half a city block.

Nothing was innocuous.

He pretended not to notice, and circled the building to the right at the next block, checking out the hotel some more, but also waiting to see if the Tahoe would turn with him. He was most likely just being a paranoid bastard.

Except the Tahoe turned, too.

He reached 2nd Street, and hit another quick right, then pressed himself into the wall at the backside of the hotel. Waited.

When the Tahoe turned the corner this time, he waited until it was even with him, then sprinted over to the passenger's side and yanked on the handle.

Locked.

"Hey!" he shouted, giving it another yank, trying to see through deeply tinted windows. The vehicle picked up speed, and he ran alongside. Abruptly, it turned left and sped off, leaving him in a cloud of Texas dust.

He trotted around the roads, moving up and down blocks, scoping things out—waiting—but he didn't see the black Tahoe again. An adventurous dog chased him briefly, but it got bored. Two ladies out walking said hi when he ran by them, and an old bald man with no teeth smiled and waved from his porch.

They'd lost him. Or maybe it was a case of mistaken identity and all that. He wondered about it, but he decided to finish his run. He had the Smithy with him, which was always a good thing, and he could handle himself pretty well.

Eventually, he found a road that led out of the backside of Marathon and the Tahoe faded from his mind, moving from the forefront to somewhere just below the surface, mostly forgotten. He followed the road uphill for another mile or so. It was hot, but he was used to hot. Enjoyed it sometimes.

When he came to another road and a couple of trails that all nearly intersected, he took a healthy swig of water from his backpack, and jogged around in a circle, enjoying the scenery. Purple mountains loomed southward like giant shark's teeth. This country was rugged, and yes, beautiful, in many ways.

He headed back to Lucy's.

*****

"How far did you run?"

Kane glanced at his watch. "A little under seven miles."

"Wow! That's crazy. It's too freakin' hot out there for walking," Lucy replied. "Much less *running* seven miles."

They were standing inside her place, at the doorway to the bathroom. She was giving him *the look*, which he figured meant sex was likely again. Soon. He'd prefer to do it before he showered, but he didn't want to be rude.

"It wasn't too bad," he lied. It was awful. By the time he got back, he'd been running for just under an hour. His already tanned arms now had a reddish tint.

"Right." She looked doubtful as she ducked into her bedroom.

Kane walked into the bathroom, pushed the door mostly closed, and took off his shirt. Peeled it off, really—it was soaked through.

"Shit," she said, pushing the door open behind him. He could hear the intake of breath ... see her gritting her teeth and squinting in the mirror.

"Yeah," he said simply and nodded. Walled himself off.

"What the..."

Kane was used to this reaction. He'd taken shrapnel in his back in Afghanistan. Shot in the left rear deltoid in Iraq. The back of his torso was like a map of crisscrossed scar tissue.

She rubbed her fingers along the puffy flesh. Sometimes, it tickled. Other times, he felt nothing. Sort of like life.

He waited for her to ask the question: *how did it happen?* But it never came. Instead, she turned him around and kissed him. She no longer had the *we're-having-sex-soon* look in her eyes. Compassion had replaced it. Or sympathy.

When they pulled apart, she pushed his chest and said, "Shower. You stink."

"Right." He could smell himself, and he agreed with the assessment.

"Then we'll eat at the Burro," she said as she closed the door.

*****

"I told you. Can't go wrong with the Famous Burro's Blue Burro burger." Lucy smiled. It was broad daylight, not the hazy interior of Bob's, and he realized she was even better looking sans makeup. Those emerald eyes twinkled across the table at him.

He nodded his head, mouth full of burger.

"What do you think?" she asked.

Kane barely heard her, mumbled something, and gave his head the old vertical movement, north-south, north-south.

"Great," he tried again, after finishing a mouthful. Grinned at her. It was amazing he'd retained any manners at all after his eight years in the Army. Guys pissed in bottles, shit in holes, and went for days or weeks without showering when they were deployed. Becoming accustomed to that changed a person forever. Not always for the better.

On their way out of the restaurant, Lucy and Kane passed two men in jeans, black button-up shirts, and black sunglasses. As they were getting into his truck, he said, "Did you see those two guys?"

"In the Burro?"

"Yeah." He laughed. "They looked like the bad guys in *Road House*." He snickered and continued, "The young tough who worked for the main bad guy, Wesley. Remember? He was sort of feminine. Prissy looking."

"*Road House* ... who's in it?" she asked.

"Are you serious? Sam Elliott? Patrick Swayze is hired to be a bouncer at a bar that's having trouble?"

He looked over at her, but she just shook her head.

"Shameful," he said, shaking his head as he pulled away from the curb. "How old are you?"

"Twenty-six," she said. He was thirty-one.

"Hmm. I guess you just missed when it was popular, but I don't see how you can grow up in southern Texas without seeing *Road House*. It's a classic. I wouldn't be surprised if Sam Elliott walks into Bob's tonight."

She giggled. "Maybe we can Netflix it."

"Maybe," he agreed. He wasn't sure—didn't know much about Netflix since he was usually on the move.

Kane crossed Highway 90 without looking back. He never noticed the two guys staring at him from the window of the Burro ... or the black Chevy Tahoe parked down the street.

CHAPTER 6

Sheriff Bigsby and Deputy Slidell were almost to the post office, on their way to get some pizza. A Ford F150 with a camper crossed 90 in front of them as they passed, and Bigsby recognized the kid Bob hired to sing at his place. *Pretty good, too,* he thought. Hadn't heard anybody worth a damn at Bob's for a while.

The radio crackled to life. "Deputy Slidell, this is Dispatch."

"It's Harriet," Tom said.

"Yep," the sheriff replied.

They were silent for a moment.

"Probably a cat in a tree," Tom said as he reached for the radio. He could see the amusement in the sheriff's eyes, though Bigsby's face remained expressionless. He'd never been one to laugh too much, even when he thought something was funny, but those eyes couldn't hide the mirth.

Harriet usually found a reason to call them on the radio a couple of times each shift. Small things became emergencies. And, despite how well they all knew each other, and the size of Marathon, she insisted on using all the proper titles and radio phraseology.

"Go ahead, Dispatch," Tom said into the handset. The sheriff always drove, which meant Tom always handled the radio.

"Tom ... I mean, Deputy..."

Tom and Bigsby looked at each other. Harriet's voice was shaky, and she never called him Tom. She was near tears, from the sound of it.

"Dispatch," he started, but then tossed protocol out the window. "Harriet? What's the matter?"

"Oh, Tom..."

"Well, go ahead," he urged her quietly, but firmly. "What is it?"

"It's the Wilsons," she began. Her voice cracked.

"Yeah?"

"Someone took their baby!" she cried out. "Dave called. He's in Alpine, driving back now. He said Laurie called him, hysterical, saying someone went in their house and grabbed Colby. Just went right in the house and took him out of the crib, Dave said..."

For about two or three seconds, the only sounds in the SUV were the hum of the engine as they rolled eastbound on 90 and the sound of the Ford's tires on the highway. The calm before...

The storm broke—Bigsby braked hard and spun the twenty-year-old Bronco sharply left to make the turn onto Avenue G. Slidell gripped the dashboard in one hand, and the radio in the other, and told Harriet they were en route to the Wilson home.

One advantage of small-town living was that everyone knew everyone else. That was also a disadvantage; however, it worked in Sheriff Bigsby's favor this time because he knew exactly where the Wilsons lived. They cruised by the Wilson home, and every other home in Marathon, for that matter, a few times each week as they patrolled the town.

Tom had the lights and sirens on. Dirt followed the Bronco down Avenue G like it did Pig-Pen in *Charlie*

Brown. It only took them about thirty seconds to get to 8th Street on the north side of town.

Bigsby hit the left turn hard, and there was a moment when he thought the Bronco was going to flip. In the space of that second or two, he was flooded with different thoughts and adrenaline as he recognized he was on two wheels, prayed to God for help, and turned into the curve. It was fearfully close—and the relief was immense when his side of the vehicle hit the ground again with a bounce.

Good ol' damn Bronco, he thought. Never failed him.

They squealed to a stop in front of the Wilsons' house, recently repainted, probably Dave's idea of welcoming the baby. Women decorated the bedroom; dads like Dave built cribs from scratch and painted the house.

There was a new dually parked cockeyed across the front of the yard. It belonged to Pat Wilson, Dave's father. There were a couple of folks on the porch, and two more at the edge of the yard. Bigsby wasn't sure what to think. Extra help could be good. A bunch of hotheaded vigilantes running amok would be bad.

When he got near the porch he could hear Laurie Wilson. Crying. Moaning. Wailing. They were sad, awful sounds.

"Sheriff…"

"Sheriff."

The two guys on the porch greeted him. Perfunctory nods of two heads covered with cowboy hats. Older guys. Button-up shirts tucked into their jeans despite the heat. Men raised to respect the law that the star on his shirt represented.

He'd come up with one of them: Bill Ames, a friend of Pat's. Caroused a few times when they were younger. If it weren't such a shitty situation, they'd stop and chew the fat for twenty minutes to cover the normal stuff: weather, sports, trucks, and women.

Bill and Pat worked on heavy equipment together. They were wiry guys, used to using their hands.

"Sheriff," Tom said, motioning at the two in the yard. One of them was Bill's son, and he carried a shotgun in his right hand, dangling toward the ground.

"Bill," he said as he pulled open the screen door. "Tell your boy to put away the gun. I don't want any accidents." Bigsby didn't wait for a reply, and he and Tom entered the Wilsons' living room.

Laurie was on the couch, but she stood and hugged Bigsby hard when he entered. She was from Marathon and had known him her whole life. With a population of less than five hundred, they only had a handful of kids born each year, and he knew them all, to a degree. There'd been numerous times he escorted a pregnant mother and high-strung father-to-be over to the hospital in Alpine, lights going the whole time to clear what little traffic might get in the way.

He might not be able to understand women, but he had learned through the years that he had a knack for calming people down, women and men alike. Cheryl used to tell him it was because he was such a good listener. She was usually right about things.

Damn, I miss Cheryl, he thought.

Bigsby gave Laurie a minute to get it out, to let all the raw, emotional turmoil flood out of her. She vomited out the words like someone who'd just had that last shot of whiskey that put them over the edge. It was disquieting. Unsettling.

This wasn't Houston or Dallas, but he'd seen a lot in forty years: snakebites; runaway kids; ranch hands who lost limbs or died; and maybe the most common ... the case of the disappearing spouse. Husbands vanished with surprising frequency, but usually reappeared after a day or two.

Still ... it never got any easier seeing loss. Or pain. Or sadness.

"Tell me what happened," he finally told her. "Exactly what happened, step by step."

His direction refocused Laurie, who calmed down enough to give them a rundown.

"Colby was in his crib. Just went down for his afternoon nap. He's such a good little sleeper, you know?"

"I know," he replied in a soothing, yet authoritative way. It was hard to strike the right balance between comforting her as a victim, and using enough force to keep her on track. "And you were in the living room?"

"I was in the shower. I heard Colby crying on the baby monitor, but then he stopped, so I thought he'd just calmed down or something," she said, eyes watering.

"Go on," Bigsby pushed.

"I got dressed and went into his room ... and the window was open ..." Laurie Wilson started to break down again. Pat appeared by her side, and eased her back down to the couch.

"Let's take a look in the bedroom."

Tom followed the sheriff into the rear of the house, where they easily found the child's room—the door was open, and Winnie the Pooh beckoned them in. Crib bedding, crib mobile, changing table ... all decked out in Pooh. Eeyore curtains shifted slightly in the breeze from the open window. A canister of baby powder lay, contents strewn across the floor, in front of the window.

Bigsby squatted down and studied the floor. "Boot print," he said.

"Uh-huh," Tom said. Took a few pictures with his phone. "Partial, looks like."

"Right," he agreed. They were careful not to touch anything. "Just the top half. No heel. Looks big, though."

"Hmm."

The sheriff stood. The creases in his shirt betrayed the fastidious care he displayed in all his doings. Small town didn't mean less professional. He kept his shirts crisply starched; today was no exception. The khaki material sometimes made little scratchy sounds when he moved, but he didn't mind. Just evidence of the pride he took in his uniform. He noticed that Tom had started starching his shirts, too. *Good man*, he thought.

Without another word, they walked through the living room where Pat was caring for Laurie. Remained silent. Went out to the front porch.

"Tom, get on the phone and have Harriet call the boys in Alpine to give us some help. Today. While there's light."

"Roger," Tom replied. "Want me to have her get hold of the FBI?"

"No." Bigsby squinted and rubbed a hand over his mustache. The screen door shut behind him. Without turning around, he knew Pat had joined them.

"No? But Sheriff..." Tom began.

"No, Tom. Feds won't make it out today, and I don't want them tightening the leash long distance. Let's stall for a couple of hours. See what we can do first. Get a team out here to look at the bedroom, too. Pat?"

"Sheriff," Pat rasped. He tugged off his Stetson with his right hand, and then ran his left through silver hair. Icy blue eyes peered out from beneath the crew cut he'd had for about three decades.

"Gather your guys," he told Pat and glanced around. "But keep the guns tucked away—this ain't a posse—just good citizens looking for a boy."

"Aye, Sheriff." Pat replaced the hat. Jumping off the porch, he went down into the yard with Bill and his son. Phones came out and calls were made. They were men who could be counted on in a crisis.

Bigsby felt something like pride as he walked back to the Bronco. These were his people—good people—who would band together. Despite the situation, he allowed himself to feel hope as he leaned against the SUV and monitored the conversation between Tom and Harriet.

Maybe we'll get Colby back before nightfall, he thought.

Twenty minutes later, there were a dozen men beneath the big tree in the Wilsons' back yard. Dave was still a few minutes away, according to Pat. Bill and his son were smoking, talking about the local terrain and distances. Tom stood with his arms crossed next to the sheriff, loyal as always.

"Okay, boys," he began. "Here's what we're going to do." He devised a plan he hoped would cover ground fast and laid it out for the men. He spoke sparingly, as always, but left no doubt as to what they needed to do.

Within minutes, they were spread out, searching.

CHAPTER 7

"See you gotcher Trans Am runnin'."

Bird motioned with his head toward the faded blue car parked beneath the old Exxon sign.

"Hell, yeah, Bird!" Mikey got excited, fast, when he talked about that car. "Eastbound and down, loaded up and truckin'. We about to do what they say can't be done..."

Bird grunted in amusement, and then fired a stream of tobacco juice off to his side. Some landed on his arm, but he didn't notice.

There weren't many people Bird liked—*really* liked— but Mikey was okay. He trusted him. Almost like a little brother. Plus, they shared all the same interests: guns, cars, and pussy.

"Right as rain. Yessir. Found the parts I needed at the junkyard in Odessa."

"Yeah?"

"Yeah."

A Chevy Malibu rolled in and parked at the far pumps. Mikey and Bird watched, disinterested, as the door opened and two pale lavender heels dropped to the ground. They were somewhat thick and unwieldy shoes, not sexy—much like the body that emerged from behind that open door.

Pear shaped and stocky, it wasn't the lady's height or weight that made her dimensions seem larger than life, but just everything added together. A flowery dress covered her from neck to calf, the kind older ladies wore to church—not that Mikey or Bird had much experience with church.

Gray hair resembling a beehive. *Tall old gal ... looks like one of the Golden Girls*, Bird thought. He couldn't remember Bea Arthur's name. Only remembered the show because reruns played on the television when he was a kid. She popped in her credit card and started pumping gas. Bird laid down some tobacco juice to the left again. It was natural for him to go left with it.

"Many people today?" he asked Mikey.

"Here and there," he replied. "'Bout normal."

Bird considered Mikey for a minute. Wondered if he was skimming a few bucks from the ol' cash register sometimes, and concluded that he was. Hell, it was what he would do. He decided it didn't matter as long as he was still seeing greenbacks every day.

Besides, he didn't pay Mikey shit anyway.

"Freddy?"

Bird froze. Mikey didn't even seem to notice—too busy digging the blade of his knife under his fingernails.

"Freddy, is that you?"

Bird furrowed his eyebrows at the old lady as she approached. He could sense Mikey's confusion. Heck, he hadn't heard his own name for years, and here was some stranger, calling out to him.

"Crazy old bat," Mikey whispered under his breath.

Then Bird exhaled as if he'd been punched; twenty-five years disappeared in the blink of an eye. He was back on the elementary school playground near the tire swings, surrounded on all sides by kids who were either shocked, scared, or disgusted. That's when Ms. Parker busted through the others, grabbed him by the ear, and hauled him off to the principal.

That was the day he became Bird.

"Ms. Parker," he finally said. He could almost hear Mikey's head swivel toward him—could see his mouth hanging open out of the corner of his eye.

"Freddy, well, look at you! Completely grown up now." She reached out, put a hand on his right arm, and looked at him. Bird found her smile disconcerting and he shook his head ... tried to shake off the feeling.

"Yes'm, I guess I am."

"You look nice. Big and strong, like your dad. I remember when I taught Zeke, too, if you can believe that," she said. "How's he doing?"

"He passed."

"Oh." She paused. Sympathy was written across her face. "Well, I'm sorry to hear that." She patted his arm and gave him an understanding look. Bird wanted to be angry, but found himself almost sad. "Do you work here now?"

"Yes'm," he began haltingly. "Well, it's my place. I mean, I *own* it..."

"Really? Oh, that's great! Good for you, Freddy." If she was doubtful, she didn't show it. She seemed genuinely happy for him—unlike most the assholes from town—and Bird started thinking that maybe, just maybe, Ms. Parker was okay.

He grunted in response ... could see Mikey off to his side, watching the entire exchange with what appeared to be great interest. And pleasure.

"So you taught," Mikey looked slyly at Bird, "*Freddy*? In, like, grade school or something?"

Bird clenched his jaw. Gave Mikey the stink eye.

"I sure did, young man. Years ago…" She trailed off, and looked out at the highway, before turning back to them. "What was I saying? You know, I think I just had what my friends call a *senior moment*. It's been happening since I passed birthday number seventy. It's like my thoughts just detour off the highway in my brain for a moment," she said and laughed. "All right, I guess I'll move along. You take care of yourself, Freddy. I'm just here to see an old friend for a few days. Then it's back to Austin."

"Huh," Bird said. "Um, well … good to see you," he managed. He wasn't exactly built for small talk.

"Yes!" she agreed. "And if you're ever in Austin, look me up."

Bird grunted an affirmative.

When the Malibu was back out on the road, Bird looked at Mikey. "You're lucky I don't knock that fuckin' smirk off your face," he told him.

"Sorry." Mikey looked nervous. Bird wasn't one to joke about that kind of thing. He had knocked plenty of fucking smirks off faces. Of course, Mikey was young, and prone to making the mistakes that young guys make, and despite Bird's threat, he couldn't stop himself from saying, "So, you mind if I ask why they call you Bird?"

Bird glanced at him, and then loaded up with some more Red Man since he'd swallowed the last little bit when Ms. Parker was there. It was as if he were a kid again, and he hadn't wanted to spit in front of her. So, he had just swallowed it down.

The gas station lot disappeared as he drifted back in time, and he found himself on the elementary school playground. It was recess in the fall, so it was actually pretty nice outside. He remembered that it wasn't cool that day, but it wasn't hot either.

He and another rowdy kid had been taking turns spinning each other as fast as they could go in the tire swing when he noticed the kids circling up nearby. Naturally, he'd gone to check things out ... see what the big damn deal was.

When he pushed his way closer, he saw that everyone was staring at a bird on the ground. It was looking around frantically, flapping one of its wings, but something was wrong with its legs—or the other wing— because it could only move a fraction of an inch at a time.

It was making little squawking noises laced with panic. Nobody moved. Bird looked at them with no small measure of contempt. *They're all yellow,* he thought. *Yellow-bellied ... no guts at all.*

Nobody stopped him or said a word when he stepped forward and slowly made his way over to where the bird flopped back and forth on the ground. As he hovered over it, the creature's panic intensified, the beating of its one good wing reaching a manic crescendo.

Freddy Taylor studied the bird for a few seconds. Then, without warning, he raised his right boot and brought it down in a single, crushing blow on the bird's head and neck. The bones were pulverized, death certain.

Several of the girls began crying, and most of the kids avoided eye contact with him. No one knew it just then, but Freddy Taylor had just died. Bird was born, and Bird found that he enjoyed the fear that spread through them all like the Black Plague. He grinned, daring anyone to say something. Do something. But none of them did.

That was when Ms. Parker got ahold of his ear, and the rest was history.

Bird looked at Mikey. He thought about stomping that bird's head into bits, and said, "Mikey, just shut. The. Fuck. Up."

So Mikey did.

CHAPTER 8

Kane watched Lucy slide her legs into a pair of blue jeans. They went on easy at first, until they got to the base of her butt. Then she did this little back-and-forth shimmy maneuver a couple of times to bring it up those last few inches. It was one of those woman things that he found cute and endearing and sexy, all at the same time.

"Hey, what are you looking at?"

He grinned from across the room. "Busted. Totally busted. I was watching you get dressed ... doing that little dance to get into your pants."

"Oh, yeah? Little dance?"

"Yeah. So why do girls always wear tight jeans?" he asked. "I mean, don't get me wrong, I think it's great, but it can't be convenient. Or comfortable."

She laughed. "It's not so bad. I don't even notice, really."

A red blouse came next. It hid Lucy's flat stomach and the little pink-and-blue bra she was wearing. A sad state of affairs, indeed.

"What are you going to do?" she asked.

"Well," he said. "I guess I'm going to find a place to stay."

"Not many of those around here."

"Apartments?"

She laughed. "In Alpine."

"How far is that?"

"Twenty-five minutes," she answered. "Eve owns the B&B on the west side of town ... she might have something. She rented out the room over her garage for a while when her son moved."

Kane considered that for a little bit, hands steepled together in front of his face. Bob had mentioned something similar, about having an extra room he could rent. Kane's needs were minimal, but he wanted to keep work separated from his personal life.

But, it wasn't just that.

In the Army, he'd been conditioned to have low expectations. Sleeping on cots so close to each other that he could extend his arm and touch the guys' feet on either side of him was the norm—they slept head to foot to prevent the spread of germs—and things either got better or worse from there.

They lived out of rucksacks, cleaned up with baby wipes instead of taking showers, and ate the same lame food over and over again. For months. None of that bothered him. It was like an extended camping trip, one that lasted for twelve or fifteen months, but the time aspect of it never concerned him.

The privacy thing. That always got to him, though.

Privacy was the single most important freedom of which he'd felt deprived. Dudes created makeshift tents to crawl into on their cots or bunks, just so they could be in their own world. A visit to the port-o-john might get pushed an extra ten minutes, despite the malodorous atmosphere, just for a few freaking minutes of solitude.

Kane couldn't say he never complained—hell, soldiers excelled at complaining—but he promised himself privacy when he got out. A place he could hear himself think. A place where the only farts he heard or smelled were his own.

"You know…" Lucy began, sitting down next to him, "You could always stay with me for a while. Just until you find a place, of course." She put her arm around him and smiled broadly.

And there it was.

She'd put him on the spot, and there was no going back. Ninety-nine percent chance she wouldn't understand if he tried to explain it to her. That he craved his own space—that it had nothing to do with her. Women only heard rejection in situations like this. Maybe on some baser level, that was accurate—it was a rejection. Except, the way he felt extended across all women—across all humanity! *It's me, not you.* That sort of thing. Except, it was the truth.

Kane sighed inwardly. Big boy. Grown man. His drill sergeant asked how tall he was, and when he replied 'six-one', that swarthy little man had bellowed, "I didn't know they stacked shit that high!"

Those seventy-three inches were gone in the blink of an eye, he felt so small. Powerless. About to cave and give in to another female. Men everywhere were sacrificing at the altar of some beautiful woman in their life.

"You know what?" he told her finally. "That sounds nice."

She leaned in and kissed him. Maybe giving in to a beautiful woman was okay, now and then.

"What time are you coming in?" she asked. It was almost 4:00 p.m.—her shift started soon.

"I'll be there around eight," he said.

She took her hair and pushed it back in a ponytail. It was thick, like something that one might pull and expect to hear a gong in the background.

"You look like the genie in *I Dream of Jeannie*," he told her. "With the blonde hair and the ponytail..."

"Who's that?"

He groaned. "Oh, my God ... you don't know *I Dream of Jeannie*?"

"Is it on Netflix?"

"What the Fu ... Netflix? What is it with everyone and Netflix?"

"Netflix and chill," she said. "That's what they say now."

"Who?"

"Everyone." She shrugged and smiled. "Everyone born in the last thirty years." She giggled. He tugged lightly on her ponytail and they made out like teenagers for a few minutes on the couch.

Things could be a lot worse, he thought. Privacy would just have to wait a bit longer.

He did, however, plan on using her Internet to check out the rental situation in town. His old first sergeant used to say that a man without a plan was just a man with his dick in his hand. Kane was pretty sure that meant a man should have a plan. And a backup plan.

"The PS3 is hooked up to the Internet, but I'll leave you my Wi-Fi password, too," she told him. "You can check out Netflix while I'm gone. Look for that movie with Patrick Swayze."

"*Road House.*"

"If you say so. And the genie show. It might be on there."

"Sure," he agreed. He had an iPod that he could use for Wi-Fi, but it mostly served as his jukebox while he was running. He wasn't *completely* behind the times, no matter how hard he tried.

Lucy gave him a key to her place, a kiss on the face, and was off to Bob's.

It was curious to him that he was trusted so quickly. She'd given him a key to her home, and they'd only just met. In a bar. Yesterday.

Almost as if dragged by cosmic hands, he walked through her house and looked around. There was an entertainment center in the living room with a flat-screen television, just across from the couch where they'd made all that magic—twice—the previous night. A PlayStation 3 sat nearby, and he noticed she had ten or fifteen games.

Call of Duty, Black Ops ... he was surprised, but amused, when he noticed she mostly had first-person shooter games. He knew them well—he'd seen grown men playing them in day rooms, barracks, and USOs all over the world. Had tried it himself a few times, but it was a lackluster experience, after some of the things he'd seen.

Lucy was pretty feisty, though; he could imagine her playing them. That, or the games were remnants of some dude, abandoned when he discovered Lucy was a manipulative ice queen and ran for the hills.

Joking, joking...

He didn't care what she'd done before—that was all water under the bridge. In the middle of her bedroom was an empty space. She'd told him she sold her childhood double bed six months ago—meant to upgrade—but never got around to it. The carpet verified Lucy's story. Despite the stripes that crisscrossed the floor where she'd recently vacuumed, there remained the faint outline of a bed. Deep circles indicated where the headboard and footboard had been. She was right: it was a small bed.

There was a teal chair next to the window with a matching ottoman. He sat down and discovered the view wasn't too bad … in that South Texas roughing-it sort of way. A Nicholas Sparks novel was open on the floor.

"Hmph." He thought about that for a few minutes, and then chuckled to himself. "Beautiful blonde with sea-foam green eyes. Enjoys games where you can blow shit up and kill people. Open to finding Mr. Right. The enigma wrapped in a mystery."

He pulled out his iPod to play around on the Internet for a little bit before work. There was no longer any urgency to finding his own place, and he only gave it a half-hearted go before he was looking at guitars and thinking about his playlist that night.

Work? Getting paid to play the guitar? *Get out of here.*

*****

"Hey, Kane…"

Bob sidled up while he was unclasping Honey's case, clapping him lightly on the back.

"Mister Bob. How are you doing?"

Bob looked thoughtful. "Doing okay," he replied finally, but Kane could tell something wasn't right.

"Not many people out there," he said. It was almost 8:00 p.m. and while Lucy had predicted twice the number of people from the previous night, there were actually half. Maybe it was opposite day, as kids say.

"No. Not too many. They had some trouble in town today."

"What sort of trouble?"

"Little boy was kidnapped…"

Kane's blood ran cold. "You serious?" he asked Bob.

"As a heart attack. Word is that it was some big son-of-a-bitch climbed in through the window and grabbed Dave and Laurie Wilson's boy, Colby."

"Somebody saw him?"

"Nope. Nobody saw him," Bob replied.

"How do they know he was big?" Kane inquired.

"Well, see, they got a partial boot print. Estimating size thirteen to fifteen shoes," Bob told him.

He saw Bob's eyes shift down to his boots. "Eleven and a half, Bob."

"Oh, right, I didn't mean to…"

"It's okay. New guy in town. I understand … I'd look at my boots, too."

"Right…"

Bob walked off to do whatever bar owners do, and Kane gently removed Honey from her velvet-lined home. He started plucking strings and adjusting the tuning pegs. *Honey burst*, he thought. The color was an off gold, with an orange aura in places, subtly done, harmonizing perfectly. Beneath the color, there was a hint of wood.

There weren't many things in this life that were completely and disarmingly satisfying, but he had to admit, this damned guitar topped the list.

"Psst!"

Lucy smiled from down the hall, wiggling her fingers at him. Her smile was just a little bit crooked, but he thought it only made her look better. Imperfections could accentuate. He wiggled his fingers in return and she went off to sling drinks.

It was time for him to do something that he just might have been born to do—take the stage, armed with his guitar and gumption.

Two handfuls of people greeted him from the bar. A few looked happy to see him, which he appreciated. Who didn't want to be wanted? Despite that, the atmosphere was certainly more reserved than the previous night.

In sync with the mood, he started with Alan Jackson's "Living on Love," then moved into Glen Campbell's "Galveston." Mellow soft rock, pop, and country songs were what was for dinner tonight. Some Foreigner, Styx … nothing too sad and nothing too upbeat. In the middle—even keel.

Gradually a few of the tables filled as folks trickled in.

As he worked through the chords for "Hotel California," two guys came in and grabbed a table in the rear of the room. They were decked out in the same black shirts and jeans they were wearing at the Burro earlier that day, at least as far as he could tell. The pouty bad guy from *Road House* flashed through Kane's mind, and he smiled while he was singing.

Kane had always had a mind for details. Things got analyzed and broken down. All the little tidbits and morsels were compartmentalized and stored in the recesses of his brain. He sorted and recalled things quicker than most people.

The guys in his unit had nicknamed him Data, like the guy from Star Trek, and he was frequently their Johnny-on-the-Spot in determining how much heat a situation would bring. Information went in, and a prognosis came out.

So damn reliable. That was what they thought about him. Like a metal detector for danger. Never failed, they said. Their lucky rabbit's foot.

Man, were they wrong.

The pain burned through him on stage for a minute at the thought of that moment. Bile momentarily rose in his throat. That critical moment in time when he'd let them all down was the worst of his life.

While he played, the guys in black watched him. And he watched them. They pretended to be in conversation, and he pretended to be into the music.

As one of them turned, he noticed the odd angle of the man's shirt. It jutted out, like there was something extra tucked into the back of his pants. The irregular outline made him think Pouty was packing a piece at the small of his back. Purely a guess, but the bend of the cloth made him think it was bigger than most concealed gun owners would tote. A full-sized pistol, maybe.

This was Texas, and even though carrying a firearm in an establishment that served alcohol was illegal, some folks did it anyway. Could be the Texan ideology on gun rights, Kane considered. Maybe even forgetfulness. Probably happened all the time and came to nothing, and tonight might be no different. People drove five over the speed limit all the time and nothing happened.

Except … something felt strange. Off. Not quite right.

"Back in about fifteen," he said into the microphone. He cued up a radio station through the sound system and left the stage.

It was nearly 11:00 p.m., and people were straggling through the door in ones and twos after nearly an hour of stagnation. The newer patrons seemed tired and distracted, and Kane wondered if that boded well for the night.

"Wanna burn one, Kane?"

It was a young guy named Dan who worked as a barback at Bob's Saloon. His dirty-blonde hair was pushed back with gel, and his teeth were the kind of clean and white that people paid money to get. A pretty boy. Girls probably loved him, and he figured Dan knew it.

"Sure, Dan. I need some fresh air."

Dan led the way through the small kitchen and out the side entrance where he propped the door open with a brick. "Locks if it shuts," he explained, digging into his pocket and pulling out Marlboro Lights.

He held the pack out to Kane, who just shook his head.

A single bulb cast pale off-white light in a ten-foot radius from the door. Shadows surrounded them … patches of darkness pressed against an empty keg, some boxes, and stacks of crates. The trash dumpster was steeped in gloom thirty or forty feet out. A spot on top seemed darker than the rest. As Kane's eyes adjusted, he could see it was just the opening.

"You really can play," Dan told him. Admiration was written all over his face, little brother enamored with big bro for winning the hometown game. "Takin' it kind of easy tonight, huh?"

"Just seemed like the right thing to do," Kane replied.

"Yeah. Holy shit, I can't believe someone kidnapped Dave Wilson's kid."

"Know much about it?"

"No, but the people who just came in, they were talking about it. They were helping the sheriff search the area…"

"They find anything?" Kane interrupted.

"No, they didn't find anything. Nobody saw anything. Which is really fucking weird because everybody sees everything in this little podunk town."

Kane nodded. Small-town life.

He could only see the last couple of vehicles in the parking lot from where they stood. Kane wandered out from the doorway, so he could get a peek at his truck—a long-time habit—while Dan worked on perfecting a couple of smoke rings. He cracked his knuckles as he walked. They stiffened up on him sometimes when he took a break from playing.

The parking lot, unsurprisingly, was a sea of trucks. Not one single car. He found his own F150 in the middle of the lot, in the back. Everything looked good, and he turned to leave, when something else caught his eye, and synapses started firing like the Fourth of July inside his head.

A black Tahoe was parked at the other end of the building.

"What's the matter?" Dan asked when he saw the look on Kane's face. The glare of the light reflected and refracted off the smoke, leaving a semi-transparent shroud around him.

"Do you know who those two guys in the black shirts are?"

"The guys close to the door?" Dan asked.

"Yeah."

"No. They aren't from Marathon, I know that much," he said

"Alpine?"

Dan laughed. "Alpine's a bit bigger. I know some of the kids over there and people my parents know, but not everybody. They could be from there or maybe work at one of the ranches." He knocked the cherry off his cigarette, tossing it in a large coffee can on the ground that was half full of them, then followed Kane as he went back inside.

Dan peeled off to the bar, but Kane took the back hallway around to Bob's office. He was inside rifling through papers on his desk, but looked up when Kane popped inside.

"Everything okay?"

"Well," Kane started, "I don't know. Probably nothing." He thought about dropping it, but then went ahead and asked Bob about the two guys.

"In the back?"

"Right."

"No, I don't," he said. "I looked at their feet though, and they weren't big enough to be the guy who took the kid."

"Hmm, that's not why I was asking," Kane said with a squint of the eyes, thinking. "Of course, that doesn't mean they didn't have anything to do with it. Two new guys in town at the same time a kid disappears."

"Three new guys in town," Bob corrected him.

Kane just looked at him.

"But I see your point," Bob added.

"Maybe it's a coincidence. I don't know. The reason I was asking was because I think one of those guys has a pistol in the back of his pants. And I can't be sure, but they might have been following me when I was outside for a run this morning."

Bob thought it over, and then nodded. While Kane watched, he unlocked his desk drawer and pulled out a .38 snubby, stood, and tucked it into his pants.

"Let's check it out," he said.

They walked casually back into the bar. Kane wished he had his own gun with him, but it was out in the truck. One day, being a law-abiding citizen was going to screw him. Hopefully not today.

A couple of folks glanced up at Bob and Kane when they came out, and then went back to their conversations. Through the JBL speaker system, Carrie Underwood advised her female listeners to 'get to getting on' their goodbye shoes. Pouty and his buddy were nowhere to be seen, so Kane scooted around people and tables toward the entrance.

When he looked outside, however, they were nowhere to be found. And the Tahoe was gone.

CHAPTER 9

Deputy Slidell was worn out when he fell into the Bronco's passenger seat, and his mind wandered.

Most days, he was up by 5:30 a.m., working out in his garage-turned-gym. Tom preferred lighter weights and higher repetitions, which suited his slim build.

Free weights and a cheap bench occupied one corner. The weights were very old school, of the plastic-coated-concrete variety, and were already well-used by the time he'd gotten them off a graduating senior when he was just a sixth grader.

There were machine weights he'd purchased at the Academy Sports store in Midland on the left side of the garage. He preferred working with traditional weights— didn't everyone?—but the machine was convenient, and with a 250-pound stack, he could push himself without a spotter.

Finally, in the center of his little concrete man area ... the heavy bag.

If the weights were a hobby, or a means of fitness, then the sixty-five-pound punching bag was his passion.

For years, he'd wanted one. Talked about it randomly since before he and Steph got married. Then, one year, he came home on his birthday, and there it was, hanging in his garage.

A gift from Steph.

She enjoyed keeping her car in the garage, but gave that up so he could have that punching bag he always talked about. Plus, he got a man cave out of the deal. A win-win situation. The following year, he added a carport to make up for it.

After thirty or forty minutes of weights, Tom would stretch out, lie down on his mat and do crunches, then bicycles and flutter kicks. AC/DC provided the mood music, pulsing through his little Bluetooth speaker at half-volume so as not to wake Steph.

After the old abs were burning, he'd put on his wraps and gloves and move to the bag. He varied the exercises, varied lower and upper body or push and pull muscles, but always finished on the bag. Cake first, icing last. Eggs first, bacon last. He'd done that his entire life: saved the best for last.

When Steph surprised him with the bag that first time, he'd been so excited that he didn't even change into workout gear, just started beating on it in his uniform. Fifteen minutes later, out of breath and nursing bloody knuckles and a sprained wrist, he realized just how out of shape he was, and that he had a lot to learn about boxing.

Tom never told anyone, but he signed up for some boxing lessons in Midland, to get the basics down. This old guy they called Buster taught him the ropes. Had to be in his sixties, snow-white afro atop a lanky frame, but he was still tight and muscular, and he had these long arms that gave him incredible reach.

Buster taught him how to make a fist, how to hit, and how to wrap his hands.

"Gotta protect those hands, baby," he'd told him. "Protect those wrists. Protect the fingers from breaking.

Tighten things up so that when you make a fist, it's like everything is connected. Like a hammer."

"A hammer?" he'd echoed dumbly.

"You got it, Johnny Law Hammer!" Buster laughed at his own joke, which got Tom laughing, and he didn't stop until his stomach was aching. Johnny Law Hammer. After that, they became good friends. Buster and Johnny Law Hammer.

The day had been status quo. Nearly eighteen hours earlier he'd wrapped his wrists just like Buster taught him and commenced to whaling on the bag for fifteen two-minute sessions. He'd finished by 7:00 a.m. ... then sat down to coffee and a light breakfast with Stephanie.

"Tom..."

They enjoyed having breakfast together. It gave him the opportunity to observe the little things about her. The graceful line of her neck. How she pushed the hair behind her ear—but only her left ear—never the right. Always thought about asking her why, but he was afraid she'd stop doing it.

"Tom."

His eyes opened. He'd dozed off. Dave Wilson's house was right in front of him, every light on, people congregated in a living room that should be dark and peaceful at this time of night. A toddler's toys lay sadly here and there. Inside, a father was filled with confusion, anger, and sadness. The weight of it settled on him again like a solid punch to the guts.

The sheriff was in the driver's seat. He had what some might call a thousand-yard stare. A look filled with unwanted knowledge—things better left unlearned.

*****

Bigsby watched the house. Little bugs danced erratically around the porch light in patterns of an indiscernible intent. Pat, his wife, Dave, and Laurie were all inside. The entire Wilson family minus little Colby. He'd seen guys lose limbs and people die, but somehow none of it hit him as hard as this. Just the other day, he'd contemplated retiring when they found that dead couple down at Big Bend, and it crossed his mind again now.

Maggie and Don Johnson, he remembered. That was the name of the couple attacked by the snakes. They'd boxed up and mailed their personal items to the next of kin only this morning, and when they got back from the post office, he realized they'd forgotten the GPS. It was sitting smack-dab in the middle of his desk. He stopped and shook his head when he saw it.

Pat was suddenly framed by the front door. He motioned at them, not quite a wave, and shut the door. Bigsby doubted there'd be any sleep to be had in the Wilson home that night.

"Day'll start early tomorrow," he said.

It wasn't a question or command—just something to say. They usually took turns covering standby on Saturdays, but there was no question they would both be going to work. It was part of the fabric of the men they were and what drew them to that work in the first place.

"Did they get a good mold of that tire track?" Tom asked.

"Yeah. Probably tell us it was a truck," Bigsby replied.

Tom grunted. That would narrow it down to pretty much everybody in the entire southern half of Texas.

"No witnesses. Guess all we've got is a boot print," Tom said.

"Maybe."

Tom tilted his head, like an inquisitive dog.

"Might get a fingerprint," Bigsby said. "Didn't exactly look like professional work today."

Tom looked doubtful. It was how Bigsby felt, but he was hoping for the best. It was never possible to know what was going to happen in this business.

"Want me to take you to the house?"

"Nah. The shop is fine. I'll pick up my truck and drive it home."

The sheriff nodded. It wasn't something he needed to ask—he knew the answer—like before, it was just something to say.

CHAPTER 10

Unhurried footsteps echoed across the chamber.

Three-foot squares of stone comprised the floor—ancient, 250-pound slabs—married to one another for three hundred years or more. The stones were smooth like the pebbles at the bottom of a river, and an ominous gray, like thunderstorm clouds about to rupture.

That chamber floor had seen sunlight only once in those centuries. Arson. A fire meant to destroy everything. But the flames were squelched. And the darker element prevailed.

Giant wooden beams supported the ceiling at nine-foot intervals, giving it a ribbed appearance, like an upside down and underground Noah's Ark. Despite their age, they showed no sign of weakening. On the contrary, they exuded strength and permanence.

There was a fairy-tale quality to the structure, a rugged beauty and charm like that of a king's great hall. It could have been a place of merriment, dancing, and jovial conversation—the location of celebrations and marriages—if it were anywhere else.

The walls were made up of the same stones as the floor except in the vertical. Nothing adorned them ... no paintings, no tapestries, and no oversized stuffed game animals. They were smooth and gleamed as if they'd been polished.

Centered between entrances, away from the wall, was that which eventually drew the attention of all that entered—an altar. Cold and hard, it blended with the motif of unwelcoming lifelessness. A lone monolith on an arctic glacier.

A person had to look at it; they were compelled to, which the room's sole occupant did upon reaching the middle of the room. It was almost as if electricity connected them. Then, with a flash of teeth and eyes and an audible crackle, the walking continued and the connection dimmed.

The footsteps stopped, and then the echo of the footsteps faded as the visitor reached the other side of the room. A gloved hand rapped three times on the enormous oaken door that barred the way, and it swung open in response.

The sound of a child crying immediately shattered the silence.

The clack-clack-clack of the footsteps resumed, and the visitor opened the door to one of the three smaller rooms inside. The volume of the child's crying intensified—cutting—slashing like a scythe.

"Shhh…" the figure commanded. Three cages were lined up on the opposite side of the room. Chicken wire stapled to wooden slats. Crude, makeshift homes. There was movement from only one of them, the cage on the far right, where a child lay swaddled in old patchwork blankets. Angry red splotches dotted the pale skin.

"No one to keep you company?"

The voice resonated like a harsh wind through mountain passes, unyielding, and carrying with it some deeper wisdom of the unimaginable. A harsh knowledge of time and places from the past, and those to come.

The toddler's crying waned, replaced by small spasms of upset. "Shhh..." it said again. A thumb went to the mouth, the spasms ended abruptly, and only the slurpy, rhythmic sucking remained.

It was happening. Light flickered across a face that seemed to morph and change repeatedly, man to woman, old to young, good, and then evil. An unpleasant smile spread across that face, and for a moment, the canine teeth were exceedingly long and sharp. The kid began to whimper and soiled himself.

"Soon," it promised. A different voice this time. Deeper. Gravelly and dangerous, like the steep descent into a cave straight to hell.

CHAPTER 11

Bird woke up Saturday in his yard.

It wasn't the first time. Three or four times each year he got too drunk to open the door of the trailer. Or he fell off the steps and blacked out. Sometimes, he just tumbled off his chair or the picnic table ... no memory of how or why.

This was, however, the first time he'd woken up with his pecker pulled out. "Some Texas Anaconda crawlin' around out here," he said out loud, and then snorted with laughter. There was a slick spot on his jeans about the size of a half-dollar coin, and he laughed some more.

"Looks like I shot myself!"

He realized from the thick feeling in his head that he was still a little drunk. Which was fine—he didn't mind at all. Bird rolled over on his back and was met with one of the clearest and bluest skies in his memory. Thinking ceased behind the Neanderthal-like bulging forehead, and he almost drifted off again ... until *she* flashed through his mind.

Red.

Slowly, the details of the previous day came back to him, and snippets of that vivid dream, the one that had him discharging his weapon onto the leg of his pants. Oh, Red...

He had done exactly what she asked. It wasn't any trouble. Not really. At first, he was concerned by what she had asked him to do that night she appeared to him by the backside of his trailer (in his dream?), but she convinced him she would make it worth his efforts.

Then he'd gone to work Friday afternoon, and the whole Ms. Parker thing happened. That had thrown him for a loop. Big time. Seeing her was like seeing a ghost or something, and it had him thinking about life in ways that had been absent for as long as he could remember, if they'd ever existed at all. There was no time in Bird's memory when he'd cared about anyone except the guy in the mirror. That wasn't an idea he articulated to himself—it was simply how it was—but something changed Friday with old lady Parker.

When he told her he owned that gas station there was this weird light in her eyes that was completely new to him. He was normally on the receiving end of suspicion. Fear. Disbelief. He was intimate with reactions guided by those feelings in other people who mostly approached him about missing property, or allegedly siphoned gas, or a slashed tire or two. His entire life, he'd been the object of bad feelings from teachers, the police, and even passersby.

Ms. Parker's look was foreign. She had been ... *proud* of him. The closest he'd ever come to receiving a look like that, before that moment, was when Zeke had watched the video he had taken of him banging the blonde.

Bird's dad looked just like the guy in the old Amityville horror movie, and in his own way, with that crazy light and grizzly satisfaction in his wild eyes, he had been proud of Bird. For about thirty seconds, anyway.

It didn't cross Bird's mind that he hadn't done anything to deserve Ms. Parker's affection.

But, strangely enough, having felt that warm glow of positivity, even just for a few seconds, was like sunlight falling upon a flower, leaving the bloom eager to receive more of that life-giving energy. There was the subconscious realization that life could be better.

Something new had awakened inside of Bird.

It was nothing so dramatic as to completely reverse a lifetime of lying, cheating, bullying, stealing, and so on, in one shift at the gas station. He was still Bird. There was beer to drink and women to ogle; he didn't think twice about counting back the wrong change to tourists and pocketing extra dollars throughout the day.

But, the cogs were turning. He didn't have the words or the objectivity to fully describe the change, but in his own way, he suspected he hadn't made the best decisions. Maybe for the first time ever, he considered the legitimacy of other people, their decisions, and their right to live life in a certain way.

He'd never been in a more thoughtful and ponderous mood. After he closed up the gas station Friday evening, he went home and pounded some beers at the picnic table in his yard. When the old thing almost collapsed under his weight, he got out a hammer, some nails, and some scrap wood and reinforced it in a couple of spots. His mood was legendarily fine, at least for him.

Bird might even have been whistling, though nobody could prove it. The tree falling in the forest without anyone around didn't make a sound, so they said.

Every time he'd finish a beer, he would huck the can across the yard as far as he could. Then he'd reload his Smith & Wesson 500 and unload on it. His aim improved through beer seven, then it began to taper off pretty rapidly, but he was having a good time just feeling the massive power in each shot.

The Beach Boys had once talked about good vibrations, and Bird was feeling good, good, good .... good vibrations. He was in rare form, indeed. Felt cleaner—pure of heart, relatively speaking—ready to join the other knights at the semi-round table.

Something like that.

Then Red came along, except this time ... he hadn't been dreaming. *Or had he?*

He didn't think so. She was suddenly there next to him—scared the shit out of him—and she'd leaned over and grabbed his pistol by the barrel. He waited for a reaction to the hot steel—it was surely burning the shit out of her hand—but she didn't so much as bat an eyelid. She set the weapon to the side and smiled at him. He'd say the smile was wicked, but that didn't do it justice ... evil was a better word.

"You're not finished," she said.

The majority of his internal struggles before that moment revolved around whether he should buy Natural Light or Pabst. Red's voice was silky, like satin sheets—he almost felt hypnotized.

He shook his head to fight the spell she was putting him under.

That's it, Bird thought, watching Red, who was now sitting on the tabletop. *I'm done with her. I don't care how hot she is; I'm not doin' shit else she says.*

She started laughing. It confused the hell out of him, and he found himself angry. Who did she think she was?

Did she have any idea what he could do to her? He could crush her windpipe with one hand…

And, yet, she started laughing even harder, and he found it difficult to master the fear that was determined to replace his short-lived confidence. It was still morning, but he realized he was sweating something fierce. Red, on the other hand, may as well have been in the air conditioning. That beautiful skin was as dry as the dirt in his yard.

"You're not done with me, Birdie Boy. And … you're *going* to do all the 'shit else' that I fucking say you will."

Hearing her repeat his thoughts back to him turned his blood cold. The saliva in his mouth vanished, but his sweating doubled, and it drained from his unkempt, nappy hair down to his unkempt, nappy beard.

"But I'm going to give you a gift, Birdie. Something to help keep you motivated and doing what I need you to do."

After that, she'd grabbed the barrel of his *other* pistol and done some serious damage. The old anaconda hadn't been worked that hard since he visited the brothels across the border a few years earlier, and maybe not even then. *Old Red had herself a* magic *tongue,* he thought.

Magic.

Bird was pretty sure she'd read his mind. *Read his fucking mind!* Either that, or he was going batshit crazy. He grunted … it was possible. An argument could be made that the entire Taylor line was a little on the crazy side.

Of course, he'd also killed more than a rack of beer, but he didn't think it was an alcohol-fueled burst of imagination. The only conclusion he came to was that she knew magic. Maybe she was a witch or something.

A white bird soared by, high above. For several seconds it moved in a straight line toward Marathon. Then, it began to yaw to the left, a heading change that would take it to *The Bends*. There was something comforting about the bird making its way from one horizon to another.

With a sigh, he put away one pistol, grabbed the other from the table, and went inside for a shower. The water that left his body was dark, but he showered so infrequently that it wasn't something that fazed him. The water was always dark.

Something had changed inside of Bird. Maybe it was nothing. Just a bump in a road that led nowhere, soon forgotten.

Or maybe it was more than that. Even a break in the mightiest of dams starts with the smallest crack. Maybe, just maybe, Ms. Parker had been that crack.

Bird whistled his way through a hot shower, and then made his way down to the gas station for the Saturday afternoon shift.

CHAPTER 12

"Hey, you slept in today."

Lucy had been watching Kane tiptoe through the living room, on his way to the shower.

He laughed. "I guess I did … it's almost ten. Day is already half gone! Which means you're up early." Lucy smiled sleepily at him. She was propped up on an elbow, head framed by a serious case of bedhead. Without makeup, without any cosmetic enhancements to the hair, the face, the nails, the eyes, the lips … he always thought that was when a woman was truly her most beautiful. He leaned over and kissed her on the neck.

"Pee-yew!" she cried out and wrinkled her nose. He laughed. "Come see me again after you shower."

"Yes, ma'am," he told her. "By the way, why do they call this place Marathon if I'm the only guy ever running out there?"

"It's too hot for running," she said, but her head was buried under the pillow and the words were muffled.

When he got out of the shower, Lucy's breathing was steady and loud, but not quite snoring. *Not that she would snore in anything but a feminine way,* he thought with a quiet chuckle. He laid down next to her on the sofa bed and started reading a book on his iPod. In the Army, he always had a hundred books loaded on his Kindle app that he wanted to read, but he didn't have the time. One of the great things about his nomadic life, aside from making the old six-string sing to people, was that he had more time to read.

Books were exercise for the mind. P90X for the brains.

He cracked open the virtual pages of *Salem's Lot*, picking up where he'd last left old Ben Mears. Just as Father Callahan was on the verge of drinking Barlow's blood, Kane Montgomery entered his own netherworld and drifted to sleep.

*****

Kane was walking fast, almost jogging.

Not in his Asics, and not for exercise.

At first glance, it was as if he were in an English lord's manor—a taxidermist's wet dream. The heads of animals adorned the walls, along with birds in flight, and the largest racks of antlers a person could imagine.

Size does matter, *he thought, but he didn't linger or stop to check them out.*

He moved quickly through connecting hallways. There was even an alcove with a warrior's garments on display, but it wasn't English. To his untrained eye, he thought it might be Native American, which seemed out of place.

He was looking for something. Or someone. He wasn't sure.

That, and he thought that he was being chased, though he wasn't sure who was doing the chasing. Or why.

He came to a room with a large fireplace and scanned the walls. Where next? A fire crackled in the hearth, but when he went closer, he didn't feel any heat. It was as if it weren't real, but a life-size screen saver you'd see on a computer.

The fireplace poker looked strangely out of place, so he grabbed it to get a better look. Instead of pulling free, it was connected to the floor. Strange. He pushed and pulled, and finally, it slid several inches. A lever of some sort.

A panel of the wall next to the fireplace swung inward.

With only the slightest hesitation, he entered, and the door closed behind him. Instead of blackness, the entry was lit by ... he couldn't fathom it, but there were actual torches in the wall. In front of him, stone stairs spiraled down out of sight. There was a rhythmic thumping from below accompanied by another sound...

Am I trapped in an episode of Scooby Doo? he wondered. If it wasn't for those pesky kids...

He started walking down, slowly, because ... well, what else was there to do?

It dawned on him that he was hearing the beat of a drum, and chanting. He cocked his head and listened, and the hair on his arms and neck went to attention.

Where was he? And just what the hell was going on?

*****

Kane awoke with a start.

He was confused about where he was, but that was nothing new. His combat tours had forever changed him, as cliché as that might seem to an outsider. Sometimes, he woke up thinking he was in the backseat of a hummer, moving through streets littered with people who wanted to kill him. Or that he was catching a nap at a raid site. As a soldier, there were times he didn't sleep for two days, and caught naps anywhere he could.

It wasn't long before his eyes adjusted to the dim room.

There was the familiar outline of heavy curtains with that rectangular vignette of sunlight bordering them. Refrigerator sounds punctuated the silence across the room, and there was the soft exchange of oxygen for carbon dioxide from the beautiful woman on the mattress next to him.

Feeling around, he found his iPod and checked the time—almost noon.

"Lucy," he said softly, but she didn't respond. He moved the blanket aside, intending to slide in closer to her. Instead he found himself transfixed, like walking into one of those bear traps where the sharp teeth snap shut and clamp down on the legs.

Lucy was wearing pink-and-blue lace underwear that arched over each side of her rear, not really covering the cheeks, but just sort of skirting around them and dipping down in a "V" in the middle. It was too sexy for words, and Kane found himself overcome by baser instincts—the inner caveman—and he wakened her with rough urgency.

An hour or so later, they jumped in her Toyota Tacoma.

"Ready for the grand tour?" she asked.

"Heck yeah. I am … *excited*. This is pretty much the moment I was hoping for my whole life, only I didn't know what it was, but I do now, because *this* is *it!*"

She slapped his leg, "That's what I'm talking about. Enthusiasm."

"Oh, yeah."

"Smartass," she added under her breath, and they laughed.

Lucy drove around Marathon, pointing out various historical landmarks, and he found himself impressed with the local history and lore. He was so eager to leave his own hometown in the middle-of-nowhere Nebraska that he never bothered to learn anything about the place, at least not beyond what his teachers paraded out for everyone in school. World's biggest ball of yarn sort of information. And the majority of that was long forgotten.

"That windmill was Marathon's first jail," she said, pointing at the landmark on First Street. "They'd chain people to the leg of it."

"Really?"

"Yep. Later on, they built a real jail with jail cells donated from Alpine."

"Hmm. That's cool."

At his insistence, they got out and took a closer look at the Gage Hotel. In the lobby, the receptionist, Debbie, gave him the rundown of their amenities: spa, swimming pool, full service bar, and twenty-seven acres of garden.

"We have everything you could want, hun! And our concierge over there can arrange anything you need in the local area." Flawless blue eyes, broad white smile, and an oversized bosom gave Kane the impression that she might have been a former beauty queen of some type. Or a sorority girl.

"Sweet tea?"

"I thought you'd never ask, Debbie," he replied, and she winked at him.

Lucy smiled politely at Debbie, but when she turned her back to pour the tea, Lucy shot warning daggers his way, and he grinned mischievously.

They drank sweet tea and talked about the weather. Kane guessed this was as everyday as it got in Marathon, easygoing and friendly.

"Well, we sure appreciate your hospitality, Debbie." he told the receptionist as they were leaving, and Lucy discreetly pinched his arm.

Lucy and Kane made a detour and strolled through the Gage Hotel gardens on their way out. He realized that he was feeling enchanted by his Marathon experience. There was a great deal of charm to be found in the town and its people.

"Douglas MacArthur was here in 1911 during the Mexican Revolution to establish a military command post to guard from raids."

"*The* Douglas MacArthur?" he asked

She looked at him and smiled. "I don't know."

"The five-star general and medal-of-honor winning Douglas MacArthur?"

"Probably? They make a big deal out of it here in town, so I'll say *yes*. Sure. That's the one. *Definitely*."

"Huh." He was impressed. "That's kind of cool, I guess. Little old Marathon was a regular hotbed of activity."

"Indeed. But they replaced him."

"With who?"

"George Patton."

Kane groaned loudly. "Are you serious?" He opened his mouth, and then shook his head. "Oh, never mind."

Lucy laughed. "Kane, I'm fucking with you. I know who MacArthur and Patton are."

He groaned again and nodded. "Well played, Luscious Lucy."

"Thanks!" she chirped.

When they got back to her truck, they took off down the road and she pointed out Marathon's lone pizza joint. "Big Bend Pizza. I think they came up with that name all on their own."

Kane laughed.

"Looks like we're going to have to get gas."

They were going east on 90. A few minutes outside of town, she pulled over at a gas station and parked at the farthest pump.

"I'll get it," Kane said and jumped out. He popped the nozzle into the truck and gripped the trigger a few times. "Come on," he pleaded, and silently cursed the sluggish flow.

While he berated the pump, he noticed a huge dude standing at the door of the station. Kane wasn't a shrimp at 6'1", but this guy had him by five or six inches and a good fifty pounds.

Okay. Maybe not a *good* fifty pounds.

This guy looked strong, but in a rough, untrained way. Some guys said you never can tell from appearances whether someone is better than you, but Kane disagreed. He could usually tell; and, he figured he could take this guy.

From behind his Oakleys, he analyzed people and situations for threats. Perhaps it was some strain of PTSD from the service. Or maybe it was why he was always such a good soldier.

Almost always a good soldier.

Or, I'm just paranoid, he thought, but if that was true, perhaps a little paranoia was a good thing.

The automatic shutoff finally clicked, and he put the nozzle back in its metal slot. *Pump number four,* he noted to himself.

"Howdy," he said when he walked up to the big guy. "Got twenty-two bucks on number four over there."

Kane handed over two twenties. He waited while the guy stepped inside and rang him up on the register. When he came back out with change, the big guy fired a wad of chewing tobacco out of the corner of his mouth, off to the side, and Kane noticed there were dozens of tobacco juice stains all over the place.

He dropped a stack of bills in Kane's outstretched hand.

Kane counted it out quickly in his head. Seventeen dollars. He started to leave, but then turned back.

"Hey, looks like this is a buck short," he said.

They stood there for a couple of seconds, looking at each other, and Kane wondered if something might happen. His pulse quickened slightly and he counteracted it by slowing his breathing and allowing his body to go loose. The sickly-sweet odor of chewing tobacco filled the space between the two men.

Then the guy grinned somewhat savagely at Kane, leaned back in the store, and handed over another dollar.

"My mistake," he grunted out. Kane doubted the sincerity of the apology, if it could be called that, but he just nodded.

"Right." He was about to turn, when he noticed something that made him stop a beat. Huge feet. Massive boots spilled out from beneath worn jeans. Kane recalled what Bob said about the boot print found at the scene of the kidnapping, and he wondered how many guys were wandering through this area with feet that big.

Couldn't be that many, could it?

"Thanks," he said finally and walked away.

Back in the truck, he said, "That guy looks just like the freaking Undertaker."

Lucy laughed, threw the truck into drive, and got them back out onto 90 heading west. "Good call. That's Bird ... he totally looks like The Undertaker."

Kane could see in the side-view mirror that Bird was just standing there, watching them leave. He thought about those feet again, and considered finding the sheriff and mentioning it, but then he just shook his head. What were the odds he had just stumbled on the kidnapper? This wasn't a television show, and life was never that obvious. Besides, he was sure that Johnny Law didn't need any help doing his job.

After he mentally climbed out of the well where those ideas lurked, he turned to Lucy...

"So you know The Undertaker, but not *I Dream of Jeannie*?"

CHAPTER 13
Saturday

In the last forty-eight hours, they'd made zero headway in the search for Colby Wilson or his abductor.

The Amber alert had gone out immediately, and hundreds of officers in the southern half of Texas were looking for the boy, but outside of a few false-positives on sightings in nearby towns, they hadn't gotten anything. Nada. Zilch.

They questioned every person within a five-block radius of the Wilson's home, but nobody saw or heard anything. The bustling metropolis of Marathon, Texas, seemed to be completely absent of witnesses.

All the fingerprints in Colby's room matched family members—no extras—which didn't surprise Bigsby. He'd hoped for a break, but as his daddy had said, hope in one hand and shit in the other and see which fills up first. No luck.

While parents and family members were always suspects in these situations, they had airtight alibis that had cleared them. Not to mention, unlike the reality-crime shows on TV, Bigsby had the advantage of knowing everyone personally. You don't know how small five hundred people is until you've lived there among them for five or six decades.

All they really had was the partial boot print.

A shoe sized thirteen to fifteen had come down on the floor beneath the window. Bigsby wasn't sure what to make of that. It meant that an awfully big son-of-a-bitch hauled himself up and through that window. Or a small person, with clown-sized feet.

Bigsby leaned back at his desk, closed his eyes, and stroked his mustache, deep in concentration.

He supposed that the boot print could have been faked. Either someone intentionally wore large boots, or they carried along an extra, oversized boot, and left a fake print. While he couldn't rule it out, it seemed unlikely. What would be the criminal's objective—to serve as a decoy, or to divert suspicion toward someone in particular?

There had been no other boot prints at the scene. No sandal prints. No penny loafer prints. Not outside the window. Not where they suspected the perpetrator's vehicle had been parked. Nothing. Nowhere.

Mentally, he started tallying off some names of big guys in the area: Dean Smith, Zachariah Dillon, and Bird Taylor. Almost everyone he thought about was an ex-Marathon High School football player. They were a small school with mostly average-sized kids, but the boys that played ball were usually the biggest the town had to offer.

Dean was older and lived with his wife. Both in their sixties. Hard to pin down a motive for him.

Zachariah had probably been the best football player they'd had in the last thirty years. He'd gone off to Lubbock on a full scholarship and played at Texas Tech. People speculated at the time about whether he would go pro. He didn't, though, and he eventually moved back and took over his daddy's ranch. There was a mean streak in Zach, and he'd heard gossip that the ranch wasn't doing too well. Still, he couldn't see it. Mean and broke didn't make a criminal—it just made for an asshole.

Then there was old Bird. Bird Taylor was like all the Marathon Taylors, and generally amounted to two things: jack and shit; however, Bigsby couldn't think of any motive there, either. Bird had inherited the gas station and some money from his old man, and despite it being of questionable origin, there was no evidence of anything illegal. Since then, Bird Taylor had kept his nose clean, and dropped the petty crimes, and all the little misdemeanors.

Well, at least as far as Bigsby knew, anyway.

There were some other blue-collar townies, maybe, but nobody he considered seriously. Maybe some ranch hands he didn't know about, too.

You didn't know what you didn't know.

Then, there was the most likely scenario—that the kidnapper wasn't local. Could be anybody. It wouldn't be difficult at all to slide right across the Rio Grande through Big Bend Park. Escape into Mexico.

He sighed and called out, "Tom?"

"Yeah, Sheriff?"

"Let's go out for a while. Talk to anyone around here that might have big feet." It made his blood boil that there was a child missing in his town. He needed to get out and *do* something.

Deputy Slidell poked his head in the doorway. "We already talked to a lot of people," he said.

"Well, we'll talk to them again," Bigsby replied.

*****

Bigsby and Slidell canvased the area, ranches first, followed by Marathon proper from west to east, asking questions.

And looking at feet.

Texas ranch hands trend toward the nomadic due to the seasonal nature of the work, however, there was almost always one full-timer who was steady through the year—a foreman—the owner's right-hand man. The guy behind the guy. Bigsby knew most of the year-round guys. They managed men during the busy times and made repairs or did other projects during the down season. Not a single one had any missing men. All had been present and accounted for Thursday.

Or so they claimed.

They skipped the obvious people: the elderly, kids, and the infirm. Everyone else was fair game. Word spreads faster than celebrity tweets in a small town, and Colby's last name may as well have been Kardashian, because everyone knew all the details already. Even the partial boot print was common knowledge, and Bigsby knew it had only taken a few guys from the search party running their mouths to spouses and friends before all 487 residents of Marathon were informed. He couldn't have spread news any faster if he tried.

Whether that was good or bad ... he didn't know.

"Let's go on out and see Bird," he told Tom.

Tom nodded behind his knock-off Ray-Bans. They were of the variety worn by the cast in *Top Gun*; Deputy Slidell looked more like Goose than Maverick, though.

He'd trimmed his mustache that morning, so it didn't resemble the sheriff's near-walrus as much.

"You ever think about Zeke Taylor?" Tom asked.

Bigsby tossed that around. He swished it around like wine, checking for impurities, and tasted it. "Yeah," he replied. "I was thinking about him earlier."

Tom looked sideways at Bigsby, waiting.

"I guess ... I never felt right about Zeke." He shook his head. "We couldn't find any evidence to the contrary, but I don't think Zeke Taylor would have killed himself. He was one crazy and mean son-of-a-bitch, but he never struck me as suicidal."

"Me either. *Homicidal*, definitely, but not suicidal," Tom said.

"That's right," Bigsby said. "That's right."

They popped out past Big Bend Pizza, and entered a gradual curve in the road. A mile later, just as the town went out of sight, they came upon the Marathon gas station. The pumps threw jagged reflections from the sun at them as they pulled in and killed the engine.

Bird was perched, immobile in his regular chair, legs spread out in front of him. As they opened the Bronco's doors, he unfurled a nearly continuous jet of spit that landed on the ground beside him.

Tom glanced at the shotgun when he saw Bird watching them. There was something about the man's eyes that bothered the deputy. They were twin pools of murky blackness, lacking in some vital, human way. Peculiarly distant. Unblinking atop a bulky frame that dwarfed an oversized patio chair. Crows and ravens had more spirit. With a final glance, he left the shotgun in its rack, but he did unsnap the strap that secured his firearm in its holster as he walked around the far side of the Bronco.

"Hey, Bird." The sheriff propped a foot up on the curb a few feet away from Bird.

"Sheriff," he replied—squinted—spat.

"Hadn't seen you much lately."

Bird grunted. "Stayin' outta trouble, Sheriff."

"Yeah?"

"Uh-huh. New man. A *bid*ness man now."

Something smelled odd, like spoiled milk, and Tom glanced around, expecting to see an overflowing trashcan nearby. Maybe something rotten. But, he didn't see anything except Bird.

Bird.

He caught another whiff and realized the smell was either Bird or the tobacco with which he'd painted the ground. Probably some sour combination.

Oily hair crowned Bird's head, long all over, and glistening in a dirty way. Deputy Slidell could imagine bugs living in it, crawling around, eating bits of organic protein. Tom suspected his musing was closer to reality than not.

"Business good, then?"

"Yessir, Sheriff. Good 'nough," he replied, and itched himself through his jeans, first his crotch, then his head.

Bigsby nodded. He'd heard the rumors that Bird cheated people in different ways, but nobody ever made any official complaints. From behind his aviator shades he looked down at the boats on Bird's feet. They were definitely big enough to have left the impression on

Colby Wilson's floor. The hair at the base of his neck prickled at the thought.

Tom was off to his right with his left hand up against the front corner of the Bronco. Keeping a little distance. Wanted plenty of room to pull his weapon, Bigsby reckoned.

"I'm sure you heard about the Wilson boy," Bigsby said.

Bird grunted, "Damn shame, yessir." He nodded his head in reproach, then shot a quick blast of brown nastiness to the side.

"It sure is," Bigsby agreed.

Bird's words, though inadequate, weren't what bothered him.

As sheriff, he'd talked to Bird and Zeke Taylor dozens of times through the years. Crimes and scuffles surrounded the name Taylor in Marathon, Texas. On the surface, Bird was a changed man. He supposed that was possible. Highly unlikely, but possible.

But what was going on below the surface?

Not getting caught didn't mean Bird was suddenly honest. He was likely just hiding his transgressions more carefully. Bigsby knew that a liar sat in the chair before him, and he knew that Taylor truly did not give a shit whether Colby Wilson had been kidnapped.

"Well, we're eager to get the Wilson boy back to his folks. Where were you at on Thursday? See anything suspicious around town?"

"Oh, I was right here, boss. Yessir," Bird told him. It rolled off his tongue so quickly, somebody might think he'd rehearsed it.

"Working? Alone?"

"My boy Mikey was working, too. I's doing paperwork and such, in back, while he was on the register."

Bigsby glanced at Tom who gave him an almost imperceptible shrug of the shoulders. The alibi was perfect—or nearly so—but they'd still check it out as soon as they were on the road.

"And you didn't see anything strange?"

Bird looked thoughtful.

"You know, Sheriff, now that you mention it. Mighta saw a car come speeding out of town on Thursday. Yessir, *real* fast."

"Really," Tom piped in.

Bird gave him a bashful grin full of stained teeth. "Hey, Deputy Tom, not sure I saw you hiding o'er there."

Tom tried not to let his annoyance show, which was somewhat more difficult than he would have imagined. He knew Bird was yanking his cord. "You noticed a speeding car while you were doing paperwork in *back* of the store?"

"Mighta taken a bathroom break and come up front," he replied and sat forward. "Yessir. Car speedin' away fast. Shucks, you think that mighta been the kidnapper?"

Tom fought the urge to slap cuffs on Bird and drag him to the station. He thought it might be a lot of fun to put this guy face down on the concrete first, though. Maybe wipe that shit-eating smirk off his face.

"Make and model of that car?" Bigsby asked him.

"Hmm. Sheriff, I believe that car was blue. Maybe a Toyota or Nissan. One of them Jap-o-nese cars."

"Don't suppose you got a license plate..."

Bird actually chuckled and shook his head, and Tom moved his hand to his pistol and took a step forward. He didn't know if the son-of-a-bitch had anything to do with Colby Wilson, but his casual attitude about one of the children of Marathon going missing angered him.

"Did you just laugh? Is that funny that somebody's little boy was taken?"

Bird's face went dead, and the cold, hard marbles in his head watched Tom.

"Calm down, boss. I ain't laughing about the kid, I just don't look at license plates or nothin' is all I'm sayin'." Bird squinted at Deputy Slidell, and looked down at the hand he had placed on his sidearm.

Icy stares passed between the two, and current rippled through the air.

"All right, all right," Bigsby broke the tension. "Tom, let's go check out our other leads. Bird, you call us if you remember anything."

"'Course, Sheriff."

As they pulled away from the station, Tom said, "I don't trust him. Not for anything. Did you see that? He was grinning underneath that ignorant exterior. I could feel it."

"Yeah, I know, Tom. He's as high as anyone on the list of suspects, but we need some evidence, anything, before we roust him. Why don't you get that kid Mikey's phone number? Better yet, we'll swing by the kid's house so we can see his face when he talks to us."

"Sounds good, Sheriff."

Bigsby sighed. Bird was a real prick, but they couldn't let the macho posturing get in the way of what was really important: whether Bird knew anything about the kidnapping. Desperation and hopelessness were starting to war inside of Bigsby. They needed a break.

CHAPTER 14
Sunday

Bird felt like an artist contemplating a piece of raw material, about to create his masterpiece.

Light wasn't visible on the horizon when he pulled his dad's old truck into the Villareal driveway, snug as a button against Hector's new truck. The final few blocks had been driven with the lights out. The way he figured, Zeke's truck had been sitting behind his trailer, mostly unused, for years. It hadn't been registered in a long while ... and he doubted anyone would remember it if they saw it. If anything, they'd probably subconsciously push it from their mind, not wanting to be reminded of Zeke Taylor in any shape, form, or fashion.

The driveway was positioned in such a way that neighbors couldn't see him. The sound of crickets was the only thing that greeted Bird when he got down from the cab of his old man's truck. He reached in and hauled out a faded green, Army-style duffle bag, something his dad either "acquired" or got at the Army surplus store since he'd never served anyone or anything besides himself in his entire damn life.

With a soft click, he pressed the door closed.

Bird stood in the dark and watched the Villareal house for any sign of activity. Two minutes passed. Five minutes.

Nothing.

He gave it longer, just to be safe. *Nothing stirred, not even a mouse*, he thought and almost laughed.

Slowly, he walked to the back entry, and gently pulled at the storm door. It opened with the slightest squeak. Behind it, he found the main door locked.

He reached into his bag. A terrible smell escaped, and he sifted through the contents until he found what he wanted.

Out came two things. The first was an ordinary pencil. The other was a special little device that he'd come across years back. It had a small suction cup in the center, which he stuck to the glass pane nearest the doorknob. Gently, he squeezed the little finger pump until it had a tight seal with the door. Attached to the suction cup was a device that resembled a protractor with a blade at the end. Again, ever so gently, he rotated it around the suction cup, creating a very fine cut in the windowpane.

If their bedroom had been on the first floor, they might have heard the scratch of the blade on the glass. If the Villareals had an alarm, or a dog, or if the kitchen door had a double-pane window, Bird might have been busted.

In the end, nothing interfered with Bird while he worked the blade around that bulb seven or eight times, until he was relatively certain of success. With one hand gripping the handle and bulb, he smacked the eraser-end of the pencil against the glass, top then bottom. They were sharp, quick jabs, just like his dad used to do with his fists into Bird's kidneys, making him piss blood for a week.

Tap! Tap! Pop!

The glass popped free, and he eased it back through the hole that remained. There hadn't been much noise during the process beyond some scrapes and taps.

Even so, he waited and listened.

His vigilant ears were met with a bored and distracted silence. It was the lazy noiselessness that settled upon Marathon every night, akin to the response you get when you knock on the door of an empty house.

Confident that no one had been alerted, he continued. Taking it slow and easy, he disengaged the glass from the suction cup, and then put the little glass-cutter device back in his bag, along with the pencil. He tossed the glass into the crawlspace underneath the house.

His oversized arm didn't want to get through the opening. Two fists like canned hams eventually became forearms that Popeye would envy. Sausage-like fingers danced around, looking for the lock. Bird considered moving to Plan B, which was to smash the fucking door down, when his fingertips brushed the deadbolt. He turned it carefully, quietly. Pushing with his body, the door swung inward, and Bird found himself in the Villareal kitchen.

Some kids were afraid at night—scared of the dark. When the lights went out, the blankets came up, pulled tight over their quivering heads until morning, a magical shield against things that went bump. They held full bladders through the hours of deep shadow and squeezed their eyes shut in the hopes that whatever demons or boogeymen were lurking just inches away in the dark ... that they might remain powerless if they weren't seen.

Bird was the justification of that fear; he was the demon in the night.

Downstairs, there was a metronomic tick, which manifested itself as a grandfather clock in the hallway near the stairs. Three steps up, and the floorboards groaned in such a way that Bird considered a modified Plan A, but before he took any action, the clock started its hourly toll. Four heavy strikes. Without further hesitation, he rushed up under the cover of the benign bongs of that looming timepiece.

There were two bedrooms, doors fully open, on either side of the upstairs hallway. A shared bathroom faced the stairs, its porcelain shrine gleaming in the moonlight from scattered windows.

He could make out a crib and rocking chair in the room to his right, dimly lit by a baseball-shaped nightlight. He chose to go left instead, stepping casually through a doorway that was, no doubt, left widely open so that Hector Jr.'s nocturnal cries could be answered swiftly.

Bird lumbered over to the foot of Hector and Maria's bed, where he stopped, and watched them.

He found himself curious ... curious to a point almost beyond his intellectual limits. His feelings were like the scientist who has just adjusted the key variable in a study to cure cancer, and this was the big "it" moment when he'd discover if it worked.

It was thrilling to study two people in these intimate moments, guard completely down, absolutely no idea they were being watched. Peaceful looks adorned their tan faces, and Bird tilted his head slowly, like a dog trying to decipher the words of his master.

The Villareals had always struck him as a little stuck up, but then again, most people were, in Bird's experience. Everybody was always looking down on him. Looking at him funny. The church people said judge not, but they were always judging him.

Bird's eyes fell on Maria's cotton nightgown and his breath caught in his throat. White strings darted across her swollen cleavage, back and forth from left to right, in and out of eyelets, like the laces of running shoes, except these laces were spread widely open and untied.

There, poking out playfully between the white strings was three quarters of Maria's right nipple.

Savage desire coursed through the intruder. He stared intently at the dark brown areola as it moved slowly up and down with her every breath. His mouth went dry and he licked his lips to moisten them, and he fought the intense urge to go closer. Touch it. Kiss it...

Bird groaned and moved right to improve his view. As he did, the floorboards creaked loudly.

Hector rolled over, turning away from his wife. Bird stood silently at the end of the bed, watching as Hector's eyelids fluttered, then opened. Hector rubbed his eyes with his right hand, then stared ahead of himself. Maybe he was looking at the clock or just staring off into space.

Then he rolled onto his back...

"Hey, what the hell is going on here, man?" Hector cried out. Maria came awake beside him and for one brief and beautiful second, Bird saw her nipple break free completely. Then she saw him and screamed and grabbed Hector's leg in a vise-like grip. They pressed against one another tightly and, sadly for Bird, she pulled the blanket over her chest.

"Shhh!" Bird held his right finger up to his lips. In his left hand, he held an old eighteen-inch pipe wrench, cast iron. It weighed about six pounds. The Smith & Wesson 500 rested on his right hip like a Civil War cannon.

"Please, please, sir, we won't make a sound and we won't tell anyone. Take what you want; just don't hurt my family. Please..."

"Shut. The. Fuck. Up." That mewling and whimpering—the pathetic begging—pierced Bird's brain like an icepick. The lusty ecstasy he'd been feeling just moments before disappeared. The kid started crying in the other room, and his eyes blurred from the intense pain in his skull.

"My baby," Maria screeched. She started to get up from the bed.

"Down," Bird growled at her. "Sit yer ass down. Now." His free hand went to the holster and rested on the butt of the oversized revolver.

She reluctantly obeyed, the hot flow of tears streaming down her face.

A crescendo of pain hammered inside Bird's head. Something snapped, and he looked around as if he didn't realize where he was, or how he'd gotten there. Then there was the other voice that kept telling him what to do. Breathy and satiny, the forked tendrils wrapped themselves around his brain and squeezed.

Do it!

"No!" he told the voice—grabbed the right side of his head, wincing.

*****

Hector's eyes widened as the big man seemed to argue with himself. He recognized the giant from the gas station outside of town. Knew they called him Bird, but he didn't know much else about him.

Hector remembered Bird's dad had committed suicide some years before, and from the looks of it, whatever river of craziness that led dad to do that ran fast and deep in their family.

He debated whether he should go for the pistol in his nightstand. He looked sideways at the drawer. The .38 was loaded—all he had to do was open the drawer, grab it, aim, and fire. No more than three seconds and he could put the Sasquatch down.

When he shifted his eyes back to Bird, he found the big man staring at him. Hard, dark eyes glittered like shiny black rocks in the light that tiptoed in through the window.

"I wouldn't be thinkin' bout that, Hector." Bird paused and brought the wrench up to about waist height in front of him. His forearms flexed as he tapped the head into his other hand, slowly eyeballed it, and then let his eyes dance over to Maria before he looked at Hector again. "Unless you want me to introduce Maria to this wrench."

Hector's blood ran cold, and his bowels suddenly felt loose.

"Maybe after Maria, I could introh-deuce Hector Jr. to this wrench, and he could play with it, too. Or maybe it would play with him. Huh, Hector?"

Paralysis gripped Hector, and he simply nodded his compliance.

"Smart fella, Hector. Little uppity, but I always knowed you was smart." He grinned in the dark, cold and humorless.

*****

The sun was just poking its head up when Bird backed out of the Villareals' driveway. One little reddish-orange sliver grasped the atmosphere and shook it, making a tremulous horizon out of the otherwise calm desert landscape.

Hector Jr. lay quietly in the passenger seat, wrapped in blankets, and seat-belted the best that Bird could manage—he'd wanted to be gone by daylight, but things took longer than he expected.

Don't it always? he thought.

The fire needed to burn long and hot, but there also needed to be a delay before it started. Among the many despicable actions that made up his life, Bird was a semi-skilled arsonist, having burned two buildings for a crooked insurance firm in Odessa.

One of the places was an empty warehouse, and he only made a few hundred bucks.

The other was a well-insured deli. He wouldn't have made much on that one except the apartment above the deli was inhabited by a little old lady, and she had burned along with it. He didn't even know she was up there, but that didn't stop him from shaking down the insurance guy when he found out.

Nobody played Bird.

He needed a good couple of hours before the fire started. There were several stops to make and only so much time to do it. Everything needed to work out just right.

CHAPTER 15

Kane got up early after another late night at Bob's, followed by an even later night at Lucy's. The Hungry Ranger inside him shoved down another couple of breakfast bars when he discovered extra boxes in the little pantry.

Sweat leapt to the surface of his skin seconds after stepping outside. So much for dry desert heat. It was hot and getting hotter. And humid. Seemed like he worked in the sun, played Army in the sun, or ran with the sun watching over his shoulder.

All hail that fiery orb.

He'd read once that the sun was nearly five billion years old, and that it would last another five billion years in its current state. Which was good. There were enough things to concern a guy in the modern world, without worrying about a failing sun and the dramatic end of all life on the planet.

The small things, right?

Tracing the previous day's route, he took it easier than usual. Tried to soak in all the dry and dusty details of the town. Kane didn't know how long he would be there, but he wasn't planning on leaving any time soon.

As he moved up and down the streets, he wondered if any of the homes that he passed might be that of the missing child. They were mostly weather-beaten wooden homes, green or white or brown. Every fifth or sixth place was a faded red brick. Or a trailer. He couldn't discern a "good" or "bad" neighborhood.

Porches were mostly empty, people finding refuge indoors from the heat. Or maybe they were watching the local news, hoping for answers about the lost member of their tribe. He saw nothing unusual, no people gathered, and no law enforcement personnel anywhere, so he assumed the Wilsons must live elsewhere.

As an outsider, he didn't know the local dynamics. He didn't know what rivalries existed between families, or whether Joe had a grudge against Bob. Maybe someone needed money, and they kidnapped the kid in hopes of ransom.

Or maybe it was a drifter. Someone just passing through who capitalized on the opportunity to snatch a kid. The Army had forced him to take annual computer-based training on human trafficking. It was the type of training everybody hated because they all saw it as pointless; they'd never seen it, heard of it, or suspected anyone of selling human beings.

But that was when something happened, right?

Juarez was only four hours away, and if what he'd seen on TV was true, it was one of the most dangerous cities in the world. Multiple drug cartels inhabited Juarez, and it was home to a modern-day slave trade.

Hell of a time to be the new guy in town, he thought.

If he'd looked behind himself, he would have seen a cartoonish trail of dust as the wind grabbed what his feet kicked up and tossed it around in the air, where it jumped around for a while before drifting back to the ground. It was hot, but not like the Middle East, even though the humidity was worse. He took a slug from his CamelBak and let his mind drift back to the sun.

If he remembered correctly, the sun would eventually transform into a red giant, some five billion years or more into the future. Kane couldn't remember what a red giant was—only that it produced energy differently. That, and in the case of the sun, it would expand gradually until it encompassed Mercury, Venus, and the Earth.

There were times he'd talk about science or astronomy when he was on active duty, but the younger guys weren't very interested unless it involved booze and women, though a lot of them would read action books on deployments. The Senior NCOs seemed to be primarily of two stripes: extremely career focused, or deep into fringe hobbies, like collecting ammunition casings, building models of cities, or Live Action Role Playing.

LARPing.

That's what they called it. He'd never heard of it until a new guy in his company started talking about it one day and then never stopped. They were like the guys who dressed up in Civil War outfits, and reenacted battles, except it could be for any kind of crazy thing.

He was forced to confer only with himself on most science topics. Which was fine since he considered himself a damn good listener.

Of course, there was one of his old E-9s—Sergeant Major Reilly—who found him with a copy of *Big Bang* by Simon Singh. Kane was reading it in the back seat of a hummer in Kabul, waiting on someone, when Reilly peeked in and discovered his nose shoved into the paperback. After that day, Reilly was like a heat-seeking missile, impossible to avoid, and he'd find Kane so they could discuss the universe, but with a science fiction bent: interplanetary travel, wormholes, and end-of-the-world scenarios.

Kane laughed at the memories. It took all types. Most sergeant majors swaggered around "enforcing standards" all day, bitching at small flaws in how the soldiers wore their uniforms, stating the obvious in a very loud, abrasive manner, like, "Hey, when the garbage can is full, we *change* the bag." One of their primary duties, it seemed, was to parrot whatever the commander said, like the repeat button on his iPod. He sometimes wondered what value most sergeant majors really brought to the fight aside from being hard-asses.

At least Reilly had a personality, even if it was steeped in Star Trek.

Back at the house, he wasn't surprised to see that Lucy was still knocked out. *Classic princess-beauty-sleep scenario with Lucy*, he thought, but that was okay. It was nice to be around a girly girl, even if it meant there was no space for his shaving gear in the bathroom.

"Hey, you smell delicious!"

Lucy hugged him from behind when he came out of the bathroom. She pulled her head away, and he could feel her inspecting the scars on his back, but she didn't say anything.

"Thanks," he finally said. "I *think*."

"No problemo, amigo. Is there something you want to do today, since Bob's is closed?" she asked.

"No. I'm game for anything."

"How about horseback riding, down in Big Bend? We could rent some horses over at Rising Sun and go do some exploring."

"Do you ride?" he asked. He had done some riding as a kid, but not much in the last fifteen years or more.

"You bet your butt," she replied, ripping his towel off his waist. They sparred for a few minutes in that playful way that couples do, then he pushed her down on the couch, where the real *sparring* began.

Things got a little wild, but they kept the rough stuff to a minimum.

*****

"It's beautiful country," Kane remarked.

Rugged terrain zipped past the passenger window of Lucy's Tacoma. For a man who thrived on being minimalist, who felt it helped him focus on what was important in life, Kane couldn't deny the comforts of a vehicle brought to life in this century: soft seats, cold AC, and a ride so smooth it may as well have been a Cadillac. The fun and playfully angry sound of Pink washed over them, full and rich, from an upgraded stereo system. Lucy's head moved in sync with the music.

"God's country," she replied automatically. It was a canned response, rehearsed and delivered without hesitation. Undoubtedly something she told tourists and visitors. It was probably taught in their elementary school textbooks. Painted on the town water tower.

People said the same kinds of things about Nebraska.

Except, he also suspected that Lucy believed in it. It would be a tough place to settle otherwise, and Marathon held limited career prospects. He doubted slinging beers at the bar was her dream gig.

Anemic scrub and grayish-green Creosote bushes dominated the landscape on either side of the highway. Sporadic mesas poked their flat heads up, begging to be climbed. Rolling hills and mountains lay across the horizon, waiting to be painted.

A stretch of fence kept pace with them on either side of 385, punctuated by the occasional gate or dirt road. The fence was the simplest display of carpentry work imaginable—two to three wires strung between what looked to be small tree limbs that doubled as fence posts. Kane couldn't imagine any purpose other than deterring trespassers or defining property lines; it didn't look strong enough to hold cattle or horses, especially if they spooked.

"So, I have a very important question," he said.

"Oh, yeah?"

"Yes. Are you ready?"

"Shoot."

"Here goes—why is it called Big Bend?"

"That's the big question?"

"Yep."

"You're a deep thinker Kane Montgomery, but I'll give it a shot. This is going to blow your mind. Wait for it … wait for it. It's named Big Bend because there's a really *big bend* in the Rio Grande. Right here, right next to Big Bend National Park."

She looked over at him, nodding and grinning, and he stared back at her.

"Pretty anticlimactic," he said.

"Yeah," she agreed. "What else you got? Ask me some more questions."

He thought about that one for a second. He considered asking about her parents, opened his mouth, and then reconsidered. Bob had mentioned Lucy's dad in the past tense. *Knew* her daddy. *Was* a friend. If her dad had checked out of her life, or passed away, he didn't want to be the one to bring that up. It would be better if she did.

Plus, she was a local. Her parents had to be locals, or were at one time. Just seemed reasonable she would have mentioned them already. Or that they would have called or stopped by the house. That was what small town families did.

The next thing that crossed his mind was that he didn't think Lucy would be quite so cavalier about shacking up with a guy if her parents were around. Unless, of course, it was something intentional, to piss them off.

"Okay. We're going to this Rising Sun place at Big Bend, so I know there's that, but what else is there around here to do? Where do the tourists go? Marathon seems to have a pretty steady flow of people coming through."

"Hmm. Well, most people go to the park. There are a ton of places to hike ... canyons, trails, and along the river. You can ride donkeys or horses or go on guided tours. There's rafting and biking."

She paused, clicked her tongue.

"There's climbing ... we get a lot of people who are super fit and geared up with moisture wicking, brand-name shirts, and skinny little shoes with grippy soles. All types go camping, though. You get the stereotypical outdoorsy people, aging hippies, and families. Every season there is someone who almost dies from dehydration, or because they get lost. Kids go out there to get drunk and stoned."

"Really?"

"Duh. Most of 'em aren't tourists." She laughed. "Just local kids getting away from their parents, the ranches, and the daily grind. Except for maybe spring break. All the campgrounds fill up on spring break with people of all ages, from all over."

"I guess that's what I expected ... except for the illegal drug activity," he said.

She laughed. "Drugs are easy to get around here, so the parents clamp down pretty hard. That's why kids go down to The Bend, or *The Bends* as they call it—'to get bent.' They keep it pretty low key, though ... don't cause *too* much trouble."

He thought about that for a minute.

"Do you hike?"

"Sometimes. I used to a lot more, when..." She trailed off without finishing her thought. He wondered what she was hiding. "When I was in high school," she said finally.

Kane guessed it had to do with her parents or an ex-boyfriend.

"There's a trail near Crown Mountain called Pine Canyon Trail. It's really beautiful. We can go sometime, if you want?"

"Sounds cool."

She flipped through a few channels on the radio and stopped on a U2 song.

"Oh, I forgot to mention that we have a ghost town." She opened her eyes extra wide at him. Spooky eyes. He couldn't tell if she was kidding.

"A ghost town? Are you for reals?"

"Yeah." She laughed. "I'm totally for reals. I haven't been since elementary school. Maybe fifth grade. We took a field trip there. Terlingua."

"Terlingua? Isn't that Spanish for turtle?"

She laughed. "That's *Tortuga*. Terlingua is the name of the town, and it means three languages … for the Spanish, English, and Indian languages that the inhabitants used in the area."

"Cool," he said. He preferred science, but any good Army guy was interested in history, too.

"Cool, but not cool. They didn't exactly live together peacefully."

"Who does?" he said.

She nodded. "I know, right? But these guys were really bad. I don't know much, but our librarian knows *everything* about the local lore. I guess two or three different Native American tribes, Mexicans, and Europeans would routinely fight over the area. Ms. Tate—that's the librarian—told us it could be gruesome. Entire villages slaughtered. Rape. Human sacrifices."

"Wow," Kane said.

She was thoughtful for a minute, eyes on the road. "Yeah. Scary stuff. Like, why would anyone fight over Big Bend? Most people fight to get *out* of this place. You might have noticed the shortage of people."

"Now that you mention it..."

"Exactly."

They approached a sizable pile of rubble on his side, and he tensed slightly. IEDs, or Improvised Explosive Devices, were a daily hazard in Iraq during his cumulative twenty-six months there. He wondered if he would ever stop thinking about them, back in America.

"Do you speak any Spanish?" he asked her.

"A little bit."

"So you can habla us some Española if we need it?"

"Sí."

He laughed. She flashed her pearly whites at him. He loved that her smile went just a little higher on one side, giving it a sexy tilt. It made him think of the Maroon 5 song that talked about the girl with the broken smile, and he started humming.

Kane had been drifting around for the better part of two years, running from the ghosts of the friends he lost, and blaming himself. Logically, he knew it wasn't his fault, but that didn't stop him from feeling guilty. He was their good luck charm gone bad.

None of that crossed his mind as he hummed along with the music in his head and snuck glances at Lucy. For the first time in too long, it felt like his life was almost sort of normal.

"Almost there," Lucy told him and winked.

CHAPTER 16

Sundays in Marathon were usually pleasant.

Most residents went to church; there were more to choose from than an outsider might consider possible in a little town of (almost) five hundred. There was Sunday brunch and lunch at the restaurants. Families gathered, and kids played. Tourists did what tourists do.

Bigsby usually kept to himself on the Sabbath, but this was no average Sunday ... not when Marathon was missing one of its kids.

Sheriff Bigsby was busy in his office, typing on the computer. Watching him sitting there, fumbling around on the keyboard, was something painful to witness—awkward—like discussing sex with someone's grandmother.

For one thing, Bigsby had outgrown the desk. The girth of his body had increased over the years, and what used to be a good fit had become something resembling Pac-Man eating the desk, or a sideways taco, as his stomach both overlapped and underlapped the desktop.

Then, unlike his burgeoning middle, which got wider just thinking about food, his eyesight had been deteriorating, making reading difficult. The words started line-dancing whenever he sat down with a book, or at the computer. Not one to visit doctors, he'd invested in reading glasses from the spinning rack at Walgreens. He'd developed the habit of tilting his head up and back so he could look at books or the computer screen through the bottom half of the lenses.

The icing on the cake was that his keyboard cord wasn't long enough, and he had to perpetually lean forward to type. He made some half-hearted attempts at moving the CPU years before, then simply resigned himself to everything residing just outside the bounds of comfort. Through the years, he had developed a hunch in his posture from it.

Bigsby had fantastic instincts and people skills, but technology eluded him. It was one of those things Cheryl had taken care of for him. He leaned forward, rolled sleeves inching up and catching in his underarms. Cheryl would have taken care of the keyboard and bought him new shirts. He would have rolled through life blissfully ignorant of the byproducts of his "growth."

He took a break from staring at tire tread comparisons and leaned back in his chair, thinking about Cheryl.

She was his wild redhead, subdued freckles all over the place, and friendly to the point of contagiousness. He rarely laughed, merely smiled; she laughed enough for the two of them—and it was like hearing a sunrise. If there was something more beautiful, he'd never come across it.

Her daily uniform consisted of a straw hat, jeans, and most times, a sleeveless cotton shirt. She dressed that way because it was comfortable, without a care in the world of what other people thought, but Bigsby could vouch for the *fact* that she wore it like nobody else.

He imagined her there with him, sitting on the edge of his desk, legs swinging. Bigsby reached a tentative hand out and placed it on her jeans and *she was really there!* His mind raced. He realized he should be startled, or frightened, maybe ... his Cheryl had been gone for half a decade, from cancer.

The magic reminded him of his first record player. Now *that* was hearing music—real music—feeling every scratch and all the little peccadillos embedded in that vinyl disc. Feeling it in the body as well as hearing it in the ears. Knowing it didn't get any better. He moved his hand up and down the soft jeans, and she smiled at him.

"Sheriff!"

"Bye," Cheryl whispered at the sound of Tom's voice.

"No," Bigsby pleaded softly. "Don't go."

She winked at him ... and then disappeared. The sheriff opened his eyes and blinked a few times. Nobody there. *Must have dozed off,* he thought, quickly wiping at his damp cheeks.

Tom appeared in his doorway, strung tight like a coil. "Sheriff, Hector Villareal's place is on fire!"

Bigsby sat up fast. "Fire guys responding?"

"They're on their way, but it looks rough. Don't think they can stop this one. Guys from Alpine are coming."

"Okay. Let's go see if we can help." He grabbed his hat, and they headed out the main door. There was one hallway that led to the other end of the small building and a soundproof booth: the dispatcher's post.

"Learn anything about the tire tread, boss?"

"Yep," Bigsby replied.

Tom looked at him expectantly as they jumped in the Bronco.

"I learned that it's available on just about every damn truck out there, and on some cars, too."

Tom grunted. "Figures."

The Villareals lived on the southeast side of town. It was a two-story bungalow with a pair of windows that poked out like eyeballs from the slanting roof. It was bright yellow, and Hector dutifully repainted it every other year. Whenever Bigsby saw him up there on a ladder with his brush, he remarked to Tom about the obvious pride Hector took in caring for his home.

Hector and his wife Maria had moved from Alpine about fifteen years before, and the old folks around town still referred to them as "that new couple." They were in their twenties back then, without kids, and after a while, everyone assumed that parenthood just wasn't going to happen for them. People talked about it here and there— a given in any small town—but not openly.

Naturally, everybody was surprised, but happy, when Hector Jr. came along the previous year. Maria and Hector had just turned forty, so there wasn't a second to spare.

The Villareals lived as far from the sheriff's office as a person could in Marathon proper ... so it took them a full two minutes to get there.

Bigsby's heart ached as soon as he saw the flames. The Marathon fire truck, affectionately nicknamed *The Little Fire Engine That Could*, had arrived and two volunteer firemen were getting it hooked up to the extinguisher: Jim Herring and Joe Morales.

"You boys need some help?" Tom shouted.

"Yeah, when I grab the hose, just fall in about five feet behind me and help hold it in place," Joe replied.

The three men jumped into action, affixing nozzles and unhooking the primary hose. Jim donned additional protective gear on the fly.

The heat was intense, even at a distance, and Bigsby trotted in a wide circle around the house until he could see the end of the driveway. Right away, he recognized Hector's Chevy 4x4 tucked into the carport. While he watched, one of the timbers of the carport roof crashed into the bed of the truck, sending up a blast of fiery embers that danced erratically in the wind.

"Do we know if anyone was home?" Bigsby shouted over the almost deafening roar of the blaze.

Morales looked grim. "Don't know, *Jefe*," he shouted back. "We checked the house as soon as we got here, but there's no way to get in there. All the windows, the doors … the fire is too bad!" Bigsby nodded, and Joe turned away from the sheriff, focusing again on the fire. He made his way closer and Tom followed him. They had donned the protective coats, but Tom was still wearing his work pants.

The sheriff opened the passenger door of the Bronco and leaned in for the radio, "Dispatch, this is Bigsby."

"Hi Sheriff, are you on site at the Villareal home?"

It was Doris, the part-timer. Harriet never worked on Sundays.

"I am, Doris. Need you to call Marathon Baptist and see if the Villareals were at church."

The line went silent. Bigsby was about to ask if she'd copied that when she replied, "Are they inside, Sheriff?"

"Don't know, Doris. Just call the church. If they don't know, call around and see what you can find out."

"Okay. Copy that, Sheriff.

Marathon didn't have enough people or infrastructure to warrant a full-time fire department, so they relied on a volunteer crew that received a pittance for a stipend. A truck slid to a stop on the shoulder behind the Bronco, and another of the volunteers went running by in his church clothes.

The pumper truck finally had water pulsing out of it. Bigsby knew that once it hit peak flow, more than a thousand gallons a minute would be forced out, at least while it was hooked up to the fire hydrant. While he watched, they moved the water along the base of the fire in front of the house and to the left side, toward the nearest neighbors. Bigsby assumed they were trying to put up a barrier between the homes even though more than an acre separated them.

Despite what seemed like an incredible amount of water, the flames continued, growing brighter and higher in defiance, angry tendrils shaking their fists into the sky.

The radio squawked: "Sheriff."

"Bigsby," he answered.

"The pastor at Marathon Baptist says that the Villareals did not make it to church this morning. He tried calling because they never miss a week, but nobody answered."

He thought about that. Never missed a week. Devout people.

"Doris," he said, "Can you look up some family phone numbers for me? They have people in Alpine, I think. Hector's mom. Same last name."

"Copy, Sheriff, will do."

As he reached out to put the microphone back, there was a tremendous thud—*Whump!*—and the ground shook. He ducked instinctively, and his free hand went to his hat. A ball of smoke and flame ascended behind the house, roiling and churning as it climbed higher and higher.

The truck, Bigsby realized.

"Sheriff, you okay? Sheriff?"

He reached for the speaker microphone, but then realized he was still holding it, and pressed the talk button, "I'm here, Doris."

"What was that?"

Bigsby counted the men outside. Joe and Tom had dropped to the ground, but they were back up, spraying. The other two were safe. "Looks like we had a truck explode."

"Oh, my God," Doris said. Bigsby said nothing, but he silently agreed with her. He could hear a phone ringing on Doris's end of the line when she said it.

"Sheriff," she said a few seconds later. "I've got Hector's mom on the other line. Someone called her, so she called us."

Bigsby felt an awful weight settle on him. "Okay, Doris, get me the number so I can call her."

When they finished talking, he shut the door, and then cranked on the engine to get the AC going. Dehydration, the heat, and the phone call he was about to make all conspired to make him pass out, but he hung tight.

With a heavy heart, he called Hector's mother.

CHAPTER 17

Bird slid the double doors shut at the warehouse, then wrapped the heavy chain through the handles. He gave it a quick tug to make sure things were tight before he pushed a new padlock through the links and locked it.

One delivery down, and one more to go.

A cyclone fence surrounded the property, rusty and worn from the elements, but still standing mostly straight. Bird considered for a moment that the padlock on the fence had been broken for several years. Adding a new lock might arouse the suspicion of anyone that came up here and knew about the old busted lock, but considering what he'd just stored inside, he had to do something.

He looked around the yard—thought about moving some pallets or other debris and blocking the fence—then figured it all amounted to the same. He hauled another chain and padlock from the rear of his truck and snapped it onto the fence.

Bird hustled back to his truck and jumped in. The baby next to him was gripping the little white stick of a completed Dum Dum's lollipop and cooing over and over again.

"Ahh-oooh," Hector Jr. said to him.

"Ahh-oooh," Bird replied, then grunted. He reached into his pocket and pulled out a fresh Dum Dum for the kid. It was sour apple, his favorite, so instead of giving it over to the baby, he grabbed the Solo cup from the cup holder and spit the rest of his chew into it. Some of it missed and dangled from the cup in a long sinewy strand, but Bird paid it no mind—he frequently missed—and put it back in its place, some of the liquid mess falling unnoticed to the floor. Then he popped the lollipop into his mouth and smiled. It had been years since he had a sour apple Dum Dum and it tasted like his youth.

"Da-da," Hector Jr. said.

"Right," Bird replied. He reached into his pocket and pulled out another sucker. This one, he noticed, was cream soda. "Nasty," he said, then chuckled, "You take it little Hec." He pried the chewed up white stick from the baby's hand and replaced it with the fresh lollipop, which instantly disappeared into the kid's mouth.

Cream soda was as nasty as black licorice, Bird thought as he peeled away down the dirt road, but when he looked, the kid was devouring it, cheeks coated in saliva.

"You like that shit, uh, Hec?"

"It!" Hector Jr. answered.

Bird guessed the kid was about a year old. It didn't look like he could walk, but he was sure trying to talk. He didn't know much about child development, but he thought the kid seemed smart.

"Shit!" Bird said and whooped.

"It!" Hec replied, and Bird just laughed.

It took him nearly ten minutes to get back to 90 from the abandoned warehouse. It was uphill and northwest of Marathon proper, lost on snaking gravel and dirt roads that were becoming overgrown with desert shrubs. As far as he knew, nobody ever went there any more. You could hardly tell there was an entrance from the highway. There were no road signs, and even the kids in town seemed to have forgotten about it, and they generally sniffed out any place where they could drink beer, shoot their 22s, or smoke some weed. The *cool* ones, anyway, he figured. The dorks were all playing *Pokémon Go* these days.

Fucking Pokémon. That was something he didn't understand at all, but from what he heard people say, there was a Pokéstop right there at his gas station. How the hell did that happen? He couldn't see it, but people said it was there, and they'd stop by just to get it.

When he was little, his dad would crack open a beer, and sit down and watch Wiley Coyote with him sometimes. Old Zeke would laugh louder than he did, and offer him beer. He hated the taste at first, but came to love it.

He grunted, thinking about those crazy foreign cartoons. They were probably the reason kids were so messed up these days.

After just a few minutes on 90, he cut right onto 385 toward Big Bend, and opened it up to about eighty miles per hour. A black cloud exploded from the exhaust, and the truck shuddered for a few heartbeats. He wondered briefly if it was going to make the trip and what he would do if the truck died, but it was too late to be concerned about that now.

As he sped towards his next stop, he glanced in the direction of the Villareals' house. He didn't see any smoke, yet, which was good. It meant that the delay he'd concocted was working. Or at least he hoped it was. The other possibility was that the fire hadn't started, and it never would start, and then he'd be fucked because he hadn't worn gloves and his fingerprints were all over that place.

"Shit," he said, and swerved to avoid a two-by-four in the road. The last thing he needed was a flat tire from a nail, but as the truck went sharply one way, and then back the other, the laws of physics kicked in and tossed the kid onto the floorboard of the passenger side.

"Ah, shit," he repeated, utilizing one of the key words in the Bird Taylor vocabulary, then followed it up with another favorite: "Fuck!"

He whipped over to the side of the road and leaned down into the well of the passenger side. All he could see were blankets; the kid was upside down. He was going to be in serious trouble if the kid was hurt. Not knowing what to expect, he snatched up the little bundle, turned it around, and was surprised when he saw the little guy laughing.

"Tough little bastard, ain't you?" he said, and placed him in the passenger seat. He tried to fasten the seatbelt around him, but it kept slipping off. After a brief struggle, he yanked some extra belt out and looped it a couple of times around the kid.

"That oughta hold ya, bud."

There wasn't any traffic, and he was able to get back on the road without any additional delays. He knew there wouldn't be any cops out, so he pushed the truck up to eighty-three—it wobbled dangerously at eighty-four—and settled in for the drive.

*****

"You ready, Hec?"

"Eddy?" Hector Jr. repeated. He kicked his legs out and laughed, and Bird just shook his head. He didn't really like kids. At the gas station, he saw a dozen kids each day, crying, angry, and asking where the bathroom is, near to pissing themselves.

He shook his head.

There was something about this one, though, this little twenty-pound punk with the pile of black hair on his head. He smiled at Bird in a way that nobody smiled at him. Not ever. Including what little he remembered of the woman that was his mother.

He was parked in the rear of the building, out of sight of anyone else. There were several black SUVs nearby, as well as the red Audi.

"Ah-right, bud," he tucked Hector Jr. under his arm, and pushed the door shut.

Hector started laughing and said, "Shit!" which made Bird laugh. He'd pronounced it perfectly.

Maybe I wouldn't be such a bad parent after all, he thought.

Hidden in an alcove, behind an exterior wall, there was a door that blended with the stone walling on either side. If he hadn't been told where it was, he's not sure he would have ever noticed it. Which was the point, of course—whatever they had going on, they sure wanted it kept secret.

Bird rolled up to the door and lifted his hand to ring the bell, but faltered. His head had grown cloudy when he reached the property, like he was dreaming or something, but it was twice as strong now. Why was he doing this? He glanced down at the child under his arm and wondered how he'd gotten there and what it was he was doing...

By concentrating on the door, he was able to push away the cloud. Not completely rid himself of it, but his head cleared enough to recognize Hec and remember just what the hell he was doing there.

He reached out for the bell again, but this time, the door opened before his hand reached it. Inside, one of the weird guys in the black clothes motioned him forward, then closed the door behind him.

CHAPTER 18

"Here we are," Lucy announced. "The Rising Sun Lodge."

A wooden sign stood upright, perpendicular to 385, with the name emblazoned across both sides. Large white rocks surrounded it. Scrub brush poked up at two-foot intervals around the rocks. She turned the Tacoma onto a well-kept lane off of 385.

"Interesting name," Kane said.

"You mean because of that book, the one written by the Jurassic Park guy?" she asked.

"Michael Crichton? I didn't know he wrote a book with that name, but I did read Jurassic Park. Liked it.

"Me too."

"I'm surprised I never read anything else by him," he said.

"Yep, same," she told him. "What were you thinking about, then?"

"I can't remember for sure, but I think that's what the Japanese flag was called. Maybe not, though."

"Boring," she said, and then laughed.

"Yeah, it is boring," he agreed. He pointed ahead, "Is that Lone Mountain?"

"Yep. The lodge is tucked away on the backside of it."

The road twisted back and forth, but it was in great shape—much better than 385. Kane figured they'd paved it recently, in the last couple of years. Gradually, as they circled around to the southern side of Lone Mountain, the lodge itself came into view.

It was a grand old place, large in a sweeping sort of way that reminded Kane of the hotel in The Shining, and he told Lucy as much.

"Hmm. Sort of, I guess," she replied. "Except *that* place was fancy and people were dancing in tuxedos and there were luscious gardens. This place is rustic, and packed with cowboys, horses, and people that haven't showered in days."

"Semantics," he said, and she laughed.

They stopped when the access road emptied into a traffic circle with exits on the other side. Matching wooden signs pointed people in three directions: rentals, cabins, and main lodge.

The main lodge building was straight ahead of them through the first exit, and it was three stories tall. Privatized balconies jutted out, with half-walls on each so that people didn't have to see their neighbors when they stepped outside to smoke cigarettes, fool around, and stargaze. Once guests discovered the extraordinary number of pinpricks that dotted the inky sky each night, they gravitated to the balconies when it was dark so that they could get lost in it.

Following the middle road, cabins were visible in the distance. It was hard to be certain, but it looked like ten or twelve individual units.

Off to the left was the sign for rentals, but nothing could be seen over the rise in the road.

"Looks like a really nice place," Kane said.

"Yeah. It's been a while since I've been here, but I swear, everything looks nearly new. Like, it hasn't aged at all." She shook her head incredulously.

"Do you know which exit?" Kane asked.

"Of course, it's the..."

Lucy stopped talking and stared as a truck came barreling up from the lodge. Kane guessed it was fifteen or twenty years old—it resembled the P-O-S that he was the not-so-proud owner of.

The truck slowed almost imperceptibly as it got to the roundabout and started around. Lucy edged her Tacoma over to the right side of the road to protect her truck and give the other one more clearance.

As they watched, the other vehicle's tires went off the side of the road. The truck danced back and forth and slowed considerably before the driver got things corrected, and the vehicle jumped back in to the circle.

It swept by them, side mirrors missing each other by less than a foot, but the driver didn't even seem to notice—he was completely focused on the road, and paid Lucy and Kane no attention. Kane heard the engine rev as it picked up speed and passed them.

"That looked like The Undertaker," Kane said.

Lucy laughed. "Yeah, it was The Undertaker. Bird Taylor."

"Guess he was in a hurry."

"Yeah. Weird," she said, watching his truck disappear in the rear view mirror, before she turned her head to Kane. "It looked like you two were sizing each other up when we were at his gas station."

He looked at her and pursed his lips thoughtfully, "Is that what it looked like?"

"Yeah, it did. You two looked like the guys in the boxing ring before the fight, doing the stare-down thing," she said. "You know, the kids around town have a nursery rhyme they sing about Bird. He's their boogeyman—the grim reaper of Marathon."

She paused and looked at him—smiled—and reached out a hand and brushed her fingertips along the scruff on his cheek. He smiled back at her.

"The funny thing is," she continued, "That I don't think you were scared of him at all. He's a giant—this huge dirty ogre—the object of all the local kids' nightmares. Most of the adults are afraid, too—he always makes me nervous when I'm getting gas. But you didn't look worried at all. You just studied him like a specimen in the lab."

Kane gave her a half laugh and shook his head. He looked out the passenger window and studied the landscape. In this area of the world it had the strange ability of looking the same and, yet different, every time he saw it.

"Hey, look at me. I mean, am I right? You two were sizing each other up. Was it, 'who has the bigger thing' or something else?"

This time he chuckled a little bit. "Maybe," he told her.

"Maybe?"

He thought about how to answer that, how to sum up what amounted to a diverse and critical analysis of anyone that he considered a possible enemy, without sounding like a complete nutcase. "I guess you could say that I was evaluating the odds."

"What odds?" she asked.

"That he might try something. What his move would be. How I'd react. Whether I could take him."

She watched him for a minute with narrowed eyes, then relaxed and nodded her head. "I guess I understand. You come from a different world than I do." She moved her hand down to his shoulder and he saw her eyes flicker to his back and then back to his face. "I don't really know everything you have gone through, growing up or in the Army…"

He made some noise between a grunt and harrumph, and she sighed.

"You know what, though?" she asked.

"What?"

He waited for a reply, but she said nothing.

They sat in silence for a little bit, then she put the truck in drive, and turned in at the rentals sign. The road rose for a while. When they crested the top he could see stables and another building in the style of the main lodge in the distance, but smaller.

Lucy turned to him and nodded her head slightly, then looked back at the road. Then she glanced at him again and smiled, "By the way … I get the feeling you could take him."

He laughed, thankful his eyes were hidden behind his sunglasses. There were some things he just didn't talk about. Call it superstition. Or, perhaps he was just being cautious. Hedging bets by staying silent.

He wasn't going to say it out loud, but inside, he had reached the same conclusion: he could take him.

*****

The old man gave their horse tack straps sharp tugs, and visually inspected the harnesses, saddles, and bridles once more. His tanned arms were all wiry muscle and veins, and his mustache matched the snowy grey hair on top of his head, hiding his mouth completely. The bushy mass on his upper lip puffed outward as he talked, woolly filaments moving up and down.

"Guys, I think you are *all* set!"

To Kane, it sounded like he said they were *owl* set, his accent was so thick.

"Thanks, Buck. It was good seeing you again," Lucy told him.

"You too, baby girl," he said. "Next time, don't be such a stranger."

"I won't."

Lucy and Kane got their horses moving down the trail that led away from the stables; fifteen or twenty minutes later, they passed a sign that announced they'd entered Big Bend National Park.

"So … you knew Mustache Man back there?"

Lucy grinned. "Yep. I told you I came here as a kid."

"I know, he just seemed really excited to see you," he said. "I mean, it was kind of hard to *understand* him…"

"Oh, hush," she told him. "You know, if you haven't noticed, you have an accent, too."

"Really?"

"Sort of Midwestern, and a little Southern, but faster. Like a Yankee. And clipped sometimes, which is probably from your time in the Army, right?"

He was unused to being analyzed and found himself at a loss for words. Finally, he said, "That's pretty good—you nailed it, I guess."

The trail became less defined as they moved from flat terrain to what might be considered hilly, but with an overall incline as they drew closer to the Chisos Mountains.

They came upon a mesa that stood proudly ahead and to the right of them, and Kane felt the interlacing harmony, something equally rugged and magical, in the physical attributes of the world that surrounded him. Rock faces rose up to greet them in hues of burnt orange and brown and yellow. A jackrabbit bounded up nearby, thought twice when it saw them, then shifted its heading and bolted away on a new course. Lizards, butterflies, and other small critters scattered as they moved deeper into the park.

They sauntered along in comfortable silence for the better part of an hour, carving their path like a slow and lazy river, the sun dampening their jeans and long-sleeved shirts with sweat.

It was better to sweat than become a victim of the elements in other ways.

Lucy periodically reached into her saddlebag to sip bottled water, while Kane had his trusty CamelBak that he took the occasional pull of water from. He wasn't sure about the national park's laws on carrying a firearm around, but he didn't care; he had no intention of being out here without his pistol.

They found a shallow pool of water in a glen between two rocky outcroppings, and decided to stop and let the horses get hydrated. Kane climbed down from his mount, then held a hand out to Lucy so she could do the same.

"My lady," he said, bowing slightly as she climbed down. When she got to the ground, she brushed her lips lightly against his, and then looked up and gave him sexy eyes.

"Thanks," she said.

"No problem," he told her.

After they led their horses to the water, Kane shed his outer shirt and tied it around his waist. Lucy removed a Ziploc baggy with apple slices from her saddlebag and fed the horses several wedges in turns as they were drinking. She ran her hand around the horses' necks and heads, and talked softly to them while they rested. Lucy's horse was named Spirit, and he heard her use the name several times in their human-to-horse conversation.

"How do we know the water isn't bad for them?" he asked.

"They wouldn't drink it if it was bad."

"You sure about that?"

"Yes, silly guy. Horses are smart and have better senses than humans."

"If you say so," he was doubtful. "I think we give animals too much credit for knowing things sometimes. Maybe they're just lucky."

"I'd rather be lucky than good."

He watched her while she rubbed down the horses. "You got me there," he said, reflecting on his own past. He used to be Lucky Kane, the human rabbit's foot, which even seemed to be true for a while. Until they foolishly relied on his luck, and his buddies died.

We should have known better, he thought with a deep sigh.

The sky was dazzling blue above them, and Kane breathed deeply and relaxed, letting the past recede. He closed his eyes and savored the relief of the shade. "So, when was the last time you came out here?" he asked, drinking water, and pouring a little over his head.

"Hmm," she considered it as she applied some more sunblock to her ears, neck, and around her glasses. "Eight and a half years."

He took the sunblock as she passed it to him and slathered it on the parts that pained him now and then: nose, ears, and neck. "Eight and a half years? That's a pretty precise timeframe," he said.

"It is," she agreed, and when he saw her face, he sensed the moment had transformed from easygoing to … something else, tinged with sadness.

"Okay, that's cool," he said gently. "Why don't we keep going?"

She looked off in the distance, and seemed to return to normal. Kane thought to himself for the hundredth time that she was beautiful. While he watched, she slowly nodded in agreement. "Sounds good. Let's keep going."

"All right, Gorgeous…"

She gave him a kiss.

They put away the sunblock and water, climbed back on their steeds, and started moving again. Kane played the scene over again in his mind, wondering what was bothering Lucy, but in the end, he decided that she would tell him when the time was right.

Or not. You never could tell with women.

They clopped along at a leisurely pace, pausing now and then so Lucy could take selfies with him, or to allow the horses to drink. It was Kane's kind of day.

They'd been out for about three hours when they came to a path between two sheer faces that loomed twenty feet or more above them. They looked to either side, but there was no obvious way around. The slice in the rock was about ten feet at its widest point—plenty of space to ride through on horseback—but it looked to be a couple hundred yards to the other side.

"Cut through here, or go around?" he asked.

"Oh, let's just keep going. I'm pretty sure this pops out at a good place."

"Cool."

They moved forward on their horses, keeping side-by-side when possible. Lucy took the lead whenever the trail narrowed.

About midway through, the walls pushed in tightly, and they got into their front-and-back formation. They were clopping along slowly when Kane heard a noise out in front of Lucy. It sounded like something wet slapped the ground. Then he heard the noise behind him, and when he looked back, something that resembled tree limbs began falling, hitting the ground around them two, three, then five. He glanced up and thought he saw the outline of someone poised up above … someone familiar. The sun washed everything out, but little bells rang in the back of his mind.

Then he heard the rattling, and sensed the movement all around them. Those weren't tree limbs that fell down.

Rattlesnakes surrounded them.

"Stay calm," Lucy said. Kane slid his CamelBak gently around to his front, drew out his Smith & Wesson, and chambered a round. The horses were getting skittish as the snakes inched closer. "Calm," she repeated.

Kane's horse neighed and shook its head and he leaned in, "Shhh." It didn't seem to help much. Lucy was a much more experienced rider, and he asked, "What do we do?"

"I'm trying to urge her forward, but she isn't budging. If I could get her to move, we'd just go."

Sounded reasonable. The only problem was that they weren't moving.

Just then a snake struck at Lucy's horse. Spirit reared and Kane grabbed for the reins, but Lucy went flying. She landed hard between the horses as Spirit bolted around her at full gallop. Snakes were rattling all around her. She would be bitten any second.

His own horse, Lightning, was chomping at the bit to buck him off, too. He had the saddle horn in a vice-like grip in his left hand, his gun in his right, and things weren't looking too good. He suspected he'd be tossed if he fired from the saddle.

"Lucy!" Kane shouted, but she didn't respond. The ground slithered all around them.

One slithering devil darted toward Lucy's limp form.

"Fuck this," he whispered. He gripped the pommel to steady his aim, took a breath and squeezed the trigger.

The Smithy bucked in his hand.

The snake split in half just inches from Lucy's feet. The rattler quivered a second more then stopped. Lightning shook beneath him then steadied. "Good boy," he said quietly, sighting up on the next snake.

The Smithy bucked again, and another snake stopped rattling.

He repeated the action again and again, ending the lives of six rattlesnakes in quick succession, and only missing once. When his slide locked to the rear, he released the spent magazine, and popped in a full one. Then he let the slide go forward, chambering a round.

Small rocks rained down on him from above, and he looked up in time to see a shadow disappear over the lip of the wall to his right. Had someone been watching? It didn't make any sense. Then he remembered that he thought he'd seen someone up there when the snakes started raining down around them.

Did someone intentionally try to hurt them? A rattlesnake ambush? It seemed laughable, and yet, here they were.

With care, he dropped down from his saddle and squatted next to Lucy's prone body. "Lucy," he whispered, rolling her over, pressing his face close to hers. She was breathing and had a strong pulse. He glanced up again, but seeing nothing, looked back down at Lucy. There was a rock buried in the hard-pack near her head, so he gently checked beneath her hair with his fingers, and found the knot he expected.

Her eyes flickered open then closed. Then back open. She focused on him and smiled.

"Ouch," she said.

"Yeah, ouch," he agreed. "How do you feel?"

She sat up slowly, and winced. "A little sore up top, but not too bad."

"Think you can ride?"

"Yeah," she said. "Help me stand up."

He gave her his hand, and then checked her pupils. Both were the same size. She looked all right. His fingers lingered on hers, and he said, "Glad you're okay."

She nodded and bit her lip.

He scanned the rims of the wall above while Lucy checked on Lightning.

"Wow," he heard her saying. Snake carcasses littered the ground, and he was still holding his gun. "Did you *shoot* all the snakes?"

He shrugged.

She looked oddly impressed. "Thank you."

"You're welcome." He slid his gun back into his pack, leaving the handle jutting out slightly.

"You must be one hell of a shot," she remarked. "I guess we're down a horse?"

"Spirit said she was getting the hell out of here," Kane said.

"I don't blame her."

He policed up his brass and put the casings in his pocket, while Lucy made some quick adjustments to the horse. *Talk about a good day gone sour,* he thought, but he was glad they were safe, and they climbed up onto Lightning and moved out.

When they reached the stables, the sun was more than halfway through its daily hike across the sky. A woman was leaning against the wall beside the stable entrance. Kane furrowed his brow at her odd garb—red dress stacked over red heels—not the best gear for riding. He was exhausted and didn't pay it much mind.

"Have a fun ride?" the Lady in Red asked them.

"Not really," Kane said.

"Oh? Did you have some trouble?"

"You could say that," Lucy chimed in. "We ran into some snakes."

"I hear the rattlesnakes are absolutely devilish this year," Red said.

Kane eyed her suspiciously. Coincidental choice of words? "Right," he said, thinking, *nothing innocuous is innocuous.*

They walked past her into the stable, where Buck greeted them. He relayed that Spirit had wandered in just moments before, unharmed, which made Lucy happy.

"By the way ... who is that lady in the red dress?" Kane asked. He motioned toward the stable doors.

"What lady?" Buck moved around him, and together they walked back to the entrance.

"Huh." Kane shook his head and shrugged at Buck. The woman was gone. "I guess she left," he said, but it was creepy ... almost like she'd never been there at all.

CHAPTER 19

"There you are—someone to keep you company," it chuckled. "Perhaps you can discuss sports. Or the weather."

Colby Wilson inserted his little fingers into the chicken wire and pulled himself up in his cage. His head scraped the metal top, and he cried out and dropped back down on his butt. Despite the pain and the frightening creature towering over him, he pulled himself up again just a moment later, but there wasn't enough room to walk. This time he remained standing, hunched over, eyes wide.

"Soon, you can rid yourself of that worthless body, and serve me," the thing told Colby. As it spoke, the voice changed from a gravelly, masculine sound to something feminine and melodic.

Colby blinked, and his eyes went wide, but he couldn't turn away.

"Shit!"

Colby turned and looked at the child in the cage next to his. Hector Jr. pointed and laughed and repeated himself: "Shit!"

A swift anger descended on the boys' visitor, and the creature moved so swiftly as to almost not be visible. It was suddenly outside Hector Jr.'s cage, pressing its snarling face against the top. Colby started crying softly a few feet away.

Hands like claws reached out slowly and gripped the wire that comprised Hector Jr.'s cage. His laughter vanished, and he defecated in fear. The claws shook in rage for a few moments, rattling the contraption, before they relaxed and let go.

"Why, what's that putrid smell?"

The melodic voice had replaced the snarling one, and both kids stared blankly.

"Now that you've *done* it, it's appropriate for you to *say* it. Say it again, little Hector. Say it again," the beast prodded. "Say, 'Shit.'"

Hector remained silent.

"Say, SHIT!" it screamed, the sound echoing from the stone walls around them.

Both children cried out, and the beast's rage changed to laughter. The laughter grew louder and louder until it filled the room, deafening, an evil sound. Bulging eyes threatened to pop out of the twisted face. Then, just as quickly as it had changed, it returned to normal.

"Pathetic."

One empty cage remained in the room. It looked down at the container thoughtfully, and reflected on the dark magic that was so strong in this building—and in these very stones. Of all the places on Earth, amid all the mindless hatred and destruction, there was one location that continuously beckoned.

A lighthouse in the storm.

The power of three. Three cages. Three children with three years of life between them. The structure with dimensions in multiples of three. Everything had to be just right.

The children continued to cry, and the face, which was now feminine again, pursed its lips. "Shhh…"

Leaving the three cages and two guests, it returned to the vast main hall. Heavy footsteps bounced from wall to wall, but gradually transformed into the staccato click of heels, and by the time she reached the stone altar, it was the Lady in Red again.

"Soon," she said standing over it. Leaning over, she ran her tongue along the length of the cold, hard surface. She admired the blade resting along the forward edge, honed to a fantastic sharpness.

The time was coming. She would have it all— nothing was going to stand in her way.

CHAPTER 20
Monday

Bigsby loved coffee.

There was a time when he drank orange juice every day with something light in the morning ... sliced fruit, granola bars, or cereal. Cheryl made egg whites and turkey bacon on Saturdays, when they slept late. He'd only have a cup of coffee at work. Maybe two when the day ran long.

That changed when Cheryl died.

For a while he followed the same routines and kept the same habits. Prepared the same sensible breakfasts, except for one person instead of two. He attended church every Sunday—*religiously*—you might say. And he finished his day with a beer or two.

The drinking escalated. Two beers became four, and four became eight. Or ten. He stopped drinking orange juice for breakfast, but made up for it with a screwdriver at lunch. Two months after the funeral his boat was taking on water faster than he could bail it out. So ... he just let himself sink.

It was liberating getting drunk. No pretending that things were the same, or that he was going to be okay. He simply drank until the world disappeared.

All the booze made it hard to wake up, so he replaced those nutritious breakfasts with coffee. Strong coffee. The stouter, the better.

Tom and Steph surprised him with a Keurig machine his first Christmas as a widower.

Widower, he thought. *I never liked that word.*

Tom knew the sheriff made horrible coffee. The few times they let him near the machine at work, he burned it. Tom had laughed and said, "Imagine that, Sheriff. I didn't know you could *burn* coffee." And just in case any doubt lingered, Bigsby burned it again the next day, too.

Harriet told them she would take care of the coffee when she was at work; both men appreciated that since she crafted a fine brew—better than Starbucks.

Most Sundays he was too hungover to wake up for church and his attendance dipped from weekly to monthly, and then to spiritual holidays.

If anyone at work noticed the drinking, they never said anything to him. Cheryl's friends shared in his pain at first, but they got over it, and moved on. He was left alone with his broken heart, and a nearly fatalistic need to drink.

Eventually he reached some bizarre equilibrium between the drinking, work, and his personal life, which consisted primarily of staring over the top of his television set.

Then one day there was a knock at the door.

*****

"Hi, Sheriff."

"Reverend," Bigsby had replied, surprised to see Pastor James on his doorstep. It was Sunday, the day they usually saw each other ... back when he still attended services. He felt like a truant high school kid, busted playing hooky, but he recovered quickly and stepped aside, "Come on in, Rev."

"Thanks."

They sat at the table in the kitchen and chatted, and Bigsby wondered if it would ever end. Pastor James prattled on and eventually pulled a piece of wood out of his pocket.

"Mind if I whittle?" he had asked.

"Knock yourself out, Padre."

The following week, Pastor James showed up again. They chatted again. And out came the wood and the knife, again. Except that week, he brought a chunk of wood for Bigsby, too.

"Balsa," he told him. "Great for whittling. Nice and soft."

Bigsby didn't want to whittle, but he was too polite to decline, so they whittled.

Over time, those dreaded Sundays became the highlight of his week. Pastor James gave him some overdue grief counseling through a year-long series of whittling sessions.

Eventually he stopped drinking, but he would never give up the coffee.

*****

"Mornin', boss." Tom rolled in early, as usual.

"Good morning, Tom."

Harriet was off, so Tom went straight to the coffee machine and got a pot brewing. Bigsby was still nursing his java from home, but he was thankful because he knew he'd need more soon. Tom came over and held up his cell phone, and Bigsby read the meme out loud.

"One day on Mercury lasts 1408 hours. The same as one Monday on Earth."

Bigsby nodded and Tom cracked a half-smile, but the usual banter felt forced and out of place, overshadowed by what Marathon had suffered that week.

"Are they going to be able to rake through the Villareal's place?" Tom asked. The fire had burned longer and hotter than anyone had thought possible. Evidence collection wouldn't be possible until Monday afternoon, at the earliest. Maybe Tuesday. It appeared the entire family had perished in the blaze. Gathering the evidence was probably just a sad formality.

It was a devastating blow to the community.

"It looks like they will. Their momma just won't have any closure until they do." After he spoke to her on the phone, she'd driven over and stood crying by the ruins until after sunset. Bigsby never left her side.

"Good," Tom said. "Looks like a couple of Alpine boys are going to come over and help us out this week. We can use it."

Bigsby nodded. They were burning their candles at both ends.

The sun crept in through the windows as they busied themselves with overdue paperwork. At half past nine, the bell over the door jingled and the sheriff looked up to find Lucy Baker and the new guitarist standing around with their hands in their pockets.

"How can I help you two?" he asked, coming out from his office, and shaking hands.

"We met the other night, Sheriff. Kane Montgomery."

"I remember—I'm old, but not that old," he said. He hugged Lucy. "How are you doing, darling?"

"I'm fine, Sheriff."

"I didn't mean..." Kane began, but Bigsby cut him off.

"Just jerkin' your chain, fella." He clapped Kane on the shoulder. "You guys want some coffee? It's okay ... Tom made it."

"Sure, that'd be great."

They circled up around the coffee pot like a wagon train setting up camp. A stack of cups was opened and java shared around. "Hey!" Tom said when he came out to an empty pot. "I just made that!"

The others chuckled, and he got another one brewing.

"So..." Kane started, and looked at Lucy.

"Well, yesterday we went out to the Rising Sun Lodge," she began. "And some weird things happened."

"Very weird," Kane chimed in.

Sheriff Bigsby listened as they told their story. Mostly he nodded, but every now and then he asked a question, for clarification. They described seeing Bird Taylor peeling away from the place, their narrow escape from the rattlesnakes, and how their Sunday ended with a long and painful visit at the emergency room in Alpine, to make sure Lucy was okay.

"So you shot the rattlesnakes?" Bigsby asked.

"Yes, sir." Kane replied.

"Hmm." He parked his hands together on top of his size thirty-eight waist. "Let's keep that between us, okay?

It's illegal to shoot any animals inside the park, even if you feel like your life is in danger."

"Really?" Lucy's eyes were wide in disbelief.

"True story," he said, and leaned forward. "Stupid law, if you ask me. What the hell are you supposed to do if a mountain lion, or a black bear, or a … a snake attacks you?" He spread his hands wide past his shoulders.

Kane looked at Lucy, and she looked back at him, and he said, "There was something else. I thought I saw someone looking over the edge of that gorge, down at us."

Bigsby raised his eyebrows questioningly.

"I can't be certain. The sun was bright—very bright—but it looked like one of the guys I've seen around town. They're always dressed in black shirts and black jeans. I don't know. I can't say why, but something about whoever I saw reminded me of those guys."

Sheriff Bigsby stroked his mustache for a few minutes then called for Tom, who pulled up a chair and joined them. He knew the men Kane was referring to. "New guys," he said. "Driving around in a black SUV."

Kane snapped his fingers and pointed. "Those are the ones."

"I need to find out more about those guys. They're new, like *you*," he said. "I had assumed they were hired on at one of the ranches, but you know, we just went around to most of them, and I didn't see any sign of them. If you saw them at the lodge, I'll ask around down there."

Bigsby shot Tom a questioning look, but Tom shook his head. He didn't know who they were either.

"It was just the weirdest day ever," Kane said. "I mean, would somebody really throw snakes at us?"

"Oh, and that lady outside the stables was creepy, too," Lucy added.

"Lady?" Bigsby inquired.

"Yes. She was in a red dress, wearing red high heels, at the *horse stables* of all places. She said something strange to us, like, 'the rattlesnakes are devils this time of year,' or something like that."

Bigsby and Tom exchanged a look.

"Did she say anything else?"

"No," Kane said. "We went inside to see Buck, and when I came back out just a few minutes later, she was gone. Really gone. I couldn't see her anywhere. I remember that it made the hair on my neck stand up. Do you know her?" He asked, and shivered again a little bit, thinking about the queer look on the woman's face.

"We've come across her," Bigsby said. He thought about elaborating—his instincts told him that he could trust these two—but he held back. It was his nature to keep silent. Tom, on the other hand, was more talkative…

*****

"Oh, we've seen her," Tom jumped in, eager to discuss the strange woman that had haunted him for days. "Just once, out near that lodge. You pegged it. The way she talked to us was sort of like she already knew the answer, and was only asking us because she wanted to tease us. You know? Gave me the willies."

The knowing look that passed between Kane and Lucy indicated their experience had been similar.

Tom didn't say it out loud—wouldn't dare—but he had also thought Red was *smoking* hot. He'd had several disturbing dreams about her since that day, too. Dreams where she told him to do strange things in exchange for payment of a sexual nature.

*****

Bigsby watched Tom share his thoughts, and recognized the connection it made with Lucy and Kane. Then his deputy seemed to drift into his own thoughts, maybe something he hadn't shared with him. Between them, he felt a kindred purpose.

"Anything on the missing boy?" Kane asked. "I know you can't divulge things about the case, but you know, just wondering how that was looking."

"Not good," Bigsby said. "The trail is getting cold. We've done what we can do here, and there are people searching the area. There was supposedly a credible sighting in Midland, but..."

"But?" Lucy prompted.

Bigsby shook his head. "Someone called in an anonymous tip. A sighting. They had very specific details of Colby's garments and an impeccable physical description. Claimed they saw a woman get out of a blue Nissan Maxima with Colby."

"Whoa." Kane leaned forward. "What about the print, the big feet?"

Bigsby shrugged. "Could have been more than one person involved. Maybe a team. Maybe the big guy sells the kid to someone in Midland. Or they could all be separate links in a human trafficking chain."

Kane nodded and looked thoughtful. "How would someone get close enough to get those intimate details you mentioned?"

"Good question. A real good question. We immediately put out an Amber alert. More than 800 kids have been recovered with Amber alerts, you know."

Kane nodded. He didn't know the numbers, but he'd heard of it.

"Of course, what you're really implying is that the tip came from someone involved in it." Bigsby spread his hands in front of them. "It's possible."

"Did you trace the number of the anonymous tip?" Kane asked.

"We tried. The caller was on a burner."

"Burner?" Lucy repeated. "Like in *Sons of Anarchy*, the little cheapy phones?"

"Right. And it wasn't registered."

"Doesn't that seem suspicious?" Kane asked.

Bigsby shrugged again and ran his fingers over his mustache. His guts told him the situation wasn't right, and he debated only a moment before telling them as much. "Anonymous tips are good and bad. It gives people on the inside the chance to rat out other people, which is good. It also opens the gates for a whole herd of nutcases to drive through. Burners are the pay phone of the twenty-first century. Cheap. Easy to use. Disposable."

He paused for a bit, considering his words.

"In this situation," he continued, "the details seemed a little *too* good to be anonymous. In my opinion."

Kane had hardly blinked as the sheriff spoke. "Anything that could corroborate the tip?"

"Funny you ask," Bigsby said. "Old Bird Taylor, who you saw yesterday, reported that he saw a blue Nissan speeding out of town around the time of the kidnapping."

They all stewed on that for a few minutes. Tom grabbed the pot and topped off everyone's cup, then turned his chair, and sat back down on it backwards, arms on the top.

Lucy broke the silence. "Did Bird have an alibi for the kidnapping?"

"He did," Tom stepped in. "Said he was doing paperwork at the gas station. That kid that works for him, Mikey, backed it up."

"Interesting," Kane said.

"Very," Tom agreed.

Bigsby leaned back and stroked his mustache. "Unfortunately, that's where we're at."

"Well, Sheriff, we appreciate your time." Kane stood and extended his hand to the two officers. "Please let us know if we can help in any way."

They shook hands, then Bigsby went around and gave Lucy a hug.

"Protect that noggin," he told her with his patented almost-smile.

After they were gone, Bigsby found himself thinking about the additional pieces Lucy Baker and Kane Montgomery had added to the puzzle. He thought about

Bird Taylor, the Red lady, and Colby Wilson. The Villareal fire. The rattlesnakes and the car accidents.

Bigsby was desperate to save his town, but he'd be damned if he could see the connection between it all.

CHAPTER 21

Bird was in a weird mood.

His refrigerator looked like a poor, younger sibling of the ones that lined the back wall of his gas station. Burritos, energy drinks, chocolate milk, and beer filled the shelves, carried home from work after he closed down each night. He figured it wasn't stealing, since he owned the joint, and for once in matters of the law, he was right.

He fixed what was probably the closest thing he had to a *favorite* breakfast: An Extra Extra Large El Monterey microwave burrito with a standard size Miller Lite on the side. The trailer quickly became an amalgamation of dirty laundry, body odor, beer, and microwaved food. It was what it always smelled like and resembled the odor of the gas station, as unfortunate customers might testify.

But Bird didn't exhibit his usual ardor for the meal. He just wasn't feeling it. Midway through, he chucked the remains into the trash and finished his beer.

Burped loudly. Scratched his ass. Wandered over to his computer.

He tuned into his favorite pornography site and clicked around. There were thousands of videos and pictures to choose from, and he scrolled through them for a while, trying to find a good one.

He paused at a screen shot of people dressed up in kinky leather suits, beating one another, then shook his head and kept scrolling. There was another that boasted women inserting household items into all imaginable orifices, and he stifled a yawn.

A video starring three chicks with big knockers, and a well-proportioned dude, caught his attention and he clicked on it. Not-so-clever stage names flashed by on his monitor—Betsy Mountains, Hugh G. Rexshun, Sally Rides—all colorfully representative of the filth he'd be watching.

From what he gathered, the women were supposed to be college students and the man was their tutor. He was helping them study in the dorm room they all shared.

For clean young college ladies, they had a remarkable number of tattoos, and it took no time at all for the tutor to introduce the girls to some Longfellow. Bird tried to masturbate, but he couldn't get into it, so he put away the anaconda and surfed aimlessly.

There were some gun modification blogs that held his attention for a few minutes, and he watched a guy test out some new firearms on YouTube. The dude was firing a couple of pistols at different sized metal plates hanging around his property, and they all made a different sound. The guy banged out part of The Star-Spangled Banner.

Bored with that, he swapped over to *Inked* and looked at tattoos.

"The fuck?" He shook his head when he saw an article devoted to Pokémon tattoos. Pokémon again! It was bad enough that kids came around the station looking for Peek-a-choos or whatever. But to get tattoos of it? Made no sense.

He grunted in appreciation when he saw a link for *underboob* tattoos, and clicked there. He was soon disappointed at how lame it was. Little birds were flying around the bottoms of breasts—artsy and fruity shit— nothing worth looking at.

Glancing down, he flexed, and watched the scantily clad woman on his right forearm dance. Skulls and a black panther covered much of his left arm. Good work, done over in Midland years before.

He'd been thinking about a new one, but just never got around to it. Maybe now was the time. Bird decided he'd go ahead and get another one sometime soon.

With an uncharacteristic sigh, he stood up from his computer. Went to the fridge. Opened a beer and sucked some down. Fired his bottle cap at the garbage can and missed. Walked back into the living room, looked around, and then turned and went back to the kitchen. Looked out the window. Sighed again. Went back to the living room and sat down on his couch.

Hector Junior.

He'd be damned if he couldn't stop thinking about Hector Jr. The kid had just laughed it off when he got tossed on the floor of Bird's truck. Bird knew he'd been driving a little crazy, but time was short, and he didn't have one of those car seats he saw people using. Old Hec just laughed it off, though.

"Tough as nails," Bird said to the empty room and grinned.

He was really surprised when Hec started repeating words back to him on the drive to Rising Sun. Little man was smart. Said *Shit!* several times. And some other words, too.

Bird chuckled to himself in the empty trailer.

Kid'll probably be a doctor, he thought.

Except...

Except that wasn't true. The kid was never going to be a doctor, and he wasn't going to be smart for very long. Because whatever Red had planned for those kids, Bird knew it wasn't going to be something good.

Nope—not good at all.

Another sigh escaped him as he wrestled with his thoughts. He drained the rest of his beer. Stared at the cheap wood paneling of his walls. Pushed Hector Jr. out of his mind and told himself he didn't care.

Zeke's old truck had run better than he expected. That was something. Hell, he couldn't even remember the last time he'd taken it out. Which reminded him...

There was some business to take care of at the warehouse.

Bird rounded up supplies and some odds and ends. When he stepped outside, he saw Zeke's truck, and decided to give it a crank. Since nobody fucked with Bird, he left his keys right in the ignition of the trucks every night. He was less surprised this time when Zeke's truck turned over on the first try, with only a little feedback out of the exhaust.

In most cities, you used back roads to stay out of sight. Not in Marathon. There weren't really any back roads. The entirety of the city was pretty much one small neighborhood. Old people sat on porches. Kids tossed the ball around in the street. Neighbors talked about the weather and cussed the heat.

Bird didn't care to be seen, so he shot through the center of town on the highway. Nobody noticed, and nobody cared, at least not as far as he could tell.

The gate around the warehouse was intact. He unlocked it and pulled the truck inside, scoping out the area. It didn't look like there'd been any uninvited guests, and the only things moving were a couple of tumbleweeds, skirting the property as the wind pushed them along.

He hauled in buckets, water, and some other gear. Everything was in good condition on the inside—no surprises. He did what he needed to do, but it didn't give him the same pleasure that it had before. Something was different now. And he found he was just going through the motions.

It was almost as if he felt … guilty.

When he finished up, he stepped outside, closed the doors, and locked them tight. He went to the center of the compound and did a 360-degree scan of the area. Some junk littered the ground—barrels, old tires, and sheet metal—but otherwise there was only desert. A hot breeze was blowing, and it gave a low whistle as it snaked around the building. A bird cawed somewhere in the distance. Just another day in Marathon.

He figured everything should be safe for a while, so he jumped in Zeke's truck, and retraced his route back to the trailer.

*****

Bird's property was a quarter of a mile off the highway.

The access road curved several times as it climbed through rocky terrain. Back and forth, back and forth, tracing the slight incline of the land. At the top, it dipped back down, and formed a bowl. That's where he had his trailer—Zeke's old trailer. It was backed up against miles of nothing, something all the Taylors had appreciated. They didn't like prying eyes, enjoyed shooting guns, and kept to themselves. It was the perfect place for their lot.

As Bird rounded that last curve, and began the dip into his property, he jammed on the brakes. There, next to his trailer, was a little red Audi TT.

"The fuck?" he said to himself. He'd done everything she asked, and he thought—*hoped*—he had seen the last of her. Shaking his head, he took the nearly full red Solo cup from the holder and spit into it. Some of the contents splashed out, so he emptied the overflowing cup out his window, and put it back. Slowly, he started driving again down to his trailer.

He looked into the car, but it was empty. Bird almost kicked it, but then thought better. She could be anywhere. He peeked around the back of the trailer for her, but the only thing he found was a brown lizard. It pumped out the red pouch under its neck, and then scurried away.

Red wasn't outside. Which left only one place.

Bird lumbered up the steps to his trailer, two hundred and fifty pounds of resignation, and opened the door.

Red was lounging on his couch in a slinky red dress—or maybe a kimono—he wasn't sure. Despite his trepidation, he found it very difficult to look away from her legs. While he watched, she slowly lifted one leg and crossed it over the other, just like Sharon Stone in *Basic Instinct*. Zeke had shown him that movie when he was in second or third grade, and he'd never forgotten it. Sharon Stone might have been his first love.

Bird's breath caught in his throat when he realized Red wasn't wearing any panties and he felt the old familiar sensation down in his jeans—the beast awakening. "I was wondering when you were going to stop fucking around outside, and come in." She didn't so much say it, as she purred it.

Bird grunted, and mustered up enough willpower to pull himself away from her, and make his way to the refrigerator. He left the door open so the air could cool his overheating body. It was the rough equivalent of a cold shower. He leaned in, cracked open another bottle of Miller Lite, and knocked back half of it while he stood there. Never had beer tasted so good.

Facing her again in the living room, he opened his mouth to ask her...

"What do I want?" she said, cutting him off.

It was exactly what Bird was going to say. The words were on the tip of his tongue. He opened his mouth again...

"Damn it! Stop that!" She said, and laughed.

After a few seconds, Bird closed his mouth and shook his head. She'd said precisely what he was thinking. What he was going to say. Again. Like she was inside his head.

Red stopped laughing, and her eyes flashed gold before returning to their normal color. "I'll stop. Okay? Will that make you feel better?"

He nodded, speechless.

"Say it, Birdy Boy. You can say it."

"Yeah," he managed to choke out. The last time he felt this paranoid, he'd just gotten ahold of some bad pot from these guys that brought dope across from Juarez. The high lasted two days, and he'd seen things, and heard voices.

Red had worked him over like a marionette puppet, too, and he felt a little drunk. She just reached in and played with his mind as she pleased.

"This request is a special one. The child is special. I need you to bring me this kid, and the sooner the better. Everything is about timing, Birdy."

He opened his mouth to ask a question, but she answered it before he could speak.

"The Beckman kid. I want the Beckman kid. I'm sure you know where to find him in this little shithole of a town."

Bird knew all right. He kept his mind blank in the hopes that she wouldn't see anything, and she looked at him curiously.

"Are you trying to hide something from me, Birdy?"

He hesitated. Didn't say anything.

"You're going to get me the kid. Right?"

"Yeah," he said. "I'll git him for you."

She watched him closely for twenty or thirty seconds, and Bird tensed up. It felt like fingers were squirming around under his skull, tugging at his brain. Finally, Red's face relaxed and she smiled at him.

"Good," she said. "I believe you."

She stared at him and he couldn't look away.

Slowly, she reached her hands up to the lapels of her dress, and pulled it wide open. She wasn't wearing anything underneath.

"Now get over here."

Bird did as he was told.

CHAPTER 22

"What do you make of it?" Lucy asked.

They were in her Tacoma, leaving the sheriff's station.

Kane thought about it. "I don't know. I feel like there is something there, hidden in all of the pieces, and we just have to figure out how it fits together."

"I was thinking the same thing," she said. "Oh, hey, there's the library." She pointed down Northeast Third Street.

"I don't see it."

"There. The little beige building."

"Oh, sure." He'd overlooked it at first, tucked in among the homes on a residential street. It was probably a repurposed home, but the architecture was nice. It was yellow, like Lucy's place. "Wanna stop in?"

"Let's grab some breakfast first," she said.

"Where?"

"The Marathon Coffee Shop. They serve *amazing* breakfast enchiladas."

Kane's first thought when they drove up was that the coffee shop looked like the old Firestone tire shop from his hometown, only white instead of yellow. A ribbon of rust had drifted down the large sign at the curb, masking the first "f" in coffee. Cofee. What looked like skinny pine tree trunks held up the tin-metal overhang.

It was right across the street from the Gage hotel.

"Want to stop in and see Debbie?" he asked.

She punched his arm. "Funny. Now, come on." Sliding an arm around his waist, she pulled him toward the door, which appeared to be new—the only part of the Marathon Coffee Shop manufactured in the last century, by the looks of it.

"Fantastic breakfast enchiladas, huh?"

She licked her lips and nodded, and then they were inside.

It wouldn't be much of a stretch to say that Kane's mouth watered instantly. Frying potatoes sizzled in the kitchen. He could smell ham, beans, and tortillas. There was the subtle yet fragrant undercurrent of onions— Kane's favorite.

"I might be in heaven," he told Lucy.

An elderly lady told them to sit where they wanted. Wooden four-seat tables filled the rectangular dining area, pushed together at strategic spots to fit six or eight. A variety of Mexican and Southern art hung from the walls, and a statue of the Virgin Mary stood in an alcove by the last table.

A floor heater sat unplugged in the corner.

They picked a table near the windows and Kane scoured the menu ... two front-and-back pages sealed in document protectors. Lucy watched him study the options like a chess grandmaster looking for the checkmate.

"I'm getting Huevos Rancheros," he declared. "You?"

She just stared at him.

"Just kidding. Can I try some of yours?" he asked.

"I don't know. I like my enchiladas."

"I like *your* enchilada," he said.

"What does that even mean?" she giggled. "Girls don't have anything that looks like an enchilada."

"It would have worked out better if you'd ordered tacos."

As the old lady moved back and forth to their table it was always "You ready to order, darling?" and "Here's your drink, hon," and "Y'all doing okay?" She didn't waste any time dropping hot plates in front of them.

"We've been called darlings, honey, hon, and y'all. Every Texas vernacular stereotype has been fulfilled."

"Well, we *are* in *Texas*, Kane."

"True." As he said it, he watched Lucy mop up the last of her cheese and beans with tortilla. "I like a woman with an appetite."

"Then you're going to love me," she replied. It seemed like a normal thing to say. Right? Except her eyes lingered on his, and his on hers, and he suspected that maybe they weren't just talking about food any more.

"Ready for the library?" he asked.

*****

"Hello, Ms. Tate!"

"Well, if it isn't Lucy Baker!" Ms. Tate was tall and slender, and she apparently never stopped smiling. She was dressed conservatively, but not without style, in a white blouse and mustard sweater. Her skirt rested just above the knees. Her hair was sitting behind her head, twirled and wrapped and kept together by what appeared to be a set of plastic chopsticks. Kane guessed she was in her mid-fifties. Guessing ages was something he did unconsciously with everyone he met.

She stood up from the circulation desk, came around the counter, and grabbed Lucy in a bear-hug.

"It's really good to see you," Lucy said.

"It's been way too long," the librarian replied. She nodded her head sideways at Kane, and then winked at Lucy. "Is this your new fella?"

Lucy blushed.

Kane introduced himself and put out his hand. Ms. Tate placed her hand in his, in that gentle and feminine way that left the top facing him. There was always this funny urge for him to kiss hands offered like that, but he never did.

"Kane—nice to meet you. I'm Jennifer. Both of you call me Jennifer." She gave Lucy a playful look. "Got that Lucy? We're all adults now. I'm just a little bit older."

"Not much," Kane chimed in.

Jennifer Tate's smile broadened. "I like him."

Kane glanced around at the library while Lucy and Jennifer caught up on different things. Bright colors filled the room, and book covers greeted him from every direction. The building was riddled with chairs of various sizes. An elementary age girl was splayed across a beanbag chair, absorbed in her book, and oblivious to them all.

A giant summer reading program poster was framed near the entrance. There was a playful tidiness about the place, and it was obvious that Ms. Tate took pride in her library. It made him wish he was a kid again.

"So what are you guys doing here?" she asked them. She elbowed Kane, "Need a library card? We have all the latest bestsellers *and* the classics. I even maintain a romance section. Certain ladies in the town wouldn't have it otherwise. They desperately need the H-E-A in their lives."

"H-E-A?" Kane asked.

"Happily Ever After. It's a key ingredient in the romance recipe."

"Well, we're not looking for the H-E-A," Lucy said. "We wanted you to tell us about Terlingua. The fighting and the killing ... the strange things that have happened around here."

Her eyes shone. "Yes, the fighting. The raping and pillaging."

"Yes!" Lucy said.

"Well, well, well ... you've come to the right place *and* the right person. There may not be anyone else alive who geeks out on Marathon and Big Bend history as much as I do. Some call it passion; I call it obsession."

Lucy was nodding. Ms. Tate was a fast-talker, and had almost no discernible accent—maybe Northern, if anything—but definitely not Southern.

"Let me grab some books from the reference room, and we can powwow right at the desk."

"Thank you so much, Ms. Tate, err, Jennifer."

"Of course." Jennifer smiled at Lucy. "I'll grab my things and some drinks and be back in a sec."

*****

171

"When do you think people first came to the area, Kane?"

"No idea," he answered. "Five hundred years ago? Eight hundred? Probably before Chris Columbus."

"Way before Christopher Columbus or Leif Erikson," she said. "Try *ten thousand* years."

"Holy cow," Kane said. "That's crazy."

"It *is* crazy. You're probably wondering why they lived here, right? It's hot, it's dirty, and it isn't the easiest place to carve out a life. Not much fun. Except the climate was different back then. Bison roaming around, trees everywhere, and not many tumbleweeds. These prehistoric natives were hunters and lived off of the land, and from what we can tell, life was pretty good."

Ms. Tate stopped to check out books to a mother with two small kids. Books littered the table behind the main desk, and Lucy and Kane browsed through them while she was away. A few of the texts were old, and they handled all of them carefully.

"Check this out," Lucy said. She slid one of the books across to Kane and pointed at a picture.

"What's this?"

"A painting from a cave in Big Bend," she told him.

"It looks Egyptian almost," he said. There were clothed stick figures in the picture. One of them appeared to be a priest, dressed in black. Next to him was a person dressed in brown with long hair. They were holding a baby. Little stick figures in robes surrounded them. "Looks like a baptism."

"I don't think so," Lucy said. "The lady has a knife."

"What?" Kane got closer and studied the image. There was a triangular object protruding out from the little stick figure hand. "I think you're right. It looks like a woman holding a knife. That's freaking insane."

She leaned over his shoulder and read through the page. "They dated the painting back to the Archaic Period, roughly five thousand BC."

They were still studying the picture when Ms. Tate sat down again. "Where were we? Oh, right. First natives arrived ten thousand years ago. They were mostly hunters, following prey. Spears were *their* weapons of mass destruction. They hunted Woolly Mammoth and Bison—for food—but also to make clothing and shelter from their hides."

Lucy and Kane listened with rapt attention as the librarian ran them through the Paleo Indian and Archaic periods. Climate change thinned herds. Cooperative hunting evolved and the Mammoths went extinct. "Hunters compensated by learning to hunt smaller animals. They relied more on gathering edible plants and berries."

"It's fascinating," Lucy said.

"It is." Jennifer Tate's eyes twinkled.

"Almost forgot." Lucy slid the book with the photo of the drawing across the table. "Do you know much about this?"

"Oh, yeah." The librarian nodded. "I was here when they discovered this about twenty years ago. I was a complete and total groupie! I pestered the team at the site incessantly!"

The librarian laughed. It was a loud and boisterous sound, and it was impossible not to smile and laugh with her.

"That was on the wall of a cave that was practically inaccessible—the entrance was in the middle of a sheer cliff face."

"How'd they find it?" Kane inquired.

"Climbers came across it by accident," Jennifer answered. "It's thirty feet off the ground, camouflaged by Mother Nature. This woman and her boyfriend quite literally *swung into it* moving down their ropes."

"Rappelling." Kane nodded and clasped his hands behind his head. He had plenty of experience with that. He could almost hear the helicopter's rotary wings thumping from when he and one of his old units did a particularly hairy night insertion. Even the brassiest nerves jangled at times.

Lucy looked thoughtful. "How were the ancient people getting in and out, if it was thirty feet above the ground?"

"Ladders."

"Ladders?" Lucy repeated.

"Crazy, right? They found bits of petrified wood and some fossilized molds in the sediment below the cave, and as best they can tell, it was from ladders. Easy to make the next connection, that they used them to climb up to the cave." She nodded vigorously, then looked back at the book. "But, I digressed! What did you want to know about the picture?"

"It looks like that person," Lucy pointed, "is holding a knife. Do you think that they were sacrificing the baby?" Lucy had lowered her voice when she asked, and it came out somewhere between a whisper and the traditionally hushed library-volume-voice.

"It's possible. Human sacrifice pops up all over the world in history." Ms. Tate opened another book and flipped through some pages. "Here we go. You see this … the Egyptians and Phoenicians, the Chinese, Vikings, and a lot of other civilizations ritualized the sacrifice of people. Just south of us, in Mexico, the Aztecs sacrificed thousands of people each year as sort of a *payment* to their gods for providing them with the earth, the sun, and the means to flourish. They believed it also kept them in their gods' favor."

Lucy grimaced in obvious distaste.

"We find it abhorrent now, but they didn't know any better back then. In many civilizations it was a deep-rooted belief—a part of their culture or religion—and it had to be done."

The trio worked their way through other books, and Kane learned about the groups that had inhabited the Big Bend and Marathon areas at various times. Mexican people, the Spanish, and Apache and Comanche Indians were prevalent the last five hundred years.

"Oh, darn—it's getting late," Lucy said looking at her watch.

Kane stood and stretched. He was surprised to see they'd been talking for more than two hours.

"It's really interesting stuff, though," he said.

"Hey, wait a sec … what is that?" Lucy was pointing at another photo. "It looks like that first one we saw, except more advanced."

"You're right." Jennifer traced her finger on the glossy photo insert. "I never noticed it, but they are very similar. Another man in black holding a child. The woman nearby with the knife."

"Is that one from the Archaic period, too?" Lucy asked.

"No," Jennifer responded. "This one is a few thousand years later, from the late fifteenth century … about the same time that the Aztecs ruled most of what we currently call Mexico."

While Lucy and Jennifer talked, Kane studied the picture. Something was strangely familiar. *Like déjà vu or something,* he thought, but he couldn't figure it out. There was the priestly figure in black clothing, holding the child up in the same manner that Simba was presented in *The Lion King.* And, alongside him, the lady in the dress, evil smile, knife at the ready.

CHAPTER 23
Tuesday

"Holeee shit," Deputy Slidell whispered after he got off with dispatch. For a second, he just stared at the radio, not really seeing anything, paralyzed. Normally, he'd say a quick "Sorry, God" when he cursed, but his mind was blown.

Tom's body tingled, and he felt strange all over. Like he was coming down with something bad—a virus—the flu. Except he wasn't sick, not even close. As his dad would say, he was fit as a fiddle and trim in the middle.

They were parked outside the Villareal home. The evidence collection team was nearly finished around the house, and Sheriff Bigsby was talking to the lead man, Charlie, whom he'd worked with a few times in the past. Things weren't looking good. There was a fingerprint that didn't match anyone in the Villareal family that they were able to lift from a piece of glass in the rubble. That, the boot print, and the tire tread were their only leads. No witnesses ... at least, not any that were available or alive.

Deputy Slidell hopped out of the Bronco and landed unsteadily. His legs were spaghetti noodles. *Get your crap together,* he told himself and took a deep and shaky breath.

"Sheriff!" he called out, walking toward the rear of the house. With each step, he felt a little better, and he quickly regained his composure. A powerful sense of urgency hit him, and he started jogging. The gear on his belt was held in place pretty well, but it still jostled a bit, and without thinking he placed a hand on it as he moved, to reduce the motion.

*****

Bigsby looked up as his deputy came rushing into the backyard. From the look on his face, he knew right away that something wasn't right. "Tom?"

"We have to go, Sheriff!"

"Be in touch," Bigsby told Charlie.

They fell into a fast walk together, and Tom eyeballed the house to make sure no one was around.

"They got another kid," he said, as low as he could.

Sheriff Bigsby stopped dead in his tracks for a beat or two while Tom kept moving, then he hustled to catch up to his deputy as if they were connected by an invisible bungee cord that had been pulled taut. Bigsby scrolled through his mental Rolodex of Marathon's kids.

"Who?" the sheriff asked.

"Reese Beckman."

Bigsby clenched his jaws so tight that the joints cracked and he thought he'd broken a tooth.

"Dot Beckman's," he said, as they jumped into their truck and peeled out.

"Dispatch, this is Deputy Slidell. Me and the Sheriff are en route to Dot Beckman's trailer. Get us some more deputies out there ASAP. And get a BOLO out for Reese Beckman." He paused, and then added, "Also, please let the evidence guys know they've got another job. I didn't tell them on our way out."

The radio crackled to life.

"Dispatch copies," Harriet replied. There was eerie static—the mic was still keyed hot. Feedback whined through the vehicle before Harriet finally added, "You get this guy, Tom."

Bigsby looked over. Tom's face was flushed and his muscles twitched. "Roger that, Dispatch."

Dot Beckman lived on the southwest side of Marathon in an old doublewide trailer. Her husband died the previous year. Dot's four daughters had left town gradually through the last decade, the youngest of them, Becky, leaving her with a grandkid to take care of, father unknown.

Dot coped with it in the old-fashioned way—booze.

As Bigsby barreled across U.S. 90 with barely a glance in either direction, Tom reached down and unclasped the Beretta 1301 Tactical shotgun from its rack. He loaded a shell into the ejection port and popped the bolt forward, then put another seven shells into the magazine tube and extension. It was a semi-automatic 12-guage. The first time they fired it, Tom told Bigsby that he thought he'd fallen in love. Tom had blown off 8 rounds in just a few seconds and the target had literally disintegrated under the onslaught.

Just let me find this bastard, Bigsby thought. *I'm going to put him down.*

Sixty seconds later, they turned right onto Kate's Run, and ten seconds after that Bigsby slid to a halt in Dot's front yard. She ran outside with her hands in the air, screaming, and almost tumbled over in front of the Bronco.

Bigsby wondered if she was three sheets to the wind.

"They took Reese," she cried. Probably in her late fifties, Dot was looking twenty years older right then. She staggered, falling in Bigsby's direction, and he caught her. He could smell gin, but it wasn't overpowering. While he held Dot, Tom ran inside her place with the shotgun out ahead of him as he went.

"What happened, Dot?"

"I was in the livin' room watchin' *The Price is Right.* Reese was in his bed in the back room, nappin'. I musta fell asleep, and next I knew, I heard a noise and woke up."

Tom came out the front door and down the steps. He and Bigsby exchanged a look before he circled the trailer.

"Go on."

"I ran back to check on him, and the window was wide open!" she howled. Her eyes were watery and halfway bloodshot. "Little Reese wasn't there. I ran over to the window and I saw a car speeding off down Lee Street."

"How long ago?" Bigsby asked.

"I dunno, maybe twenty or thirty minutes."

"Did you say it was a car?" He was surprised. Not too many locals owned cars, so it would be easy to crosscheck against the residents. "Did you get the make or model?"

"No, I couldn't tell what it was. Looked older, maybe."

"How old?"

"Hmm. I dunno. Just not new."

"See the license plate numbers or what state it was?"

"No..." she mumbled and shook her head.

"Color?"

"Gray? I think it was gray. Faded..."

"Two doors? Four?"

She bit her lip and concentrated, and Bigsby felt himself growing impatient. "Oh, I don't know, Sheriff ... it was moving so fast I only saw it for a second and then I just ran straight inside to call you." She'd given him almost nothing. All he knew was that it was a car, and he could surmise that it had four wheels and an engine. No way of telling whether it was local or fell outside Marathon proper.

Of course, there were a lot of folks with old vehicles that didn't bother registering them. They sat in various yards without being used for the better part of twenty years, except on weekend trips to the Piggly Wiggly.

Despite the smell of alcohol, Dot was fairly lucid, and Bigsby believed her. He didn't think she'd had enough to drink to chalk this up to neglect. Just dumb bad luck.

"Okay, Dot. Go inside and stay put. Don't go near Reese's room or touch anything. You understand? Can you do that for me? You can't go near that room, so we don't mess up any evidence."

"Okay, Sheriff," she said. She was crying again, and he walked her as quickly as he could back to her living room and got her onto her couch.

Tom was waiting outside, and they quickly exchanged notes.

"Same as the Wilson place, boss. Went straight in through the window. Looks like he knocked the screen off on his way back out. Probably what she heard. Found this near the boy's bed."

Tom held up a Ziploc bag with an almost empty roll of duct tape inside. Bigsby raised his eyebrows.

"Maybe to keep the kid quiet," Tom said

Bigsby nodded, impressed with Tom's logic despite the awful situation. "Our guy was in a car, possibly gray. Make and model unknown. Number of doors unknown. State of registration unknown. Last seen heading north on Lee Street toward 90. Every other direction is private property, or you'd need four-wheel drive to go off-road, so it all jibes."

"Yes, sir." Tom agreed.

Stan Mitchel, one of the Alpine deputies sent to help them out, pulled up fast and parked behind the Bronco. He was a bright guy, and eager, and they quickly brought him up to speed.

"Stay with Dot, protect the scene, and wait for the boys to get here and go over the place. Find out where she thinks the car was parked, and don't let anyone mess with the area."

"You got it, Sheriff," Stan replied.

"Tom, give Stan that tape for evidence collection and let's go take us a look around."

They jumped in the Bronco and whipped out onto Kate's Run.

"Dispatch, Slidell."

"Go ahead, Deputy," Harriet answered.

"We need to get all the law enforcement personnel within about a hundred miles on the lookout for a..." He paused and looked at the sheriff. Bigsby sighed and shook his head back and forth. "Be on the lookout for a gray car, vicinity U.S. 90, suspected involvement in the kidnapping of Reese Beckman, age eleven months, black hair, blue eyes."

"Roger, WILCO, Deputy."

They cut a quick right on Lee Street. Their eyes scanned everything from behind dark sunglasses, searching for clues, finding none. A bearded guy in jeans with a plain, paint-splattered T-shirt and camouflage hat was digging in the toolbox of a truck at the curb.

"Hey, Ralph," Tom called through his open window.

"Deputy Tom. Sheriff." He offered his hand through the window, and both men shook it. A town of five hundred people was smaller than many high school graduating classes.

"Ralph, you see a gray car come through here?"

"No."

"Have you seen *any* car driving on this street?"

Ralph furrowed his brows as he pulled out a can of Kodiak and popped in a dip. "No. Don't reckon I have."

Sheriff Bigsby faced forward, nodding his head.

"This got to do with the Wilson boy?"

Bigsby looked at Ralph sharply, but then relented. News of Colby Wilson had dropped like a big rock into a small pond. It rippled through every household in a matter of hours. Everyone took it personally.

He needed all the help he could get right now.

"Ralph, I'm gonna shoot straight with you."

"'Course, Sheriff."

"Reese Beckman just got kidnapped. Dot saw a gray car leaving the scene. I want to *nail* this son-of-a-bitch and get these kids back."

Ralph's eyes went wide, and then hardened.

"Whadda you need, boss?"

"Keep your eyes and ears open. You see anybody that ain't from Marathon, check 'em out, and let me know about 'em. We have to look out for our own. You ken?"

"I'll be looking out," Ralph replied. His voice had morphed from southern friendly to menacing.

"Don't hurt anyone unless you have to ... unless you're sure."

Ralph nodded.

"All right," Bigsby said. "Call me if you see anything."

Without another word, they kicked up gravel and rolled. They both could see Ralph the Handyman in the mirrors. It looked like he was grabbing a pipe out of the bed of his truck, but instead of going back to the house, he jumped into the driver's seat.

"Think that was a good idea, Sheriff?" Tom asked.

Bigsby let out a very uncharacteristic and shaky laugh. There was no humor in it, only exasperation.

"Tom, I don't have any damned clue," he said. "All I know is that in about a week we've lost the three youngest people in Marathon."

They were silent until they got to 90. They could go left or right, but both directions seemed equally unpromising. Across the highway was the Marathon Motel and RV Park.

"Let's swing by the motel and ask if they've seen anything." Sheriff Bigsby tried to sound hopeful, for Tom, but inside ... he was losing faith.

CHAPTER 24

"Bird," Mikey greeted him, eyebrows furrowed. "Thought you needed me to close down the place tonight?"

"Yeah, Mikey, I do..."

Mikey looked at him curiously.

"Need your car," Bird told him. He had his old man's green Army duffel bag in his hand.

Mikey looked crestfallen. Bird knew that the kid worshipped that old car. He updated Bird on it every day, every new part that he installed for the last six months. However, Bird wasn't making a request.

The boy just nodded and his eyes glazed over. He had the thousand-yard stare that soldiers sometimes get when they've been in serious combat, and they become numb to the world. Mikey dug around in his blue jeans and pulled out a set of car keys—set them on the counter. He avoided eye contact. Bird almost laughed, but he liked Mikey, so he didn't screw with him this time.

"Back soon, bud," he told him. He even waited to gun the engine until the gas station was out of sight and he was down the highway.

The seat was a little small for someone Bird's size, but he didn't really mind. Busy checking out the car, he discovered that he really liked it. From the stainless steel steering wheel frame to the four-speed automatic shifter, the car was a rock star among cars. Nothing was better than owning a truck, but if you had to own a car, Bird reckoned that it definitely should be a Trans Am.

The thing had a huge set of balls on it, too. There was a six-point-six-liter V-8 engine under the hood, and when he hit the gas, it leapt forward like a big cat going for the kill.

I should probably own this car instead of Mikey, he thought, and did a combination laugh-grunt. Remembering what he had to do, he brought it back under the speed limit, and leveled off.

He passed the Marathon Coffee Shop and noticed the hot little blonde from Bob's Saloon, Lucy Baker. She was a few years younger than him, but they were almost in the same grade when he finally dropped out. Moved on with his life instead of doing the stupid school bullshit.

She was getting into her little rice burner Toyota truck with that guy from the gas station, the one who tried to stare him down. Thinking about it pissed him off. He had been completely busted shortchanging him. He didn't even need the money, just enjoyed getting the better of all these people that thought they were better than him.

There was something in the way the guy had held himself—like he knew what he was doing—and Bird had one of those rare moments where he exercised caution despite the flaring of his temper. After hundreds of fights, he'd learned to recognize tough opponents. He lost about one out of every fifty, and it was those losses that he remembered most.

Bird didn't mind pain. When you were Zeke Taylor's son, you learned about pain very early in life. Most times, he just tuned out the pain anyway. Nope, he wasn't afraid of pain … he just hated losing.

And his guts told him he would lose. So, he backed off. Maybe he could make it up to that guy some night. Maybe take a bat to his knees, then let him watch while he boned Lucy Baker. Now *that* sounded like a good time!

Half a mile later, he was in a good mood again, when he saw the sign for Lee Street and turned left.

Red wanted Reese Beckman. His good mood evaporated thinking about it. He'd already delivered two kids to the Woman in Red, from a town that didn't have kids to spare. And now he was going to grab the third.

But that wasn't what really bothered him.

Bird knew Rebecca Beckman. Becky. Reese's mom.

Every now and then, some of the local bad kids would come looking for him, to buy weed or ecstasy. He didn't deal, per se, but he always had a large personal stash, and he didn't mind unloading some. He'd often make double or triple the money he paid for it.

But, there were times he gave it away free…

Now and then, one of the local girls would come around with their friends, hitting him up for dope, and he'd invite them all into his trailer and fire up a joint. Once they were good and stoned, he'd have his way with them. If they weren't interested, he had other drugs to *make* them interested.

Becky Beckman—Becky Two Times—had been to his trailer on several occasions. She'd brought an older sister once and the three of them had partied until dawn.

Bird may not have been the smartest guy, but he wasn't an idiot. When people in town began gossiping about the youngest Beckman girl being pregnant, he did the math, and realized that the kid might be his.

Maybe.

Becky Two Times got around. When the football players needed to celebrate after a big game, Becky was happy to oblige. The fact that she'd go alone to Bird's trailer was telling. In the history of Marathon, there might not have been any girl as promiscuous as Rebecca Beckman.

It tore up her old man when he found out she was pregnant. Rumor had it that the news gave him a heart attack. Nobody could prove it, though. Then the shit hit the fan all at once: he died, Becky gave birth, and then she split and left Dot Beckman to care for Reese.

Bird wasn't the kind of guy that got emotional. He listened with mild interest if he overheard people talking around town, then promptly forgot about it.

Now he was parked on Lee Street, around the block from Dot's trailer, and he was about to see this kid for the first time. Despite his cavalier attitude toward, well, everything … he felt a little weird about it.

He cut the engine, and went to take care of business.

*****

Bird's boot got caught on the windowsill climbing out of Reese's window. His free arm pin-wheeled, and he ripped the screen down trying to brace himself. There were two seconds of peace as he fell. The quiet before the storm. Then the Earth gave him a hard kiss on his side and head, and the wind was knocked halfway out of him. The kid was tucked under his arm, facing the sky, and went unscathed, but the jarring impact started him crying.

"Shhh," Bird said. He'd forgotten the duct tape he brought to cover the kid's pie hole, so he got up and ran for Mikey's car. He knew he was going to hear someone hollering for him to stop, but it never came. He thought he saw Dot Beckman in the rearview mirror as he stomped on the gas and the car lurched forward.

Bird looked at the kid lying sideways in the passenger seat. He'd kidnapped three kids in one week, but this one was bigger than the other two, stocky and long body, wavy black hair.

The kid stopped crying and stared at Bird. Held eye contact. Unknown to him, there were only three kids under one year of age in Marathon. He'd stolen the youngest members of the city's population.

"Nana. Car. Dada. Da-Da-Da." The kid babbled in the seat next to him, but Bird didn't hear all of it. Mostly, he just heard the word "dad."

He made the right for Rising Sun and stepped on it. Traffic was never heavy, and he kept looking at Reese Beckman. Road … Reese. Road … Reese.

The right side of the Trans Am veered onto the shoulder, and the car twisted sharply. Bird wrestled it back onto 385, and cursed himself.

I'll be damned if that kid doesn't look like me, he thought.

Bird pulled the car over on the side of the road. He leaned in close to the kid and looked him over. Studied his arms. The shape of his nose and size of his forehead.

In those few minutes, he convinced himself he was Reese's old man.

There was no epiphany. No revelation. There was keen interest, like when he'd heard they were bringing back the Ford Bronco. His concept of fatherhood went no further than sharing a beer with the boy when he got old enough to stomach it.

And, yet, he was pulled over on the side of the road. *Maybe I should go on Oprah or Dr. Phil*, he chuckled to himself. *Gettin' in touch with my female side a lot lately.*

Time to man up.

Red Man was wedged into his shirt pocket. He took a second to load up a big plug, then jumped the car back up onto 385 and got it up to ninety in no time.

"Eastbound and down, loaded up and truckin'..."

CHAPTER 25

The Lady in Red watched Bird.

She stood in the shadows, looking through the small break between two curtains. The suite of rooms above the private entrance belonged to her. The surrounding rooms belonged to those that served her. It prevented curious eyes from seeing their comings and goings.

The Rising Sun Lodge's owners were her puppets. Their purpose was much like that of Dracula's manservant, Renfield. She didn't worry about their loyalty—she controlled them effortlessly. They were gofers from a long line of gofers. Having a legitimate business afforded her the freedom to operate without suspicion.

It was genius, really.

Times had changed, after all. During other periods, she'd been able to operate plainly, and openly. She treasured her experimentation with the Mexicas, or what most people called Aztecs. She'd moved into their culture and single-handedly transformed them into some of the most successful mass murderers on the planet. They ripped the beating hearts from men's chests. That wasn't a metaphor … it was literal.

Historians estimated the Aztecs sacrificed an average of twenty thousand people each year. The numbers were actually double that. In two centuries, they killed more than ten million people.

She laughed and clapped her hands together lightly.

It had been so easy. By integrating the sacrifices into their religion, she'd engineered a killing machine of unmatched proportions. And acceptance!

No need to hide anything.

Hitler got close to her numbers, but the Nazis weren't her invention. Nope, Hitler was one sick puppy, all on his own ... batteries included.

The Aztecs had been very efficient, and there was an undeniable logic to the system she put in place.

Her favorite example was the Tenochtitlan temple. The Aztecs captured enemy warriors and converted them into slaves. Those slaves were used to build the temple. The temple was dedicated to Huitzilopochtli, their god of war (and a totally magnificent invention of Red's).

The Tenochtitlan temple's dedication was an epic party! They sacrificed nearly a hundred thousand people, including those enemy warrior slaves that helped build the place.

Naturally, more slaves were then needed, so it was a good thing they had such a strong deity of war to lead them in acquiring more, bringing them full circle in the process.

But, alas, they say all good things must come to an end. The signs were there, though she chose to ignore them. There was the earthquake. Problems with smallpox. Dissent among some of their supposed Mexica leaders. The emperor himself, succumbing to a growing yellow streak down his back.

The Spanish...

They might still have survived if it weren't for the Spanish and that damned Hernando Cortés. It was foretold to her that a stranger would be her downfall. Time and again, it had been true. Cortés was but one of many.

She was tired of moving. Tired of strangers. This time would be different.

Bird went around to the passenger side of some shitty little car parked below. Gone were the days when she had her pick from the finest minds in the city, or the most beautiful people. Good help was hard to find in the modern world, and especially in a place like Big Bend.

Her powers didn't work on everyone. Subjects had to possess certain qualities and be pliable—malleable—like human clay. People with weak moral fiber and a proclivity for violence were the easiest. Intelligent and power-hungry was another good combination. Villains, thieves, liars, and thugs all had their place, too.

While she watched, Bird dipped down into the seat and emerged with another child. This one was somewhat bigger than the other two even though they were all roughly the same age.

Excellent, she thought. Everything was falling into place.

While she watched, something unexpected happened. Instead of carting the boy straight inside to her waiting minions, Bird held the child and paced around for a few minutes behind that awful vehicle. He looked down into the face of the child periodically, and it looked like his lips were moving. Was he talking to it? What was he saying?

She concentrated, but found that her ability to read his thoughts had diminished. It didn't make sense, and she found herself both annoyed and angry. He was a cretin, but then again, there was an undeniable strength under the dull, oversized exterior.

Just when she was on the verge of sending someone out to take care of it, he crossed out of her sight, and her gentlemen in black brought him inside.

*****

Red heels clicked on the giant stones as she crossed the sacred room. The altar waited silently. A ceremonial dagger gleamed, even in the dark. The polished blade was sharpened to such a degree that any pressure whatsoever would penetrate flesh and open deep fissures.

The giant stones were the same as those used at Tenochtitlan, or what people called Mexico City, now. When Cortés had begun tearing apart her beautiful city, she had simply diverted some of the supplies to her next destination. It was eight hundred miles through treacherous terrain, and most of the slaves she used died on the journey.

Too bad, so sad.

There were always more slaves in local villages along the way, more than willing to replace the ones that dropped away like flies to the elements. Cortés had too much to oversee, and his new puppet emperor was her puppet, too. Another stranger had bested her.

She bided her time.

Doors opened before her and she crossed from the sacred area into the adjacent rooms. She could hear soft crying nearby.

"Parents, please take your children into the crying room during church," she said, and her laughter filled the room. "Unless they are needed at the altar."

The features of her face contorted, changing shape and identity rapidly, like the special effects of modern film. Man, woman, dragon, and goat—the bones snapped into different positions again and again. It rotated through the many forms it had taken over the millennia. Identities shed like snake skin. The eyes glowed a fiery orange then went shiny black.

Finally, the woman in red returned. The unnamed beast had always favored that outward representation of the entity that roiled beneath.

"How are my three favorite men?"

The crying escalated briefly and she laughed.

"Shhh..." she ordered. "Just like grown men, aren't you?"

The crying ceased.

She walked slowly in front of the cages and let her burning red fingernails scrape along the chicken wire. All three cages were occupied. She could feel immense energy. Most of the preparations were complete, the stage set for another glorious uprising.

But ... what if something happened?

It was the same old thing that prevented her from being able to fully embrace the moment. She'd been watching—*waiting*—for the inevitable stranger. The interloper. He who would dare to take it all away from her—again.

There was the new man in town—the Army man. Her agents followed him. Watched his movements. Waited for any sign that he was the one. And while he didn't seem to fit the hero mold, there was something about this Kane Montgomery that worried the woman in Red.

She'd sent her guys after him the day before. Half a dozen rattlesnakes should have taken care of business, but she'd underestimated Kane Montgomery. She'd expected death, or at the very least, serious injury, but apparently he was quite the gunslinger.

Her eyes narrowed. All of her adventures had ended in failure at the hands of strangers. Investments of time, destroyed. Maybe a different tactic was in order? She stared down at the feeble little humans in their cages, and decided to try something new.

"See you later boys," she said as she walked out.

The echo of her heels ricocheted again as she crossed the outer chamber and located her henchmen, the two clad in black.

"The stranger—I want him. Bring him to me, alive." She thought it over then shrugged. "But, if he dies accidentally, that's fine, too."

CHAPTER 26

"It's sort of like an amusement park."

Lucy laughed and brought her truck to a crawl so he could get a good look at the colorful Terlingua attractions.

"Passing Wind." Kane chuckled at the large sign spread over the entrance to the property. "There's a boat … and it looks like a fake submarine sticking out of the ground. What's up with *that* place?"

"Just somewhere to hang out, I guess. It's been here for a while."

"Huh. Weird."

Lucy kept the pace slow, giving him the opportunity to ogle things and make sarcastic remarks. She already knew him too well. He motioned at the welcome sign they were passing. "Birthplace to all chili cook-offs worldwide? I thought this was a ghost town."

"Terlingua's a place with a personality all its own," she told him.

"You're right about *that*," he said.

"There are people that actually live here. A few dozen, I think. Something like that. I don't know how they do it. There's just nothing out here. Except tourists. They probably come up with stuff like these crazy little businesses and chili cook-offs just to stay sane and make a little cash."

"I heard that! The struggle is real."

She shook her head at him.

They followed the road around, passing a variety of seemingly misplaced buildings and a cemetery. There was a place with a canoe bolted to the roof called the Boathouse Bar. A pink trailer sold barbecue, and next to that: The Kosmic Kowgirl. He had no idea what that place was.

A nondescript building claimed to house a Justice of the Peace. Kane wondered what they did out here. *Chili-themed weddings?*

The land climbed upward. Away from the quirkier places nearby, the landscape was dotted with smallish buildings in varying states of decay. A few were remarkably well kept. Others were missing roofs or had chunks taken out of walls. There were multiple places where only a foot or two of brick walling remained, outlining the structure's former design.

The true ghost town ruins were almost all uniformly beige or tan. Green scrub had established itself throughout the terrain. The Chisos Mountains stood like stoic guardians in the distance, brown with spots of burnt orange.

They parked between the Starlight Theater and the Terlingua Trading Post.

Kane stretched when they got out. The drive had taken better than ninety minutes, south on 385, then cutting across on a Big Bend road that was still a derivative of 385. They'd passed the Rising Sun Lodge nearly an hour earlier.

"This is where people start," she said. "We can grab some little maps inside and give ourselves a tour. If you're extra nice, I'll let you kiss me as the sun sets."

"I am going to be amazingly nice. Mr. Rogers or Oprah nice. Sugar and Spice and…"

"Okay, smartass—watch yourself."

He ran around the truck and picked her up. There was hugging, laughing, a tickle or two, and a kiss. When he dug his fingers lightly into her sides, she giggled and threatened to wet herself.

Light gray clouds splattered the sky and a stiff breeze blew. For the first time all week, Kane didn't feel like he was going to melt.

"Feels great out here," Lucy said. "Low seventies."

"Yeah," he agreed. In this area of the world, weather wasn't just daily conversation. Well, it was, but it was also something of genuine interest. He looked at the clouds, sniffed the air. "Smells like rain, though. And the clouds are building."

Four or five horses clopped in the road, a group on tour. The guide was darkly tanned, with deep lines etched in his face and a comfortable manner. His Palomino waggled its white mane while he sat, half-turned in the saddle, talking.

"The Terlingua you see today has a population of about fifty. Crazy, I know, but you can't control what you fall in love with, and the residents love it here. I should know since I'm one of them." He was greeted with quiet laughter. He tipped his hat at Kane and Lucy, and then continued. "In the 1880s, Terlingua grew to about two thousand people, then nearly three thousand some years later. The buildings you see here are remnants from the Chisos Mining Company days. When things dried up in the 1940s, the company went bankrupt, and gradually people abandoned their homes and moved on. There was no work, and no reason to stay."

They listened until the tour ambled too far away to hear.

"That's pretty cool." Kane pulled his sunglasses into place, and slid his CamelBak onto his back. "Did you want to do a horse tour?"

She put her hands on her hips and shook her head. Grimaced.

"I think I'll stick to walking this time."

Two days earlier she'd been flung from a horse and knocked unconscious. Now he was asking her to go horseback riding. Kane slapped the palm of his hand against his forehead.

"Right. Dumb guy question. No horses today," he said. "Let's go inside and get one of those walking tour maps—check this place out."

*****

"Hey, look at this."

Kane wandered over and found Lucy staring at one of the grave markers. There was a large, flat stone on the grave, with misspelled words crudely carved on it.

They took are chuldren

"Scary." Lucy did a quick sign of the cross and kissed her thumb. It was the first indication he'd had that she was Catholic—or any denomination for that matter. She didn't attend church, there were no crosses in her house, and they'd never discussed it. It wasn't that they avoided the topic—it just hadn't come up.

Not that he minded. His own views had been fluid after his friends died. One day he thought one thing, the next it was another. He knew he'd figure it out one day, but it wasn't going to be today, so he just kept quiet.

"This whole cemetery gives me the creeps," he said finally.

The largest graves resembled the ovens he'd seen in the Italian pizzerias. Tan bricks formed grave-sized rectangles. They extended an additional foot or two vertically, forming a mini dome over the head of the grave. Carved wooden crosses extended from the domes, like bony hands reaching toward the heavens. The effect was both beautiful and chilling.

He'd seen some shitty places in the Army, but now and then they slid in a good one, like Italy.

"Let's grab an early lunch at the Starlight Theatre," she said rubbing her arms. "It's actually a little cool today—chilly weather. No pun intended."

The gray clouds around them were growing heavier, and the wind was increasing, gusts kicking up a little dust. Afternoon storms appeared inevitable.

"Sounds good."

Their hands found one another on the walk. Kane usually felt uncomfortable holding someone's hand, but with Lucy, it was a good fit. Natural.

"Seems like we're always eating," Lucy said.

"Because food is delicious," he offered. "Besides, the way to a man's heart is through his stomach. Also through his pants. Stomach or pants."

She bumped him playfully with her hip.

Inside the restaurant, Kane was pleasantly shocked to find a modern place with a stocked bar. The female servers wore cowgirl outfits and smiles. Jangling turquoise earrings. Straw hats. Most importantly—their hands wielded steaming trays of food. It wasn't long before they were seated and eating.

"I know that I make the occasional bad joke," Kane said between bites. "And I'd like to be able to make fun of this chili, but it's fantastic."

"Cornbread," Lucy said, and he nodded. Buttery, crumbling deliciousness. No need to say it. He watched her push a sizable wedge into her mouth.

Kane sipped his margarita. Went to set it down. Brought it back for another sip before it touched the table.

"The margaritas are ... sublime."

Lucy clinked her glass against his.

"Let me get one more of those margaritas," he told the waitress. "There was something strange about the first one. I just want to do some quality control on it, make sure they're all coming out the same."

Lucy rolled her eyes and gave him the crooked smile. His heart sped up a little. Less than a week, and he already had feelings for Lucy that confused him. He'd kept his distance with women after the Army—given them the emotional Heisman. For whatever reason, that hadn't worked with Lucy. But ... was that such a bad thing?

"What are you thinking about?" Lucy asked.

"Huh? Oh, what? I was just zoning out," he replied, draining his second margarita. He wondered if some weird woman's intuition thing had just happened, or maybe she'd Jedi mind-tricked him.

When they were back out on the trail, Kane was feeling pretty good.

"I have a serious question for you." His face was expressionless, the surface of a small pond on a windless day.

"I already told you why it's called Big Bend," Lucy said.

"Seriously," he told her.

She turned to look at him.

"Can we make out in one of these buildings?"

More rolling of eyes.

"Well, you can't blame a guy for trying."

They decided to zig and zag through the ghost town and check out the structures along the route to the church. Adobe and flat rocks seemed to be the primary building materials. Kane found it interesting and wondered about the miners' stories, and their wives and kids.

"What do you think drove these men to haul their families to the most remote and unfriendly places, only to spend their waking hours inside the bowels of the Earth? Was it the gamble on quick riches? The lack of anything better?" They skirted around the skeleton of a stable, and moved toward the church. "Or, was it in their *veins*—get it?"

Instead of eye-rolling, she laughed and embraced him, and they made out in the chapel courtyard. He pressed her close and let his hands move down to the butt of her jeans. The scent of her shampoo made him happy. Satisfied in some primal way. Seconds passed, and then she pulled away and smiled at him.

"I get it. You're a pretty *punny* guy."

She laughed at her own joke. He tried not to, but he laughed, too. If you couldn't beat 'em, join 'em.

The exterior of the church reminded Kane of the Alamo, in miniature. There was a mysterious aura about it. He could almost imagine those early settlers filing in. People packed closely together in public intimacy. Seating capacity of maybe thirty. Standing room only. Women fanning themselves while men sat sweating stoically. Was the preacher kind? Or, was he the fire and brimstone sort?

The sound of an approaching engine caught his attention. Low and slow. Probably one of the residents. Maybe they weren't supposed to be inside the church. It was hard to tell where you could or could not go.

The engine cut off, somewhere nearby, and doors slammed shut. Lucy was just ahead of him, where the altar would have been, looking at an engraving on the wall. He nudged some debris on the floor with the toe of his shoe.

Footsteps. Behind him.

Turning, he was surprised—but not much—to see his buddies in the doorway. The guys in black.

"Did Wesley send you?"

They looked at each other, brows furrowed, then back at him.

"I guess that makes me Dalton," he said.

Lucy's hand came to rest on his back. That was good. He wanted to keep himself between them and her.

The guy on the left with the pouty face—*Jimmy in Road House*—spoke up: "We're going to need you to come with us."

Kane shook his head. "I don't think so, Jimmy. If you hadn't noticed—I already have a girlfriend."

The guy on the right clenched his jaw and took a step forward. The other guy put out a hand and stopped him.

"You don't want things to get ugly," he told Kane.

Kane laughed.

"Feels like I'm in a B-movie. Are you two serious?" he asked.

"Dead serious."

Kane sighed and his face went stony.

"You don't have to do this—let it go. You guys go your way. We'll go ours. Nobody has to get hurt." The Smithy was inches away in his pack, but he didn't know if he could get to it in time. He couldn't get a read on whether these two goons were any good. If they were, he'd never make it.

They didn't say anything. He rolled his shoulders slightly and let his body go loose, putting his left foot forward. It was a modified Migi-hanmi, or Aikido ready stance.

"Stay behind me," he said over his shoulder to Lucy, but his eyes never left the goons, which was a good thing since the one on the right charged him.

Kane had studied martial arts for years, catching different styles whenever he could. Jeet Kune Do, Jiu Jitsu, and Tae Kwon Do.

His favorite was always Aikido, though. It focused more on the defensive, which was most symbiotic with his personality. Redirection of the attacker's energy was so natural; it felt like dancing.

The guy threw a quick right at Kane. He shifted his body to the left and slapped his attacker's hand out of the way. The obvious left came, and he slapped it away, adding a quick chest thrust, punching him center mass, and sending him back against the wall.

Pouty came in with a roundhouse kick. Kane stepped with the movement and whipped one forearm around each side of the man's knee, then he rotated, spinning Pouty facedown into the ground. Kane had been just a beat off in his movement—and he felt some numbness in his left arm where Pouty's boot had landed. He knew the pain would come soon.

The other guy was already coming at him and threw a quick left-right, which Kane blocked with his forearms, then the guy stepped in close and kneed him in the side.

Kane backed off, shaken, and the other man threw a straight punch. Kane sidestepped, snagged his wrist, and twisted toward the outside. Bone snapped, and his attacker cried out and went down awkwardly, trying to keep his wrist aloft.

He immediately turned in Pouty's direction, ready for the next attack, but he wasn't coming at him—he was reaching behind his back.

Kane rushed in.

He put his head down and rammed Pouty hard in the chest. Pouty sailed back against the side of the church and the entire structure shook. The pistol he'd been reaching for dropped to the ground, and Kane grabbed for it. Pouty landed a kick to his shoulder, and there was a burst of pain there, but he had the gun firmly in his hand, and he jumped back.

The goons made a break for it.

Kane racked it. Verified there was a round in the chamber. He could hear retreating feet outside, and moved cautiously holding the weapon in front of him until he could see through the doorway, but they were already jumping in their vehicle.

"Are you okay?" Lucy asked, following him outside.

There was a crack of thunder. Fat drops started slapping the building and ground around them. He watched the black SUV's taillights wink between buildings and brush as the truck bounced downhill to the main road. Kane considered squeezing off a couple of rounds—he was confident he could hit the vehicle—but decided not to. The rain began to fall in earnest, sheets of it blowing across that little ghost town in southwest Texas.

Seconds later, his buddies in black were gone. He shoved Pouty's gun into his pack, and looked at Lucy. She stared back at him, something new but accepting in her face.

"Run for it?" she asked.

"Sure."

They dashed downhill in the rain.

CHAPTER 27
Wednesday

"When do the feds get here, boss?"

The sheriff's office in Marathon was starting to hum. Two extra deputies were helping out from Alpine; they'd arrived in their new Chargers that morning. One of the local volunteers was also there. They were setting up some workstations in the conference room for their ... guests.

Bigsby frowned. The phone call had come while Tom was making coffee. Part of him thought he should welcome the help, but the robotic voice on the other end of the line had bothered him. Special Agent Martin seemed devoid of emotion — alien.

Take me to your leader.

"Special Agent Martin will be here this afternoon, Tom." He didn't elaborate further, but Tom knew the deal. This could be taken from them with the snap of some fingers. *And who knows*, Bigsby thought tiredly. *Maybe that would be a good thing.*

Still, all the help in the world didn't change the fact that this was his town.

"The computers are ready in the conference room. Got 'em connected to the LAN." Tom paused, then added, "Plenty of privacy if they decide to shut us out."

Bigsby grunted.

The bell jingled over the door, but the sheriff didn't look up since there were so many folks running around, in and out. Electric bill was going to go through the roof.

Just something else for the decision makers to complain about.

"Hey, Law Hammer!"

Bigsby glanced up at the man with the cottony afro, but he was looking in Tom's direction.

"Buster! Long time, no see, old man!"

Bigsby watched surreptitiously with keen interest, as the two men greeted each other. There was even one of those man hugs and claps on the back. The older man looked familiar, but he couldn't place him, and he was usually sharp as a tack with faces.

"Sheriff, this is Buster Mackey."

"Buster Mackey..."

He shook his head gently, brain in overdrive, gears turning. Where did he know that name from? The older, lined face watched him with some small measure of amusement. Finally, the proverbial lightbulb went on and he snapped his fingers.

"I'll be damned," Bigsby said.

"Don't be damned, Sheriff." Buster's face was crinkled, almost smiling, skin tight across strong cheekbones.

"I watched you box over at Fort Stockton in the sixties."

"Guilty as charged, Sheriff."

Sheriff Bigsby's dad had been a diehard boxing fan. He'd find local fights to watch and haul his boy out with him. Rooms with a ring, concrete flooring, and folding metal chairs. The smell of sweat.

They watched all the big fights on television. Bigsby was sure his pop had bought their first TV solely for boxing matches.

"Man, you were really *good* back then."

"I was okay."

Buster was being modest, though.

"Okay? I think you were better than okay. I remember watching Dick Tiger beat Giardello back in sixty-five. He got his title back that night, and my dad was excited. My old man thought Dick Tiger was one of the greats. He'd sort of shake his left hand before he jabbed with it."

Bigsby jabbed playfully in the air with his left hand, then paused, seeing it in his mind. Sitting on the floor while his dad nearly fell out of his chair from leaning so far forward during the fight.

"We saw you a few weeks later in Fort Stockton, and I remember my dad telling me that he thought you were *better* than Dick Tiger."

Buster's face remained pleasant, and he shrugged his shoulders.

"What happened?" Bigsby asked.

"Vietnam," Buster replied.

All three men were silent. Bigsby was too young for Vietnam. His dad was missing a finger and ineligible. Even though it didn't touch their household directly, Vietnam reached out and hooked its claws into the town. It took some of her finest and kept them, or returned them as different people whose little remaining innocence had been stolen from them.

"They put me in the infantry," he continued. "Did one tour. Came back for a little bit. Did another. Things were different when I got back. I was different." There was a moment when it seemed like he was looking somewhere else, some distant location outside of the room.

Then he shook his head and smiled.

"Life is good though, Sheriff. God put me here to do certain things, and I done 'em." His eyes were full of laughter again.

"Well, hey, I still remember that fight," Bigsby said with a smile. "I was only ten, but it was good, and you won. My dad said you had a dangerous wingspan."

Buster let loose with a hearty laugh.

"That I do—long arms. Gotta use them for something. Worked with your deputy here. Have you seen him box?"

"Actually, I haven't," Bigsby said. He looked at Tom, who seemed a little embarrassed to be the subject of their conversation.

"He's pretty good," Buster nodded approvingly. "Hard jab. Eager. Works out hard. Tough."

Sheriff Bigsby knew most of that already—it was the same earnest manner in which Tom attacked his work. And he knew about Tom's hobby—had seen the heavy bag—but was surprised to learn the extent of it.

"Mind if I borrow Tom for a bit? Thought we could grab a bite while I'm passing through."

"Of course. It was good to meet you, Buster."

The men shook hands warmly.

Deputy Slidell gave him a look that said he didn't have to go anywhere, but Bigsby waved him off. They'd been at it hard for days. It would be good for Tom to get away, even if just for an hour.

*****

Buster and Tom settled into the last empty table at the Marathon Coffee Shop. Tom exchanged subdued greetings with the other locals. If the tourists suspected themselves of standing out like sore thumbs, the answer was that they did, but that was nothing that the indigenous clientele held against them.

"How you been, Tom?"

"Could be better. I figure you're asking because you know about the..."

Buster nodded. "Yeah, it's a crying shame. Folks in Midland are rooting for you guys to get those kids back."

Tom sipped his orange juice and nodded his head. They'd started getting calls from reporters, asking about the kids, and whether they had any leads.

"Sheriff is taking it hard. He shoulders the weight of anything that happens around here. He don't talk about it much, but I know."

The waitress gradually worked her way over to their table. Friendly banter, coffee refills, and requests for ketchup and salsa were tossed her way in healthy numbers. Buster and Tom gave her their orders and some bad jokes, and she was on her way again.

"So what are you up to? I see that canoe strapped down in your truck ... you gonna play around out on the river a little bit?"

"That's the plan. I've got one of those cabins at the Rising Sun Lodge reserved through the weekend. Figure I'll paddle around, drink a beer or two, and relax."

Tom leaned back and messed with his mustache. It was a Bigsby move—not that he noticed. They were like the odd couple ... Oscar Madison and Felix Unger.

"Penny for your thoughts, Law Hammer."

Tom Slidell looked at his friend and debated whether he should say anything. Police work started with hunches, but civilians didn't always understand all the nuances. The public wanted everything to be done exactly right, innocent until proven guilty, and nobody better be offended in the process. They assumed there was a checklist that, when followed exactly, led to the apprehension of the criminal.

"I'm just going to level with you, Buster."

Slidell looked around the restaurant. Everyone seemed engrossed in their own worlds. Even so, he dropped his voice before he continued.

"There are new people that have been hanging around."

Buster raised his eyebrows but said nothing.

"We've seen one of them out there at the lodge. And heard of others going there. I'm just wondering if you could..."

"Snoop around?" Buster spoke low, too.

"Maybe. I don't know. Just sort of check things out and see what you see. Fill me in on it if you see something that isn't right."

"Who are they?"

"Well, there's this red-haired woman who wears red dresses and drives a red car." He thought about what happened to Lucy and Kane, and added, "There are also these guys driving around in a black SUV."

"You think they have something to do with the kidnappings."

It wasn't a question, and Tom thought about it. The waitress appeared with their food and he leaned back to give her space. Steaming plates were served up in front of both men. She asked if they needed anything, smiled, then was gone again, off to fight the good fight against hunger.

He slid in close to Buster.

"I don't know, Buster, I just don't know. But it's an awfully interesting coincidence that these people show up in the area and then kids disappear. We had a lady bitten to death by rattlesnakes out at The Bend and who is the first person me and the sheriff see? This lady lounging on her red sports car in the desert. She says something about a *snake* problem. I'll be honest, it was just damn creepy. Made the freaking hair on my arms and neck stand up."

Buster rubbed his own neck and stared intently at his friend.

"Two folks were out there at Rising Sun riding horses. Attacked by snakes. First person they see? This lady in red again. I'll tell you who else has been popping up is Bird Taylor."

"Don't know him."

"Big guy, maybe six-five, long brown hair. Looks like a biker. Always got tobacco in his mouth. You won't have any doubt who it is if you see him, but be careful if you do. He's a real snake in the grass, that one."

They ate their food in silence after that. Both men chewing on what they had covered.

"That sure is a mean breakfast," Buster said. "Like that left jab of yours."

Tom shook his head.

"You think I'm crazy, right?" Deputy Slidell sighed. "It's okay if you do. I wonder if I am myself. Makes me feel helpless, these kids disappear and we're trying to find something, anything … but what we have leads nowhere, and we're not getting any breaks."

"I've seen a lot in seventy years, Tom. I'm superstitious as hell. I don't believe in coincidences in this world. Worst case, you're cautious, they're innocent, and nothing happens. I'll check it out."

"Thanks," Tom said.

"You bet, Hammer."

They stared at each other stone-faced. Probably would have laughed if the situation were different. To Tom, knowing those kids were missing felt sort of like someone was sitting on his chest. Or something. An elephant, maybe.

A rain shower was moving through when they got outside, and Buster drove Tom back over to the sheriff's office.

"Give me a shout whether you find anything out there or not, okay? Make sure you're all right."

"All right, dad."

Buster laughed, and they parted ways.

CHAPTER 28

There they were.

Colby Wilson, Hector Villareal, Jr., and Reese Beckman were plastered across the front page of the newspapers in the machine at Bird's gas station. From his perch, he could see all three of them clearly. Almost imagined he heard Hec telling him in a conspiratorial tone: *shit!*

When Bird was young there were four newspaper machines there, and another four at the post office. Two red and two blue. They'd sell out each day. Seemed like everybody and his brother wanted a paper, women and men alike. Big Sunday papers full of coupons and cartoons.

Then the Internet came along and changed everything.

Only one red machine had survived, along with a few copies of the dinky little free paper stacked on the counter inside. Cars and appliances for sale, dating ads— stuff like that.

Bird was in his chair, mouth full of chew. Towering white clouds moved in periodically and washed the place down. His lot was looking good, and he thought to himself that oftentimes things took care of themselves if you let them. Hell, he wasn't even sweating today.

Hector Jr. watched quietly from the display behind the panel of glass. Of course … the newspaper had it wrong. The article described the tragic loss of Marathon's three youngest. Two kidnappings and one tragic fire.

A black fella was at one of the pumps, filling up. Bird hadn't seen him before. He had a bright orange canoe in the back of his blue truck. It was a fairly normal look for these parts. The outdoors stuff. They exchanged a "hello" for a "hey" and that was all before the old man paid at the pump with his credit card, and got back in his truck.

The man had only been gone a few seconds when Bird heard it.

An engine revved in the distance, something foreign, his ears told him, and he knew it was Red before he saw that Audi come blasting in from the direction of town. It came into the lot so fast that he stood up, startled, and stepped back. It was an action that looked more than a little out of place for Bird. At the last second, she slammed on the brakes and the car slid neatly into position at the pump right in front of his chair.

Not a week before, she'd come in asking him about the lodge, and it struck him that she'd already known exactly where it was, and in fact was already staying there. *She's a better liar than me,* he thought. *She was probably just scouting me out to do shit for her.*

He sighed and spit out some chew. Just let it sort of fall next to him.

"Hello, Birdy!"

Her tone was candy bars on the surface, but razor blades in the middle.

"Whatchoo want?"

She put her hands on her hips and gave him this look that made him wince, but also turned him on. A sort of knowing, slutty look.

"Do you want to take me in to your gas station, and bend me over the counter?"

Bird's mouth dried up real fast, and he nodded dumbly.

She brushed against him on her way into the store, and walked up to the counter, right next to the cash register. Sliding her hands down her sides, she eased up her dress and spread her legs slightly.

Despite a bubbling pot of feelings inside him, Bird really couldn't be expected to control his own actions in light of this. He glanced each way outside and didn't see any cars; it wouldn't have stopped him if he did.

Shaky overgrown hands fumbled with the belt buckle and worked it open. He was a teenage boy again, first time at bat, swinging for the fences.

*****

A couple minutes later, she told him, "I've got something for you to do."

He groaned. It was an exchange of goods and services, pure and simple. He'd had the goods, and now it was time to perform the service.

Should have gone home and shook hands with the sheriff instead of shaking hands with the devil, he thought.

Red started laughing.

"You know, Bird, sometimes, you are pretty fucking funny."

Bird sighed and zipped up his fly. No privacy, even inside his head.

"What is it this time?" he asked.

"I need you to hurt someone. Or kill them. Either way." Her eyes flashed yellow and he shivered a little bit.

"Who?"

"The stranger."

Bird nodded. "The guitar player."

"That's the one."

Something about Kane Montgomery bothered Bird, and he was still stinging about that day outside. He decided they had some unfinished business, and this was as good a time as any to get it squared away. This town just might not be big enough for the two of them.

While Red fueled up her car, Bird sat back down in his chair. The rain started again. Light drops pitter-pattered on the roof that covered the pumps, allowing customers to spend their money no matter what the weather. Since he'd had card readers installed, he even made money overnight, while he was pounding beers or shooting off his guns.

The pump clicked and Red jammed the handle back in place. She walked to the driver's door and opened it.

"Hey, ain't you gonna pay?" Bird hollered at her.

"Put it on my tab, Birdy," she replied. He just sat there staring, mystified, while she winked, laughed, and jumped in her car. The Audi pulled out fast, rear end sliding on the wet pavement.

"Well, fuck me," he said to himself. Shook and scratched his head. That woman, or whatever she was, just wasn't right.

Despite being stiffed for the gas, Bird was somewhat relaxed, awash in pleasant post-coital satisfaction, and his focus switched to Kane Montgomery.

Shouldn't be very hard to hurt him. Not hard at all. And it was going to be fun. Nothing more fun than throwing a good ol' ass-whipping on someone that needed it. Zeke would have agreed with that. He threw a beating on Bird pretty regularly, and Bird was a better man for it. He felt certain he was helping that guitar player—going to make him a better man, for sure!

He chuckled and itched himself. A fantastic mood had befallen Bird, and he thought, *maybe I'll have Red swing by more often.*

It lasted until he noticed Reese staring at him with disdain from his spot just a few feet away. Little Reese. Just watching him. It was a good picture of the little guy, too.

Suddenly, the euphoria was gone, and he was back in Marathon sitting on a chair in front of the gas station. It was almost like Red had cast some sort of spell on him.

"Fuck," he said out loud. Sighed. Then began to make his plans for dealing with Kane Montgomery.

CHAPTER 29

Buster couldn't believe it.

After he dropped off Tom, he glanced down at the fuel gauge in his truck, and figured a smart man would get some gas before he headed out toward Big Bend. He believed in being prepared for anything, in and out of the ring.

The GPS told him that the only gas station within twenty miles was to the east, just outside of Marathon, so Buster decided to swing over and get some petro before starting down 385. Except for doing some investigating for his friend Tom, the only plan he had for the next few days involved the canoe in the bed of his truck and the Yeti cooler packed with beer in the back seat.

When he pulled into the gas station, and started gassing up, he looked over and almost did a double take.

There was a big guy chewing tobacco. Long hair. Looked like a biker. Like Tom had said, he knew he was the guy Tom was talking about as soon as he saw him.

"Hello," he said.

The big dude—Bird Taylor—stared back at him ominously for a few seconds.

"Hey," he finally replied, then went to town scratching at his crotch.

Buster had boxed as a heavyweight, but only just barely. He tried for a while to shed pounds because he suspected he would have been deadly in a lower weight class, but 210 pounds was as low as he could get, and that weight cost him some muscle mass.

The guy he saw was scary looking, but not unlike some of the men he'd met in the ring. Or guys in Vietnam, for that matter. There was a craziness in his eyes that kept you from turning your back on him ... otherwise you might end up with a knife buried to the hilt between your shoulder blades.

He snuck a few glances at the guy, but he didn't want to draw attention to himself, so he kept it minimal. The pump clicked off while he was thinking about it, and he shook his head. If he didn't leave now it would look a little strange, so he grabbed his receipt when it popped out, then put the cap on and jumped back on 90.

Buster was still processing his discovery when a red Audi blasted by so fast that he was only barely able to register long red hair whipping around inside as it passed. His truck rocked in the car's turbulent wake.

"What the hell?" he mumbled, slowing down, and following the car in his mirrors. While he watched, it careened into the gas station and nearly took out the pumps.

That was the last thing he saw before the road took him out of sight. He pulled over in the parking lot of a little joint called Big Bend Pizza, and wondered what he should do next.

Should I call Tom? He wondered. *I didn't see anything illegal.*

He considered it for another minute, then pulled out his cell phone and gave Tom a ring. It rang five times before voicemail picked up.

"Hey Hammer, it's Buster. Just saw something funny at the gas station outside Marathon. Something you might be interested in. Call me back."

Buster hated voicemail. Always felt unprepared, which he hated, and his messages were woefully inadequate. He wanted a beer, but it was too early, and he was driving. When he was in his twenties, it was pretty normal to drive around this part of Texas with a beer open in your lap, but those days were gone. He didn't want to lose his license or end up in jail.

That was one change he thought was for the better.

Ten or fifteen minutes later, Buster was about to pull out when he saw that red car coming fast down the road. He waited and watched as it turned on 385, another stroke of dumb luck, and then pulled out after it.

The red Audi was a lot more agile than his Dodge, but he had a Hemi and loads of power, so he put it up to over a hundred miles per hour and coasted. The car stayed in his sights for a while, growing smaller and smaller, until it finally disappeared.

Oh, well. If Tom was right about where they'd seen that car and the woman last time, there was a good chance it would end up there again, the same place he was going: Rising Sun Lodge.

Half an hour later, Buster was handed a key to cabin number three. He thanked the clerk and walked back outside.

He hadn't seen the red Audi in the lot when he arrived at the lodge. That didn't mean the lady in red wasn't there. It only meant that he didn't know where she was, exactly. His gut told him she was hanging around, somewhere, and he always trusted his instincts. It was one of the reasons he'd been a great boxer.

When the sheriff had mentioned seeing him box that morning, it was as if a very old wound were sliced open—with a meat cleaver. He was a humble person, and he was modest in most ways.

Except when it came to the boxing.

He *had* been great. Fewer and fewer people brought it up as the years went by. The last time was probably two or three years before, or maybe even when he met Tom. He couldn't remember. But when they mentioned it, he would just shrug and give them an *aww shucks* smile.

Vietnam had robbed him of his shot. Messed up his right leg just enough to take away his speed. Messed with his head just enough to take away his game. A small check was deposited in the bank each month, courtesy of Uncle Sam, a little something for the damage that could never be undone.

Buster Mackey. No nickname. He didn't need one.

Best to let that sleeping dog lie, though. Focus on the present. He decided to check out cabin number three, then figure out his next move.

*****

The sun was setting when Buster woke up, disoriented. Orange light invaded his room from the windows facing west, laying siege to everything in the room, and then he remembered where he was, sat up, and stretched.

The Yeti stood resolutely in the center of the kitchenette, a tan treasure chest, shielding its precious contents from the hands of intruders and the elements.

It was also keeping his beer cold.

Buster had a weakness for Shiner Bock, and he popped the lid off of a Black Lager, and let some slide down his throat. There was also some White Wing and regular Shiner. He made his way outside to watch the light fade away and study the layout.

The cabins were half a mile from the main lodge, a paved road leading between them. He fancied he could get between the two in about six or seven minutes, if he had to move fast. Otherwise, an easy walk with a flashlight. Have to look out for snakes. Buster didn't like snakes, but he wasn't like Indiana Jones about them or anything.

Earthy ochre tones blazed in the last rays of light coming over the horizon. Meat was grilling at one of the cabins. The aroma overwhelmed him momentarily, and his concentration faltered ... some sort of sweet barbecue. His stomach growled loudly and his beer lost some of its luster. He wished he were throwing back a twelve-ounce ribeye instead.

Buster settled for a quick sandwich. He pretended it was a steak instead of pastrami on Wonder Bread. Freshly grilled, kissed by the flames until warm and pink in the middle. The perfect balance between rare and well done was medium.

The sandwich tasted nothing like steak—not even in his imagination—but at least his stomach stopped haranguing him.

Only a thin blue line remained on the horizon when he stepped back onto his porch, the rest of the sky having faded into varying shades of darkness. Except for those no-legged reptiles, Buster was comfortable in the dark. He had on a long-sleeved navy T-shirt and jeans over his boots. A baseball cap covered the white hair on his head—a freebie from a hardware store in Odessa. He brought his pocket knife and a little Maglite.

Walking quietly through the Big Bend darkness reminded him of 'Nam. Strange how the human mind worked. What you might or might not remember. At least once a week he couldn't find his truck keys, and yet, he could remember walking through the jungle wondering if Viet Cong were going to decide that was a good night for him to die. How many times had *that* crossed his mind?

Almost every day, he supposed.

It was cool and he was glad to have sleeves. Less than ten minutes later, he was in the parking lot outside the lodge. In the city, people might target a black man walking around the parking lot at night. Get suspicious and call the cops. But out here it didn't work that way, and not only because he was older. Big Bend was different in a good way.

There were people outside on several of the balconies. The cherry of a cigarette grew to an exquisite shade of orange as someone unseen inhaled, then it dulled like a dying star. He walked naturally, careful not to draw attention, though he made sure to survey the parking lot thoroughly for that Audi.

No luck up front. No luck on the side.

He continued around to the rear, and saw that there was a low wall, maybe six feet tall, that jutted from the building and ran out to the driveway. He noticed there was a camera mounted on the corner of the lodge aimed at the road, but no gate. It would be easy to walk back there, but if anyone were watching the camera, they would see him.

Why have a camera here anyway? he wondered. Didn't make much sense to him. Maybe for the guests? There was a sign that said *No Parking In Rear.*

Interesting.

Instead of walking where the camera was pointed, he took a good, cautious look around to see if anyone was watching. He didn't see a soul. With a few quick strides he ran, jumped, pulled himself up, and dropped down on the other side of the wall. Crouched and kept still.

I still got it, he thought to himself. *Kids eating Big Macs, waddling around fatter than Christmas geese these days, and I'm jumping walls.* He shook his head and almost laughed. It was a different world than the one he grew up in.

Buster stayed where he was, allowing his eyes to adjust to the terrain. It didn't take long at all before he saw the Audi, even with the moon not yet up. Something about the red paint glistened. He nodded to himself— knew he would find it here somewhere.

Sticking to the side of the lodge, he moved along the wall, stopping frequently to watch and listen. He was in no hurry—no hurry at all—and he moved with surprising stealth for an older man. Always was light on his feet. Boxing and infantry training helped. And patience. Buster Mackey was a very patient man.

Without warning, a door opened and a shaft of light knifed into the darkness up ahead, and he pressed himself back against the structure. Two men dressed in black popped out from somewhere. They walked over to a black Tahoe and opened the rear doors. While he watched, they made several trips, unloading supplies. One of them had a bandaged hand, but still hauled stuff using the other.

Buster stood quietly, hiding in plain sight, not daring to move.

The men didn't talk much while they were unloading, but when they finished, the one with the bandage said something that made Buster's heart beat faster.

"At least I don't have to change any more fucking diapers," he said, waving his wounded hand.

Buster couldn't believe his ears, and without knowing for sure, he *knew* for sure. Why else would two goons like this be changing diapers?

He hadn't known what to expect when Tom laid that stuff out for him that morning. Maybe a wild goose chase. But you always gave the benefit of the doubt to your friends. That's what friendship was all about. And it looked like Tom had nailed this one!

There was no time to waste. He needed to get ahold of Tom and let him know. Despite the urgency gnawing at him, Buster knew he needed to keep cool until Heckle and Jeckle went back inside. Man, would Tom be excited about this. They'd get those kids back to their parents and bust these guys.

The goons laughed at some joke he couldn't hear, then started inside. Just as he heard their door opening, another sound pierced the otherwise quiet evening.

Ray Charles, loudly singing "Hit the Road, Jack."

And it was coming from the cell phone in his pocket.

CHAPTER 30

Lucy yanked back her draperies, and studied Kane's arm in the natural light from the window.

"It's not too bad," she declared.

Kane blinked rapidly several times in the sudden light.

"I'm not sure I've ever seen those curtains open," he remarked.

"I closed them when I started sleeping on the couch, and I don't think I've opened them since then."

They were perched on her sofa bed, sheets in total disarray. Lucy kneaded Kane's upper arm, working gently with her fingers, trying to break up the areas where blood was stagnant—get blood flowing again.

"Hmm." Kane couldn't concentrate. Lucy's flimsy white tank top kept grabbing his attention. He reached a finger out and pulled it open a little bit, but she slapped his hand away.

"I'm working here," she warned him.

"Yes, ma'am."

Outside, dark clouds threatened to unload on the little town of Marathon, Texas. They'd run through a pretty good deluge the night before, after they'd been attacked at the Rising Sun Lodge.

She hit a sensitive spot and he winced.

"Sorry," she said. She stopped rubbing his arm, and grabbed a little tube sitting on the table nearby.

"What's that?"

"Something I put on my feet," she said. "It helps with swelling." She squeezed some ointment onto his arm and rubbed it in.

"Feels better already," he told her.

She stopped rubbing and traced her finger around his bruised arm.

"He got you pretty good," she said, then looked into his eyes. "Of course, you got him a lot better. Where'd you learn to fight like that? It looked like something out of a movie."

He laughed.

"I don't know. Took some Tae Kwan Doe as a kid. When I joined the Army, it became a good outlet for me. A way to blow off steam and stay in shape. Meditate. Maybe in a way it was like a childhood dream I was chasing. When I was in grade school, I wanted to be a ninja."

"Oh, yeah?"

"Big time! I would try to sneak up on people in the grocery store, and I would slide around under bushes on my stomach and spy on the neighbors. I had some Chinese throwing stars I carried around in a little pouch on my belt, and I would throw them at trees. I was certain if I just trained hard enough, then one day, I would be a ninja."

"Well, you're about as close to a ninja as I've ever seen."

He shrugged.

"Seriously." She tilted her head at him quizzically. "You were this flurry of hands and movement. It was amazing. I mean *A-freakin'-mazing*. But it made me realize how much I don't know about you because I sure didn't know you could do any of that stuff."

He shrugged again. "We've only known each other a week."

"I know. It just ... feels like more. You've become such a wonderful part of my life that it seems like we've been together longer or something, in a good way."

He knew what she meant.

She stood up and walked across the room, to her bookshelf. He'd browsed through the books there, so he was curious what she might be doing. Lifting her arm, she slid her hand along the very top, until she found what she was looking for, and pulled it down.

It was a picture frame. Pewter with one of those black, velvety fold-out flaps on the backside. Kane could only see the side of the frame, not the actual picture, since Lucy was standing in profile to him, but he knew something important was coming. He waited. Tried to be patient so it would come naturally.

Lucy's hands shook slightly. He saw her swallow. Finally, she took a deep breath and turned to him.

"I told you it had been eight and a half years since I was at Big Bend."

He remained silent, but nodded.

"You said something like, 'that's pretty precise' and it was. Very precise." Another deep breath. "It's so precise because the last time I went out there was with my parents. We went camping. My dad and I would go out there a lot, but my mom didn't like camping or horseback riding, so she would usually stay home. But, not that time. It was all three of us."

She sat down next to Kane. Moist eyes inspected him, then looked down at the picture.

"That's my mom and dad. And me, too, of course. Some hikers came by and my parents asked them if they could snap a picture of us. It came out really good," she said wistfully.

Kane looked down at the photograph. Lucy's off-kilter smile was beaming between the smiles of her parents, her arm wrapped around each one of them since she was in the middle. It *had* come out really good.

"We packed up and drove back that night after a full day at The Bend. A wonderful day. It was dark by the time we got onto 385, but you've seen the road ... it's in good condition and there's hardly any traffic, right? We didn't have a care in the world."

He waited. He didn't know the details, but he could guess where the story was going, and he placed his arm around her waist, loose enough to give her space, but with enough pressure to let her know he was there for her.

"Headlights appeared in the dark ahead of us. We were only three or four minutes from our turn, Airport Road, which would take us home. I saw the headlights veer onto our side of the road, coming right at us, and it was like a movie dream sequence. I wanted to scream, but nothing came out. My mom was in the passenger seat and I think she did scream. Sometimes my memory says she screamed, and other times it doesn't. My dad tried to get out of the way, but the other car moved, too. They went the same direction."

Lucy looked at Kane with a sad smile.

"My dad died instantly, they say, though I don't know how anyone could know that. Not really, you know? The two cars collided head on. Someone passing through found us in the road like that, hours later. My mom died in the hospital the next day. And I woke up in the hospital the day after that. That car ride was our last moment."

She searched his damp eyes with her own; his hand found hers.

"For a long time I slept with that picture in my hands, clutched to my chest. I couldn't tell you how many times I wished I had just never woken up in that hospital bed. At least a hundred times a day the first month, then maybe fifty times a day the rest of that year."

He pulled her close, put his arms around her, then hugged with all the emotion he had.

*****

When Kane got to Bob's that night, Lucy was taking drink orders from a table full of tourists. They were all wearing Columbia and North Face style gear, faces flushed with color from a day of outdoor activity. People tended to forget you could get sunburned even in cloudy weather. She said something he couldn't hear and the table erupted in laughter.

Smiling to himself, he passed by discreetly with Honey in his left hand. He knew she was itching to get out of her case and make music for people. In some ways, he felt like he was just her puppet, and that she was the one choosing songs.

"My man, Kane!"

Dan sidled up to him and gave him a fist bump. There was a cigarette tucked behind his ear, and a rag over his shoulder. He was sporting a green T-shirt that said *Keep Calm and Chive On*.

"Livelier crowd tonight, hoss. Are you gonna play something badass?"

Kane laughed. "I'll do my best, broseph. Definitely going to kick up the pace a notch, with this crowd."

They surveyed the room silently. Smiles and drinks everywhere.

"Smoke break?" Dan asked.

"Later," he told Dan. Not that he planned on smoking, but he enjoyed the social aspect. There were a lot of dudes that smoked in the Army, and his theory about that wasn't anything original. For one, guys learned quickly that smoking led to breaks from work. Two, it was fun hanging out and bullshitting. It seemed like a win-win, except for that whole cancer thing.

Dan moved off outside, and Kane continued to the back so he could get Honey ready for a night of badassery.

"Hey..."

Kane turned around and found Lucy behind him. A week ago, he was wondering if she was giving him the eye, and now here they were, living together, and he had some very real feelings sprouting up inside.

"Hey..."

"Hope I didn't scare you off with that stuff earlier."

"Nah. You can't scare me off."

"Good."

"Good."

She kissed him, then pulled away.

"Gotta get back out there. More people just came in. A lot of tourists tonight, but not so many locals."

"Yeah," he agreed. "Too much bad stuff going on. I actually wondered if Bob was going to bother opening. Everything is so weird these days."

"Well, this place never draws in huge crowds even when things are normal…"

"Hey, I heard that!" Bob came poking around the corner and Lucy's face turned red. Seemed like every time she was back there with Kane, she got busted doing or saying something.

"Sorry, Bob."

"Oh, I'm just messin'. You're right. This place doesn't bring in the big crowds, but I never thought it would. I just wanted a place to hang out, and I really like beer and music, so this seemed like a good idea."

Lucy laughed, then gave Kane a little wave and skipped back out to the floor.

Bob and Kane shot the breeze for a while. When Bob asked him how things with Lucy were going, Kane realized he was checking up on her, pulling surrogate father duty. It made him like Bob even more than he already did.

"Things are good, Bob. She's an awesome girl."

"Good. Well, I'll leave you to your preparations. Get out there and kick some butt."

Kane tuned up Honey for a few minutes, then he reached into his case and pulled out his ball cap with the American flag on it. He rotated it around in his hands and worked the bill a little bit. Thought about what he'd done for his country, and the friends he lost. He didn't regret any of it, even the parts that hurt. Loving his country wasn't something that required effort on his part—it came naturally.

*****

"That was completely badass, man!"

"Thanks, Dan."

"He's right," Lucy chimed in. "You were great."

They were standing around at the end of the night, Lucy and Dan drinking beers, while Kane nursed some of the sweet tea that Sheriff Bigsby had mentioned the week before, on his first night at Bob's. Dan was, in theory, cleaning up. Bob was off counting his riches, no doubt, and doing paperwork. The customers had finished clearing out only minutes before.

"Thanks, guys. I had a really good time up there, under the light. It was almost like Honey played herself, like she was a wild mare, and I just hopped on for six seconds."

"Honey?" Dan asked. "Is that your guitar's name? That's a sick."

Kane raised his eyebrows. "Sick? Thanks ... I think."

They joked around some more and finished their drinks.

"Ready?" Lucy asked, tucking herself in under his right arm.

"Yep. Let's make like a banana, and split." She giggled at his bad joke, and Kane could tell she was tipsy. Lucy was a lightweight.

Outside, the air was cool on Kane's skin. Two days of rain had done wonders for the temperature. Stars twinkled down from above, sending sparkly greetings from millions of miles away. Lucy sighed contentedly beside him.

When they stepped down onto the gravel of the parking lot, Kane stopped. There was a truck behind his, just out of reach of the lights. It wasn't Dan's or Bob's. Maybe just a customer, sleeping off one too many.

"What's the matter?" Lucy asked.

"You know that truck?"

She looked past his truck, and shook her head. "I don't think so."

It occurred to him that you couldn't rent a truck that old any more. It was driven here by the owner, and probably not one of the few locals from the bar if Lucy didn't recognize it.

Still, a lot of Marathon's visitors just drove in from other places in Texas, or the Southwest. The presence of an unknown truck meant nothing.

Right?

Except the old Kane sensors were flashing and beeping. Warning sirens in his brain. It was the Kane Montgomery home security system, continuously monitored for only twenty-four ninety-nine per month. It was the same internal system that short-circuited one night when he was deployed, and he told his patrol that everything was fine, when it wasn't. It was far from fine.

Logically, he knew it wasn't his fault, but his heart didn't believe in logic.

"Lucy," he whispered. "Stay alert. Something feels wrong."

She perked up next to him, and he walked a step ahead of her on the way to the truck. When they got close enough, he could see a bear-sized silhouette behind the wheel of the other vehicle. The door creaked open and a mountainous man dropped down from the cab. Giant black boots were visible under the open door, and when it was slammed shut, Kane was left looking at a familiar face.

The Undertaker, aka Bird Taylor. Dangling from his right hand, down the outside of his thigh, was a baseball bat. The bat looked smallish, dwarfed by the big man holding it.

"Take this. Go to the other side of the truck." Kane passed Lucy his guitar case, and she darted in the direction he indicated.

"Don't go too far, Loose Lucy. I got some'n for you after I finish with your little boyfriend." Bird's eyes glinted with malice.

Kane let himself go limp, and ignored Bird's threat to Lucy. Defense against someone with a club or weapon was particularly dangerous, and he tuned out the world around him except for Bird.

The big man moved forward and Kane went into a Hanmi stance, making a smaller target of himself. It also gave him the flexibility to strike or dodge by keeping his balance centralized.

Bird didn't waste any time. He came in swinging sideways with both hands on the bat, like he was going for the homerun. Kane dodged backwards, and the bat missed. It was so close he could feel the disruption in the air as it hurtled by his chest, and feel the shockwaves of its movement.

Bird swung again, this time from the opposite side, like a left-handed batter. His movement was awkward, and slower, and Kane jumped back again. Bird missed: two balls, no strikes, nobody on base.

Just as Bird twisted up from the swing, like a tetherball, Kane jumped forward and drove a quick left-right combo into Bird's right arm. He'd wanted to strike at Bird's nose, or his eyes, but he couldn't get close enough. The arm was a target of opportunity. Any hits at this point were good.

It was like poking a stick into the hornet's nest; Bird's eyes flared with anger as he got ready for the next charge. Kane reset his body into another Hanmi, and braced himself.

The two most effective methods for dealing with a blunt object attack had to do with distance. One, you could put yourself completely out of reach—long distance. Or two, you could move inside against the attacker, getting so close as to make striking impossible or weak. Kane was an inside guy. He waited with his left foot forward and his front hand at chest height.

Bird charged again, bringing the bat up with both hands over his head. This time, Kane's Army Combatives training prevailed. He waited until the last second, ensuring Bird was committed to his angle of movement and didn't have time to adjust. Kane sidestepped, putting his right foot out, then bringing his left in behind it, and leaned back. The bat whistled by where he'd been standing. At the same time that the bat struck the gravel, Kane moved forward, and stepped inside the attack. With his left hand, he grabbed Bird's left wrist and twisted, then jabbed Bird once in the face. He aimed for the nose, but Bird twisted, and his fist landed on cheekbone with a meaty smacking sound. Bird grunted.

Kane grabbed the bat with his hands and the two of them struggled over control of it. Bird had better positioning, and he wrenched the bat away, but Kane moved forward to stay with him and retain his place inside.

Bird backpedaled and tried to bring the bat up to swing, but Kane thrust his palm up into Bird's jaw, and he could feel the crunch as the man's teeth slammed together. Then he looped his left arm over Bird's bat-arm, pinning it between his left side and left arm. He popped Bird in the face twice before Bird roared, grabbed Kane's hair with his free hand, and yanked Kane's head sideways. Bird tripped him, and Kane fell to the ground on his back.

He stared up at Bird, who immediately swung the bat down toward him. Kane rolled right and it smashed into the gravel next to him. He scooted sideways, but the second strike grazed his arm, and he cursed from the pain. He kicked up as hard as he could and his foot landed squarely in Bird's privates.

Bird staggered and dropped the bat.

Kane stood up, keeping his injured arm close, and kicked the bat away. Bird recovered quickly and came in with a left, which Kane deflected. Then he swung a heavy right. Kane moved with the punch, grabbed Bird's wrist and twisted, moving quickly under Bird's arm, and twisting further until Bird dropped to his knees and went facedown into the gravel. It was an Aikido move called Tenkai-kote-hineri, which literally meant he was rotating his opponent's wrist to make him turn.

Kane put his boot down on the back of Bird's neck and kept pressure on the twisted arm.

"You had enough, big fella?"

Bird was breathing heavy. He was strong, but out of shape, and Kane suspected he wouldn't last too much longer even if he let him up. Not at the pace they were moving. Bird was used to things ending quickly, but it wasn't going to happen this time.

"Get off me," Bird growled.

"If I let you up, you back off. Understand?"

Bird said nothing.

"I'm not letting you up until you tell me you understand." Kane didn't trust Bird, but sometimes you had to take a chance, gamble. It was either that, or keep fighting and kill the guy.

"Okay," Bird said finally.

Kane released him and backed away, putting himself between Bird and the bat. Bird lifted himself off the gravel and glowered at him. Kane was wondering if he should have gone ahead and knocked him out, when he heard the click-click of his Smithy getting racked.

Bird's eyes shifted away from Kane, to the right, then back at Kane.

"This ain't over," he said.

"I think it's over, big fella. Take a walk."

Lucy moved next to Kane while Bird got into his truck, and she handed him his gun. He trained it loosely on Bird to let him know it would be a bad idea to try anything. Bird backed up, flipped them the middle-finger bird, then kicked up gravel as he peeled away.

"What the hell was *that* all about?" Kane said.

"I don't know."

"Damn." Kane rubbed his arm gingerly. As the flow of adrenaline ebbed, his arm went from numb with needles to a throbbing pain. "Dumb freaking luck. The Undertaker got me in the exact spot where old boy kicked me."

"Think it's broken?"

"No."

"Should we call the cops?" Lucy asked.

Kane thought about that. He was a little bruised, but nothing serious. Bird's taillights disappeared to the east, and he wondered what had brought that on. It didn't seem random.

"Not tonight. Let's go see Sheriff Bigsby in the morning," he replied. "He needs to know, but I want some time to think, first. Maybe we can figure out why we've been attacked twice in twenty-four hours for no apparent reason."

CHAPTER 31
Thursday

Tom woke up with a start, heart racing. He glanced at the clock and saw that it was 3:30 a.m.

Had he heard something in the house?

Turning only his head, he looked over at Steph, asleep next to him. Wavy hair held her face like gentle hands cupping water. She was fast asleep. A tornado could be outside and she'd still be out. He'd always envied her ability to sleep through anything. He was a light sleeper. Tended to wake up at the slightest disruption in the pattern of sound around him.

He usually slept with a fan on, to mask all the little environmental clicks and creaks, but the quiet calm of the place told him he'd forgotten to turn it on. The silence was deafening now and he waited.

There was the noise again.

Tom stood up and padded over to the chair where he always left his belt. His uniform was on a hook over the bathroom door, but his belt always went to the chair. It was heavy, and he wanted it close. He slid his revolver out of the holster.

He cocked it. His aim would be better because less pressure would be needed to pull the trigger, and he was certain he'd heard something. Tom held the weapon out in front of him, finger outside the trigger guard for now, and circled wide at the doorway so that he could survey every shadow.

Nothing.

He moved forward into the hallway, keeping low and right. The cast of moonlight from the living room made it easy to see. On either side of him were trails of family pictures running the length of the walls. When he reached the end, he watched. Waited.

The sound came again—*brrr-brrr-brrr*—and Tom stood up and sighed. He recognized the vibration of his cell phone from a missed call or text. If he had to guess, he bet it was a missed call. It was probably one of those telemarketing scams, a recording that directed him to call another number about his credit card account. A little chunk of cheese on the mousetrap.

Keeping his revolver pointed at the floor, he held the hammer firmly with his thumb, pulled the trigger, then eased the hammer forward using his right thumb and left hand, de-cocking it.

Tom strolled into the kitchen, and flipped the switch. The ethereal glow of the moonlight scurried away, replaced by the searing manmade glare of those technologically advanced spiral bulbs that had invaded their home, gradually coming to occupy every socket. Steph craved the brighter light, and Tom was just fine with changing the light bulbs only once every few years.

His phone vibrated again, from beside the refrigerator. It was an annoying sound, which he ignored for the moment.

The right side of the fridge was his cubby for miscellaneous junk. Phone and cordless drill chargers, pocket change, sunglasses, and keys. Mail that needed action. Papers they would shred. It was his version of a junk drawer, except they had one of those, too.

Must have forgotten the phone there, charging. Usually he kept it on his nightstand.

He poured himself a small glass of milk, and sipped it. There was no way he was going to be able to go back to sleep knowing that his alarm was set for just an hour later. That knowledge would grab him by the collar and slap his face repeatedly if he even tried. Nope, no more sleep for him. He was awake for the day, with only a few miserable hours of sleep to get him ready for it.

When the glass was empty, he rinsed it out on the left side of the split sink, then set the empty glass in the right side. House rules. Clear and rinse on the left, ready for the dishwasher on the right.

The phone vibrated again. It was set to do that every few minutes until it was acknowledged. *I'll have to change that setting*, he lamented. Maybe to silent.

The phone came alive when he touched the screen. There was a banner alert indicating a new text from Buster. He held his thumb on the sensor instead of entering his pin number, and a second later he was in. Tapped the messages icon. Opened the most recent, from Buster.

"Tom. Come out to Rising Sun Lodge as soon as you can. Cabin three. Hurry."

That was it. No explanation. Nothing else.

Tom tried calling twice, but he was redirected to voice mail. He texted and waited for a response, but got nothing.

Even though his friend was older, Tom knew he could handle himself. Hell, Buster still kicked *his* ass every time they sparred. Every time. They never said it out loud, but Tom knew Buster could cream him right away, if he wanted. That's not to say that Tom wasn't good—he was—but Buster was a pro, while Tom was more of a passionate hobbyist.

He swirled the information and details around, as if they were a fine wine he was tasting, checking for impurities and oddities. He analyzed them and came to a decision. It was simple, really. When a friend needs help, you help them.

Tom shut off his alarm, and slipped into his uniform, careful not to make noise even though his wife's sleep-state mirrored that of a coma. Utility belt on, gun refastened, he set out to check on his friend.

CHAPTER 32

"Hey, Sheriff?"

A volunteer deputy had poked his head in the doorway.

"Yeah, Phil."

"There's a forensics guy on line two. He sounds pretty excited."

Bigsby looked up at Phil questioningly, but he only shrugged back at the sheriff. He wondered briefly if he shouldn't pass the call along to *Special Agent* Martin and the other personality-less suit he'd brought with him. Like the Alpine boys, they'd arrived in a new car, too, which made him wonder if he shouldn't start clamoring for an increase in the budget.

Ah, screw those guys, he thought, and picked up the phone.

"Sheriff Bigsby."

"Sheriff? It's Charlie. Forensics."

"Yeah, Charlie. What's up—did you find something?"

Charlie's voice squeaked with excitement. "We did, Bigs!"

They went back. Two old dogs on the block. He knew Charlie, and knew he was about to get big news.

"Well, buried under the house, we recovered a piece of round glass. Looks like it was cut from the door at the rear of the house, and was probably the access point for our arsonist."

Bigsby grunted. "The murder suspect."

"Hmm. I don't know, Sheriff. You need victims before you can have a murder suspect."

"What?"

"Let's put a bookmark in right there, and I'll get back to the prints in a moment. The corpses. Oh, boy…" he trailed off and waited.

"Charlie, you're damn good at suspense—a regular Dean Koontz—now what about the corpses."

"Ha. Right. Well, we found three bodies, two adults, one child."

"Right," Bigsby wasn't in the mood for Charlie's cryptic delivery. He wanted to say *duh!* to Charlie.

"The dental work on the female corpse doesn't match work that Maria Villareal has had done!"

Bigsby teetered on the edge of his chair. "What?"

"Doesn't match. Not at all. And it looks like the other body's central incisors were partial dentures. Incredible, really. The teeth burned away, but the wiring was still intact."

"Partial dentures? Are you saying that Hector Villareal had dentures?"

"That's the problem, Sheriff. Mr. Villareal did *not* have dentures. It's not his corpse."

Sheriff Bigsby sat back stunned.

Not Maria and Hector Villareal?

"So, who are they?"

"Well, we're not sure about that yet. We couldn't find records of the dentures or get any sort of match on the female, but we're still trying."

The cogs in Bigsby's head were turning, turning, turning…

Then he sat forward so fast that he knocked his cup of coffee to the floor. The dark liquid spread out in a puddle that went ignored. His epiphany was both good and bad, but for an optimist like him, he had to hold out hope.

"The child, Charlie … was it Hector Jr.?"

If Bigsby didn't know better, he'd think Charlie waited a beat too long on purpose before finishing.

"It's not, Sheriff. The kid's bones are actually a couple of years older than Hector Jr. We don't have any identification on that body either, the decomposition of all three indicates a number of years—not recent."

"Well … I'll be damned." Bigsby leaned back and tried to absorb the information. Alternating left side to right side, and then back to the left side, he smoothed his mustache with the fingers of his right hand. The phone sat forgotten in his left hand.

"You there, Sheriff?"

"What? Oh, yeah, sorry Charlie. I don't think I've been this surprised in a long, long time."

"Aye," Charlie agreed.

"What about the fingerprint stuff that you 'bookmarked'?" Bigsby had been so surprised, he'd almost forgotten about that.

"It's running right now, boss-man. It was smudged and burned, but we believe there was enough to identify the person, as long as they're in the database. I'll call as soon as they get a hit."

There was silence then, as something else dawned on Bigsby.

"Call me as soon as you get the results. I just realized something."

"What's that, Sheriff?"

"Now Marathon has three boys that have been kidnapped."

*****

Bigsby paced his office.

"Phil?"

"Yeah, Sheriff?"

"Tom here yet?"

"No, sir."

"Okay. Thanks."

He stopped at his window and pushed down on one of the blinds to look outside. They were the cheap plastic ones you could pick up at Lowe's for less than ten bucks, and there was a semi-permanent crease left in the spot where he pushed them down almost every day to look out. The view was far from spectacular, but it was one that he knew very well. The mundane everyday quality of it calmed him down. Helped him think.

There was an empty patch of ground next door, but the property on the other side of that was occupied by a regular house. He knew the parents and their teenage boy, just like he knew everyone else in town. There were two bicycles dumped on their sides in the yard. One belonged to the kid that lived there, Ross. He was thirteen, but big for his age, and taller than Bigsby. Had a little gray patch of hair on the side of his head, though the rest was dark brown. The sheriff figured he'd be courted by the colleges to play football or baseball once he got to high school.

That is, if they could tear him away from hunting long enough to get him to play. Boy loved to hunt, and during deer season, he'd skip practice nearly every day.

The other bike belonged to Ross's buddy, Wayne. That one always seemed to be up to something. *He's probably over there hatchin' a plot right now.*

Bigsby paced the other way then back again.

It seemed to him that the key to all of this would be in that fingerprint. Charlie had explained that the little circular piece of window had been under the house and survived the fire. A break right now would really be good for the home team. If that fingerprint identified someone, it was game on. He'd be all over that person like gravy on biscuits.

Leaning out of his office, he hollered, "Hey, Phil?"

Phil looked up from some paperwork.

"Yeah, Sheriff?"

"Any word from Tom, yet?"

"No, sir."

"Okay."

It wasn't like Tom to be late, but he'd told him to take some time if he needed it. Get some sleep. They'd put in eighty-five or ninety hours this week, and they were both feeling it. He wasn't sure how long they could keep it up, really, but he wanted Tom there with him if he got a name from Charlie.

I'll wait another hour, then I'll call him. Tom would have called me if there was trouble.

He continued his pacing, then pushed the blinds down again, and looked outside. The bikes were gone now. Teenage boys on the loose in Marathon could be cause for concern—lots of signs *acquired* .22 holes—but that didn't cross his mind. Not then.

The coffee pot was full of good java, so he knew Harriet was in the building somewhere, and he thanked God silently for her as he refilled his stainless steel tumbler. Long days required a lot of coffee, and it never hurt to have a loaded jug somewhere. For a long time, he'd carried an oversized thermos, but he misplaced it sometime during that year after Cheryl died.

He resumed his position pacing the far side of his office.

"Sheriff, if you keep that up, you're gonna wear a groove in the floor."

Bigsby looked up to see Phil in the doorway.

"Where are our friends?" he asked.

Phil tilted his head toward the conference room. When he was gone, Sheriff Bigsby continued pacing.

Someone had wanted it to appear like the Villareals had all died. Was it a ploy to throw off the cops? It appeared so. But why? And what were the identities of the bodies in the house? He didn't think they were local. He couldn't remember a family of three dying in the past few years. Or a child that age.

Maybe the perpetrator needed the Villareals alive. Or maybe...

"Sheriff, Forensics is on line two again."

"Thanks, Phil."

He pushed the door of his office closed. A single light on his phone was flashing, and he picked it up.

"Bigsby," he said.

"Bigs … it's Charlie."

He felt his mouth dry up a little.

"Yeah, Charlie."

"We got a match on that print, Sheriff."

Charlie paused for dramatic effect. Bigsby wanted to shoot him.

"The fingerprint is that of one Fred Taylor, also known as Freddy Taylor, also known as Bird Taylor."

The boot print flashed through his mind. Two missing boys. And now he had a connection.

"Thanks, Charlie."

When he hung up the phone he called Tom's cell phone. Three times and always to the voicemail. Left a message to call him ASAP. Put in the call to Tom's house phone.

"Hello?"

"Hey, Steph. Is Tom there? It's important."

Bigsby could hear her sharp intake of breath in the bloated silence.

"Sheriff, I thought he was with you. Tom was gone before I woke up. His uniform and gear aren't here, so he must be wearing it."

"Did he leave his cell phone?"

"Hold on," she said. He could hear her moving through the house while he waited. Then she was back on the line, "He took it with him. Why isn't he answering?" she asked, her voice rising slightly in alarm.

He hated to answer that. "Steph, don't you worry, okay? Maybe he thought of a lead or something he needed to follow. Or just left his phone in the car."

"Don't worry? Tom never goes off anywhere without you or me knowing about it, and he always answers his phone..."

"Don't panic, darling. You need to stay calm. Check your phone, voicemail, and email, and see if he left you a message somewhere. Maybe a note in the house. I'll check around here. I'm sure he's just busy and he'll call one of us soon."

He didn't admit it to her, but he felt the same way. Tom was as stable as a cruise liner, but maybe he'd hit an iceberg. When he got off of the phone, he wasn't sure which he should do first: go arrest Bird Taylor, or search for Tom Slidell.

CHAPTER 33

Bird hated it when anyone beat him.

When he returned from Bob's, he carried nine guns, his foot locker full of ammunition, and a case of beer outside. Lined it up nice and neat on his table. Chugged a couple starter beers.

Then World War III had kicked off.

Bird went through more than three hundred rounds. Kane Montgomery was in front of his sights, when he bothered to aim. Over and over again the guitarist was cut in half by the rounds he fired. Imagining his enemy's head exploding brought him an intense and maniacal joy.

A lead-lined cloud formed and hovered just above the ground, surrounding the trailer and his property. When it got so dense he could hardly see, he stopped and pounded beer. That cycle repeated itself multiple times, until he was so hammered that he periodically forgot what he was doing.

As the sky in the east turned from black to blue, Bird fired a couple of rounds that hit his trailer. At first he cheered when he heard the metallic thuds, disoriented, thinking he was at a firing range somewhere, shooting at targets. By then he was seeing doubles and triples of everything. With intense concentration, he realized the so-called targets were actually the wall of his trailer, and he stopped cheering. He walked over to the holes, slightly mesmerized by the fact that he could now see directly into his living room.

Then he laughed so hard that he couldn't breathe. He doubled over, fell on the ground, and pissed himself.

Laughed some more, staring drunkenly at the sky, stinking of the warm piss quickly turning cold and sticky.

After that, he stumbled to the picnic table. He didn't bother with the few remaining cans of beer, but he swiped most of his guns into the footlocker, and hauled it, swaying, to the living room. In a series of clumsy movements, he and the footlocker crashed to the floor. Bird yawned, closed his eyes, and dove down into something far deeper and blacker than sleep.

Six hours later, his cell phone rang. And rang. And rang.

"Fuck off," he told it.

The ringing stopped. Then it started again.

"Fuck," he cursed.

He stumbled to his feet and tried to focus. He leaned forward, and his hair fell into his eyes. His knees banged the television stand and his flat screen wobbled dangerously. Through bleary eyes, he discovered he was pointed the wrong direction, and turned to face the kitchen table where his phone was going crazy. Several agonizing steps later, he reached the table.

And the phone stopped ringing.

The curse words flowed from him like water through a broken fire hydrant. His anger came out in a hellish fury once it got going.

When it rang again, he answered it, "What the fuck you want?"

"Bird, it's Mikey, man. Sheriff Bigsby was just in here with some guy and they were looking for you. I think they're going to arrest you ... they had a fucking shotgun!"

Bird heard the sheriff's engine as it crested the hill, and dropped down into what amounted to his yard.

The phone dropped from his hand and clattered on the table.

He turned and lumbered back into the living room. Tripped on the footlocker and dropped to a knee. Between his temples a drumbeat of pain began throbbing as he rubbed his eyes and looked down.

His guns.

He grabbed the Ruger SR-762 and set it aside. There were only five magazines, one full, and four empty. The sound of the engine was louder now. Bird jammed .308 rounds into the mags as fast as he could, setting them aside. Three were full when the sound of the Bronco's engine stopped outside. It was suddenly too quiet. He slapped a full magazine into the rifle, pulled back the charging handle to load a round, then set it down and continued filling the two empty magazines.

"Bird, come on outside. Now!"

Sheriff Bigsby was using a bullhorn, which meant they knew what he'd done. And he was in some serious shit. Nobody used a bullhorn for a friendly *hey-how-you-doing* kind of stop.

"I ain't done nothing, Sheriff," he hollered back, buying a minute more, his hands moving frantically.

"Bird. Don't make us come in there for you. Come out with your hands high. No weapons." The words echoed around his trailer, tinny and mechanical.

"Weren't me that took them boys, Sheriff. It was the Red lady. She has 'em. I swear to you, that's the truth!" He finished filling the mags, found a little plastic grocery bag from the gas station, and shoved the magazines inside. He lifted his head until he could just see out the living room window. The sheriff and another guy were behind the Bronco, weapons drawn. Bigsby had the bullhorn in his left hand, away from his face, and his pistol in the right. Bird didn't recognize the other guy, who was holding a shotgun over the hood.

"This is it, Bird. Three seconds. If you're not out, we're coming in there."

Bird tossed a Glock into the flimsy plastic bag with the magazines, then threw a couple of boxes of 9mm ammo after it. He wished he'd double-bagged it.

"One..."

"Wasn't me, Sheriff!" He grabbed his Ruger rifle and his bag and moved to the right in his living room, then closer to the window.

"Two..."

Fuck, fuck, fuck!

Bird raised himself up slowly and aimed. Squeezed the trigger.

The rifle was loud in the confines of the trailer. It bucked, and his window exploded into shards. While he watched, one of the men behind the Bronco dropped.

Gunshots erupted outside—one, two, three, four—then there was a pause. Bird looked over the windowsill, but both men were out of sight behind the Bronco. He aimed again and fired. The right front tire of the Bronco blew. Then the rear. Another bullet took out the front windshield.

Ducking low, he waited for return fire, but there wasn't any.

Musta nailed that son-of-a-bitch, he thought.

Bird grabbed his bag and rifle, and scooted low through the trailer. He opened the window of his old room and jumped out. His two hundred and fifty pounds thudded audibly into the hardpack. Silence was a luxury his size couldn't afford.

Zeke's old truck was there, right where he left it. The door creaked when he opened it; he clambered in, and swung it shut. Put the Ruger and the Glock on the seat next to him where he could get to them fast. Rivulets of sweat raced down his face. *C'mon, come on!* he thought, and turned the key.

The luck he'd had the previous week continued, and the old junker roared to life on the first try. Tucking his head low, he jammed on the gas, and the truck launched forward.

As he hurtled toward the road, he expected to hear gunshots or feel bullets as they panged off the truck.

But there were none.

Dust plumed out behind him until he hit 90 and jerked a hard right onto it. He wasn't sure where to go, or what to do. Things had spiraled out of control. Shooting that cop was probably the dumbest thing he'd ever done.

What the fuck have I done? It was an accident. I just didn't want to go to jail.

That was when he knew where to go. And what to do. After all, what other options did he have left?

He saw the turnoff for 385 and threw the old truck into a hard turn. It fishtailed around the corner, wheels whistling *Dixie* in protest, cutting off a vehicle in the oncoming lane. Bird didn't notice—didn't even glance at that other truck as he sped off toward Big Bend.

CHAPTER 34

Red's heels struck the stones of the ceremonial chamber like a judge repeatedly banging her gavel. The sharp sound echoed around the room. If those stones could talk, they might share blood-curdling stories of the Mexicas. Or perhaps they would lament the hundreds of Mexican slaves' lives given to move the stones to their current home near the Rio Grande.

Or maybe those stones would have hearts of—*stone*—and would laugh along with their puppeteer in red.

The door at the far end opened in front of her and slammed shut behind her.

Her three little boys were in the room on the right. She had no doubt they were defecating themselves in their miniature cages like the pathetic monkeys they were. Their purpose was clear. Through the rending of their bodies, and giving of their blood, her own power would surge.

She started as a human. Mortal. Of this world. Given life through the connection between a man and woman. Yet, she couldn't remember being fully human. The faces of her parents visited sometimes when she closed her eyes, but they disappeared when she opened them. The genesis of her current form was lost to her.

You couldn't call her need to rest, sleep. It was different. Daily, she closed her eyes for only a few hours—she grew very weak, otherwise. And over time her batteries recharged less and less each day, despite the periods when she closed her eyes. True rest—sleep—

came once every century or two, and it lasted for years. After the Mexicas, she'd slept for nearly twenty years.

The power of three was something she learned about only in the past few centuries. Christians knew the magic of three. Their doctrine called it the Trinity, or one God in three forms, but it seemed to work for her, too.

Yes. Those three little pet monkeys would feed her power.

Except, what about the stranger?

In tribal times, Red frequently played the role of shaman, which was fitting. People's thoughts were like words on paper. She read them, then cajoled, frightened, and forced people into becoming her sheep. Her guidance became religion, and she discovered giving people something to worship usually made it easier for them to swallow. Sun. Earth. Wind. She bade them worship those idols, and kill for their satisfaction, and they did it.

Humans really are sheep, she thought.

Things would be good. For a while. Then, inevitably, someone would come along and mess things up. Destroy what she had built. The pattern eluded her for a millennium or more.

Then there came a soothsayer with legitimate abilities: Paco. In fact, she thought this man might be like her—someone transformed—no longer fully human.

Paco had a thing for eating mushrooms that grew in animal feces. Red refused them when he offered to share, but she watched with great interest when he tossed them back. Paco would rant, paw at the sky, and see things invisible to her. During a trance, he revealed to Red that a stranger would be her undoing. She thanked Paco for the information; then she killed him.

A stranger.

Recalling those things, she veered left, away from her little caged monkeys. She could hear their grunting and monosyllabic utterances as she walked by and opened the door to the opposite room.

Red flipped a switch when she entered, and both men recoiled at the sudden light. Eyelids fluttered and their hands went palm out to foreheads, to shield themselves. The chains around their ankles clinked together and scraped the floor. A bright smile revealed her perfectly white teeth.

"Well, how are my *older* boys doing? It's good to see you're conscious again," she said, looking at Tom. "How does your head feel?"

"Please," Tom said. He rubbed the spot on his head where they'd hit him. His world had been black until just moments before. "Let us go."

"Tsk-tsk. I don't really see that happening, Tom."

His face went a shade whiter at the sound of his name.

"Yeah, I know who you are, and you don't really know me, do you? Everyone usually calls me Red, so you can call me Red, too. Red hot!" She laughed excessively at her own joke.

The two men had finally adjusted to the light, and were no longer blinking. The dark one stared at her and didn't look away. His face was devoid of fear, and she narrowed her eyes at him. Tried to read his thoughts. Invisible hands reached out toward him and tugged at his mind, fingers working around and around, trying to find a way in.

Buster's jaw clenched as if he could feel those fingers of hers inside his head, and yet he still didn't back down or give an inch. Red redoubled her efforts. What if the stranger wasn't Kane Montgomery, but was this man? What if it were both of them? Her eyes flashed gold fire with the strain, but he refused to budge.

It was a tiring process, and she gave up. Decided to conserve her energy. She let herself relax again and smiled at them.

"I hope your accommodations are satisfactory. Complimentary champagne is on the way." Buster shook his head. He refused to break eye contact with her. Seemed immune to her … gifts.

"Lady, why are you doing this? Let the kids go."

"Why, you ask? It's simple, so turn up your hearing aid and listen. I. Need Their. Blood. Do you need me to say it again louder?"

He sighed deeply and shook his head. Looked down at the floor. Looked back up.

"Take me instead."

"What?"

"Leave the kids alone. Take me," he repeated. "I've had a good life. A full life. Take me."

She considered the dark man with the apparent heart of gold. Every now and then someone offered themselves for their children or a loved one. Other people tried to be heroes. But this was the first time she'd been confronted with an offer of exchange. My life for theirs. No strings attached.

"I need three, Buster. Sorry, but no deal. Go fish."

Buster stared at her, but she couldn't read his face.

"Take me too, then." The deputy's chains rattled as he stood up. "I'm sure you can find one more to make your quota."

She studied the two men. Not only was it the first time she'd been in this situation, but now it was twice in one day. She walked across the room and stood in front of Tom Slidell.

"It's a fascinating idea, Deputy Tom. Very interesting. The problem is that things are going to happen in just a few hours, and I get the most bang for my buck with sacrifices who are pure of heart. Get it? They gotta be kids, Tommy Salami."

She smiled and shrugged her shoulders.

"Sorry."

For a moment nobody moved.

Then the deputy launched himself. He leapt forward, going airborne, arms outstretched. She could see the fingers of his hands reaching out. Going for her neck, maybe. Inches from her face, his body jerked as if he hit an invisible wall, and he dropped to the floor. The leg irons had stopped him cold.

Red began howling with laughter and found herself bent over double.

"Whew! That was really great. You should have seen yourself. Best laugh I've had in a thousand years."

She turned and walked out, still laughing.

In the other room, she checked on her little monkeys. The Beckman kid whimpered as she got closer to him.

"Hey, don't cry little monkey. After tonight, all of your problems will be over," she said, and laughed. "I've got you three, I've got the stranger, and a full moon is on the way."

CHAPTER 35

Bigsby stewed on the decision he had to make: try to find Tom, or go after Bird Taylor. He had no idea where Tom was, but he thought he could find Bird. And finding Bird might lead to the recovery of those kids.

He knew Tom would have done the same thing.

"Ralph, grab the shotgun—let's go."

They left in the Bronco without saying a word to Special Agent Martin. Bigsby was probably going to get his ass handed to him for that move, but he felt like time was critical.

He and Ralph raced to the gas station, but the kid working there said he hadn't seen Bird. He looked scared. They jumped back in the vehicle and made for Bird Taylor's place, just east of town. As they crested the rise just above Bird's trailer, Bigsby told Ralph, "Get the shotgun and come to my side of the vehicle as soon as we stop."

"Got it boss."

The yard was a disaster. Spent ammunition casings were everywhere. He'd never seen so many, not even at the range on a busy day. All sizes, too. It meant that Bird had himself an arsenal in the trailer, most of it probably illegal. The sheriff pulled his pistol then grabbed the bullhorn from the seat. He kept the Bronco between himself and the trailer, and Ralph ran around next to him.

"Bird, come on outside. Now!"

He tensed up, looking for any signs of movement, then Bird hollered at him from inside the trailer.

"I ain't done nothing, Sheriff."

Bigsby didn't believe a word, and he wasn't going to show weakness. Bullies like Bird thrived on weakness. He said into his bullhorn, "Bird, don't make us come in there for you. Come out with your hands high. No weapons."

Just a second later, Bird hollered out to him again.

"Weren't me that took them boys, Sheriff. It was the Red lady. She has 'em. I swear to you, that's the truth!"

That threw Bigsby for a loop. *Bird knew about Red?* He wondered about that for a moment. *Was Bird innocent?* He didn't believe it. And even if he was, they could sort that out at the station.

"This is it, Bird. Three seconds. If you're not out, we're coming in there."

He waited for a reply, but none came.

"One..."

"Wasn't me, Sheriff!" Bird called out.

"Two..."

The living room window exploded. Bigsby squatted down a little. He raised his pistol, aimed at the window, and fired off four rounds. Then he noticed Ralph wasn't next to him. He looked sideways and saw him on the ground, two feet back. There was blood all over the place.

"Son of a bitch!" he cried out.

Ralph moaned, and he dropped to his knees next to him. More rifle shots from the house and he heard the tires explode on the Bronco. Windshield shattered. He ignored that. Looked for entry and exit wounds. Found the opening at the collarbone. No exit wound. He applied pressure and staunched the flow of blood.

Bird flew by in a truck, and Bigsby cursed himself for not being more careful. For letting Bird get away. And for getting Ralph shot.

"Ralph, I need you to help me. Hold pressure right here."

He lifted Ralph's hand and pressed it into the wound. Ralph groaned and his eyes flickered open. Bigsby felt Ralph's hand go tight on the wound, and he jumped up.

"Dispatch, this is Bigsby, I have a man down at Bird Taylor's trailer just east of Marathon. We need an ambulance or medevac out here right away."

He dropped the mic and dug around behind the driver's seat until he located the first aid kit. Vaguely he was aware of Harriet responding in the affirmative. "Roger that, will comply."

He dropped down to Ralph, eased his hand to the side, and cut open his shirt. It was hard to see the wound for all the blood. He splashed some alcohol on the site, and Ralph bucked like a wild horse. Bigsby tried to calm him. He put all the gauze he had on top of the wound and taped it down. It appeared that Ralph had stopped losing blood.

"Hang in there, buddy. We're going to take care of you."

Bigsby did a quick recon on the vehicle. He had a spare, but with any blown tires, it would be a long, rough ride back, and he only had the one spare.

The radio crackled. "Sheriff, Dispatch."

"Yeah, Harriet."

"Medevac on the way. Be about fifteen more minutes. Those two deputies from Alpine are en route with more supplies. Is that okay?"

"I think so," he replied. Ralph had stopped bleeding, and even though his breathing was irregular, he didn't seem to be getting worse. Mild shock, he figured. "Do me a favor and get the evidence collection folks moving this way, too. Bird Taylor's place needs to be shut down. The gas station, too. Both places need to be combed over."

"You got it, Sheriff. Out," Harriet said and was gone.

He thought again about Bird Taylor and how he said the Lady in Red had the kids. For some godforsaken reason, he actually thought he was telling the truth. Not that Bird was innocent by any stretch. He believed Bird kidnapped the kids and sold them to her, maybe. Or she just paid him to help. Something along those lines.

The Alpine boys arrived with their flashers on, but no sound. They told Bigsby the chopper would be looking for the cherries off of 90. One of the guys part-timed as an EMT and checked on Ralph. He told Bigsby Ralph would be fine, though the expression on his face said maybe he wasn't so sure.

A few minutes later, the helicopter arrived, and they loaded Ralph onto it. He was a good guy—just a volunteer. Watching him go, Sheriff Bigsby cursed himself for having given Bird Taylor the benefit of the doubt, and hoping he would change.

He made a silent promise to himself. If he got the opportunity, he would take Bird down.

CHAPTER 36

Red flipped the lights off as she left, leaving Buster and Tom in complete darkness. Tom held his hand up right in front of his face, but still couldn't see it.

"You were right about her," Buster said. "She is one creepy woman."

"Yeah," Tom agreed.

They were silent for a while. Then...

"You were just telling me about those guys and the black SUV..."

"Right." Buster finished catching him up on what he'd seen and heard. The men. Red. The talk of changing diapers. That they were somewhere beneath the Rising Sun Lodge.

"What about you? Where did they grab you?"

"When I got to your cabin, I knocked, but there was no answer. The door was unlocked, so I went inside, and that's when they jumped me.

"How'd you know which cabin I was in?"

"Well, I came as soon as I saw your text, but I guess I was too late."

"Text?"

Tom clammed up. It never crossed his mind that the text might not be from Buster.

"They screwed us, Law Hammer."

"How did they get into your phone?" Tom asked.

"Good question."

They both thought about that.

"I'll be damned," Buster said finally. "I bet they held my thumb up to my phone. They knocked me out, then held my thumb to my phone. My thumbprint can unlock it. Know what I mean?"

"Huh." Tom had the same feature on his phone, and used it all the time. He'd thought of it as added security because you didn't have to type your code and have someone possibly see it. Now he wasn't so sure. Someone could access your phone even if you just got drunk and passed out, as long as they could get to your fingers.

"We have to get out of here, Tom."

Tom nodded at first, then said, "Yeah." He struggled to see his friend, himself, or anything, but he was absolutely blind. They were prisoners in a black hole.

"Are your chains tight?"

Tom felt the metal bracket around his leg. There was maybe half an inch of space between it and his leg. He pushed it down to his ankle—not enough room to pull free. He traced the links back to the wall. The metal plate there felt tight. He put one foot on each side of the metal plate on the wall, grabbed the chain with both hands, and pulled with maybe fifty percent of his strength. A good enough tug to get the lay of the land, but not so much that he'd get injured if he slipped or something.

"Feels solid."

"Mine too," Buster agreed. "You have anything in your pockets? Keys, buck knife, or something?"

Tom reached in his pockets and came out with some coins.

"Got some change," he told Buster.

They were silent. Tom wondered what might be crawling around in the dark with them. Anything was possible in this part of Texas—snakes, scorpions, spiders—you name it.

He could hear Buster fumbling around a few feet away from him.

"What the hell kind of place has shackles on the wall, anyway?"

"No place I wanna be," Tom replied. Something skittered by his hand and he jerked his hands into his lap. He wondered if he might have imagined it.

"Hey, do you have a quarter?" Buster asked.

"Yeah."

"See if you can loosen the bolts on the wall. I feel a groove etched across the face.

Tom felt his way back to the wall, groping around like a pantomime without an audience, he located the metal plate and the bolts. Just as Buster had noticed, there was a groove across the head of the bolt. Gripping the quarter, he wedged it into the groove and tried to turn.

Nothing.

He shifted his body, then pulled on the chain to bring himself closer. The quarter dropped to the floor and rolled.

"Shit," he cursed, feeling all around for it. Seconds passed. The total darkness was frustrating. His fingers scratched and scraped, but it was gone. He leaned back, agitated, thinking maybe he'd start hitting the wall ... when his hand brushed the quarter. It was behind him all along.

"You okay?" Buster asked.

"Yeah. Dropped the quarter. Thought I was going to go nuts for a second. It's like the world is conspiring to screw with me."

Buster chuckled across an indeterminable space. It was a good sound. Reminded Tom of going to the gym and sparring. Slapping the speed bag around. At least every other trip he'd hum the *Rocky* theme song while they worked out.

He sighed, then went back to work on the bolts.

CHAPTER 37

"Doesn't it feel like we're living the movie *Groundhog Day*?" Kane asked.

They were on the couch, curtains open, gray light cascading down from a cloudy sky. Lucy massaged his tie-dyed arm where the bruises coalesced in a series of connected splotches. The latest were deep shades of purple, sickly yellow, blue, and black. It looked like that bat had connected better than he thought when they were at Bob's.

"*Groundhog Day*? Never heard of it."

He groaned loudly. "Oh my God, I can't take it. Are you serious?"

"No," she laughed. "Of course I've seen *Groundhog Day*. Now sit still."

"Well played, ma'am. Well played."

Out came the emollient. Lucy applied it in small counterclockwise circles. The musky and minty odor was disconcerting, a combination of men's locker and hospital emergency room.

"Marathon's just a peaceful little town. Nothing ever happens here," Lucy said with an exaggerated southern twang.

"Right."

"Probably thinking about hanging around for a while," she replied. She smiled. He smiled. Then something weird happened. Those green eyes of hers studied him. Beneath the placid surface of her statement was a current that was growing stronger. An undertow of need. A subsurface flow threatening to pull their feet right out from under them.

Women's feelings were a crossword puzzle. Not the easy kind that you solve to pass the time at the airport. And they weren't medium either, or difficult. They were more like impossible, and the answers weren't going to be in the newspaper the next day. The answers weren't going to be anywhere, ever!

Kane had never had asthma a day in his life, but he was having trouble breathing, the way Lucy looked at him. Maybe he was allergic to something.

"Sure. Maybe. I don't know." He sat up a little straighter. How could he know? She'd been in his life only a week. One week! He cleared his throat. "I don't have any plans of going anywhere," he said, finally. That much was true. He didn't lie. Of course, he also had no plans of staying. He just didn't know. Kane liked Lucy—a lot—but he needed more time.

She smiled. Leaned over and put her face into his neck. For a second he thought she was going to say those three words, and his stomach did two back flips and a somersault while balancing on a high wire.

Danger Will Robinson!

Then Lucy stood up, humming, and collected her impromptu bruise kit. Deposited everything in the bathroom. Told him she was going to take a shower.

Close call.

Sooner or later, a close call wasn't going to cut it. That train was going to eventually arrive at the next station, or jump the tracks. Kane would have to figure out his feelings or brace himself for the train wreck. He knew he cared for her ... but this was too fast for him. He needed more time.

Sighing, he stood up and stretched. Like Forrest Gump, he wasn't a smart man. Unlike Forrest, he wasn't sure he knew what the hell love was. He would have to shelve this one. Let nature take its course and guide him.

Besides, there were other things to figure out, and the sooner the better. Little things like, who wanted him dead? Or if not dead—badly hurt.

It was an easy decision to skip his morning run. He wasn't afraid—matters of the heart were scarier than a baseball bat—but there was no point in being an obvious target. That was Vigilance 101 stuff. The Army shoved annual training down his throat about recognizing threats and being proactive. Vary your routes. Avoid routines. Don't make yourself an easy target. Complacency kills. It wasn't rocket science.

Kane rotated through some exercises that kept him limber, and others that served as practice for various styles of martial arts. He ran through some katas in the space between the couch and kitchen. A kata was a memorized set of movements that helped you practice, work on form, and find synergy between moves.

There were several that required a bokken, or wooden sword. He didn't have one, and neither did Lucy, so he just unscrewed the bristled end of her broom and practiced. Luckily it was a short broom, and he was able to move somewhat freely.

"Wow," Lucy said. "Aren't *you* full of surprises?"

Kane turned. Lucy was watching him from the doorway. There was a towel around her upper body, and another wrapped around her hair. *Why two towels?* he wondered. Maybe someone should write a book about it. *The Two Towel Mystery* by Every Woman.

"I'm going to start calling you Lucy Two Towels."

"Oh yeah?"

"Yeah."

She reached up and tugged, and the towel around her body dropped to the floor.

Kane whistled low. "Umm. Window is open," he told her.

"So?" She walked over to him, and pushed him down on the couch.

"My thoughts exactly," he said.

*****

"Have you done anything to make these guys angry?"

"I've never even talked to the guys in black. They were following me one day when I was out running. Over near the Gage Hotel. When I noticed, I ran over and tried to open their door, but they just drove off. Then later I saw them at Bob's. I noticed one of them was carrying a pistol, and I told Bob, but they were gone by the time we came out. Then there was our horseback ride. Those are the only times I've seen them."

"And The Undertaker?"

"Shoot, the only time I talked to that guy was when we were getting gas."

She shook her head. "It doesn't make sense."

He shrugged in confused agreement.

"And what about this Lady in Red?" Kane said. "She seems to have been in the same place as these other guys. Pops up around accidents. Bird pops up here and there, too."

"Weird..." Lucy trailed off.

Then she shot up off the couch.

"Wait a minute. Do you remember the pictures we saw at the library?"

"What?"

"The pictures. There was a figure in brown and guys dressed in black. They were holding up a baby."

As the pieces came together, Kane's eyes widened. "No way," he said. "Can't be related. Can it?"

"Maybe that person wasn't wearing brown. Maybe the cave painting had faded over time. Maybe they were wearing red."

"Freaky," he murmured.

"Let's go back to the library," Lucy said.

*****

They were barely through the library doors before Lucy called out excitedly, "Ms. Tate!"

The librarian stood up behind the circulation desk, and she put her hands on her hips.

"Lucy Baker, what did I tell you?"

"Sorry—I meant Jennifer!"

"That's better. Twenty minutes sooner and you could have caught story time," Jennifer Tate said and laughed. Her brows furrowed as she looked at Lucy, then Kane, then Lucy again. "Okay. You guys look pretty serious. What's up?"

"We need your help," Lucy replied. "Can we look at those books again? Especially the one with the Big Bend painting."

"Of course … just pull up some chairs."

Ms. Tate rounded up the books while Kane and Lucy wheeled chairs into the spots they'd previously occupied behind her desk. The place was warm and inviting, just like the other day. Two small children twirled around in the adjacent room, while their mother stood nearby tapping on her phone.

Ms. Tate came back carrying her books.

"Okay, let's see what we've got here." She slid books around the table like a New York City hustler running a shell game. She picked one and opened it. Flipped pages. Then she plunked it down in front of them. "Here it is."

He heard Lucy's breathing quicken.

There in front of them was the painting. Two men in black. Another figure clad in brown. Or maybe faded red. Holding the baby.

"Who is that right there?" Lucy pointed at the person robed in brown.

"That's probably the shaman of the tribe."

"Shaman?"

"Yeah. It's sort of like a religious leader, except more than that. A lot of earlier tribes believed they could talk to good and evil spirits. Commune with the dead. Influence the future of the tribe by communicating the requirements of gods or demons."

Kane and Lucy looked at each other, then Lucy asked. "Any truth behind all that?"

Ms. Tate eyeballed them, eyes crinkled. "Hmm. Interesting question. Naturally there are skeptics, however, a lot of the evidence we have indicates varying degrees of legitimacy. They certainly held positions of authority in their tribes, second only to the chieftain. Even then, if they were clever enough, they could manipulate the chief."

Kane pointed at the object in the person's hand. "Last time we were here, you said it was possible that was a knife, and that maybe they were going to kill the child— *sacrifice* the child."

"Definitely possible," she looked at the picture. "You know, now that we're talking about it, I would say it's more than just possible. You guys are sharp ... I think this painting depicts a sacrifice. Definitely."

"Why do you say that?" Lucy asked.

Jennifer Tate laughed. "Look in the upper corner of the painting. Do you see it?"

Lucy and Kane studied the picture. At first neither understood what she was talking about.

Jennifer said, "I'll give you a hint: silver bullets."

Kane's face pinched up in confusion, but Lucy cried out, "Ah-ha!" and she pointed at a white circle in the corner.

"What's that?" Kane asked.

"A full moon," Lucy said.

Kane looked doubtful, but Ms. Tate only nodded and chuckled. "Oh, yeah. Humans love to say they aren't superstitious, but they find everything in the world to be superstitious about. Stepping on cracks, black cats, breaking mirrors, three sixes, the number thirteen, a rabbit's foot..."

Kane winced inwardly, but nodded. He knew about superstition.

"Oh, man, but the full moon? Yeah, honey ... people connect everything to the moon. Psychoses. Homicidal tendencies. Menstrual cycles. You remember we talked about the Aztecs? They believed the moon was an evil goddess who killed her own mother."

They listened while the librarian expounded upon it further. She recited different tales of the all-too-easily impressionable human mind, and how science really didn't support all the claims.

"Doesn't stop people from believing it, though," she finished.

Kane leaned forward and asked, "By any chance, do you know when the next full moon is?"

Jennifer Tate whipped out her cell phone and tapped rapidly for a few seconds. Then she whistled.

"Imagine that ... it's tonight."

Kane and Lucy exchanged a look overflowing with words unspoken.

"Can we borrow that book?" Kane asked.

Jennifer Tate's robust laughter filled the room. "Kane, Kane, Kane ... we are a library. We exist so that you can borrow that book."

Ms. Tate offered to get a library card started up for Kane, but he declined. He and Lucy were eager to be on their way. They thanked the librarian quickly, and fast-paced it out the door.

"Does that mean what I think it means?" Lucy asked.

"That those boys are going to be sacrificed tonight?"

"Yeah."

"I don't want to wait and find out. Let's get over to the sheriff and tell him everything we know."

"He's going to think we're nuts," she replied.

Kane laughed and shook his head.

"Maybe we are, Luce. Maybe we are."

CHAPTER 38

It didn't seem right for a county vehicle to have that new car smell.

But that Dodge Charger they'd brought from Alpine sure did.

Bigsby was in the backseat, and the two deputies were up front. Despite the situation, the sheriff couldn't help but notice the cluster of controls in the dashboard. Spotless interior. The husky and muscular rumble of the engine. The ruggedized in-car computer.

More suitable for chauffeuring guests than busting criminals.

"Oh, hey Sheriff?"

"Yep."

"Just thought I'd give you a heads-up. That FBI guy—Martin—he wasn't too happy. Overheard him and his sidekick talking shit about jurisdiction."

"For Christ's sake," Bigsby said under his breath and sighed. "Thanks for the warning."

"Yessir."

Fan-flipping-tastic.

He sat back and thought about that. Bigsby hated watching cop shows on television. They always insinuated that street cops don't get along with the feds. FBI agents were portrayed as arrogant and uptight; local police were wisecracking and rough around the edges. The two fought over jurisdiction. In the end, they usually came to respect one another, with the scales tipped in favor of the city cops.

They were the underdogs, after all, and everyone loves the underdog.

From his experience, county sheriffs *wanted* federal help. They requested that help. And were frequently denied that help. No battles over jurisdiction between bits of witty dialogue.

Don't believe everything you see on television, they said, and for once, *they* were right.

"We need to talk, Sheriff."

Barely inside the door. Five seconds, maybe six, and Martin wanted to talk.

Bigsby gave him the old squint eye. Ambled over to the coffee pot, and filled a mug. Wasn't even sure whose mug it was, but he filled it up and sipped. It burned his throat in a wonderful way. Harriet the good coffee fairy had visited recently. *That woman is going to heaven*, he thought.

Nice and easy, he turned around.

The two deputies were fiddling with stuff at a desk. Straightening files, flipping through paperwork, picking up a stapler, and putting it back down. They didn't want to miss this action.

"Talk," Sheriff Bigsby said.

"What?" Martin replied. Momentary confusion.

"You wanted to talk. So, talk."

"Let's go in your office." Martin said.

"No, Agent Martin. Let's just do this here. I just watched a nice guy who helps us out around here for a pittance, bleeding in the dirt. You're not my boss or my daddy; I'm a big boy. Say what you have to say."

Martin's face contorted into something between frustration and anger.

"You should have told us what you were doing— you were way out of line!"

Bigsby nodded.

"Anything involving the missing kids, I need to know about it. That's not, hey, it's optional to tell Martin about it. That means you tell me. Period."

It was quiet. Deputy One had his thumbs in his belt, and Deputy Two had his hand on the back of his neck and was staring at something on the floor near the door. Martin stood his ground.

"You're right," Bigsby told him.

Martin's mouth opened, to retaliate against an expected argument, then he closed it again. A long moment passed with the two of them watching each other.

"All right," Martin said finally. "Okay."

Bigsby nodded and walked back to his office.

*****

A couple of hours later, the bells over the door jingled.

"Hi, can we see Sheriff Bigsby?"

He recognized Lucy Baker's voice, and went to his doorway. Lucy and Kane were talking to one of the deputies. Martin and his sidekick were in their conference room command center. Their door was closed.

"Come on back, guys."

They piled into his office, and he shut the door.

"What can I do for you?"

"Well," Kane started. "We have what is going to sound like one hell of a crazy idea about what is happening to those kids."

Bigsby raised his eyebrows.

"We just ask that you hear us out. I've known you my whole life, and I swear this isn't a joke." Lucy's face revealed nothing but honesty.

"Okay, guys. Whadda you have?"

They reviewed everything they learned with him. Some of it he had already heard, but now they were stitching it all together. Kane being followed by the black SUV. The attack at Big Bend. Red waiting for them outside the horse stables. His fight with the men at Terlingua. Squaring off with Bird outside of Bob's. And, finally, the history lesson that Ms. Tate had given them at the library.

"Just look at the picture." Lucy had opened the book and placed it in front of the sheriff on his desk. Bigsby leaned forward and studied it. "They are all there in that painting, Sheriff. The Lady in Red. Her henchmen in black. A child."

"Don't forget the moon," Kane chimed in.

"Right." Lucy pointed again. "Full moon in the corner. The king of all superstitious objects. The full moon! And, guess what?"

Bigsby's eyebrows went up, his face a question mark.

"Full moon tonight, Sheriff."

Bigsby stroked his mustache.

"What are you saying? That this is the same woman?" Sheriff Bigsby looked between the two of them and they stared back at him.

Silence.

The sheriff jabbed his finger at the Lady in Red. "Shit, she'd be damn near a thousand years old." He looked closer, then added, "If it's true, well … she can't be human."

Neither of them backed down when he said it. Lucy leaned forward.

"Sheriff, I swear it on my *parents*."

After her parents died, he had kept an eye on Lucy. Feared she would … do something she'd regret. The loss of her parents was so senseless. A tragedy for Marathon and the young woman in front of him. Until that moment, he'd never heard her mention them. He swallowed to get rid of the lump in his throat.

"That is a whopper of a story…" He stood up and walked to his spot at the blinds, and peeked outside. He saw things, but he didn't see them. Was he convinced? He wasn't sure, but maybe anything was possible. Then an idea struck him. "It could be that someone else knows about these sacrifices, the ones in the books. Maybe some sicko is out there reenacting this stuff from the past? Might not be anything supernatural to it at all."

The way they looked at him, Bigsby could tell they hadn't considered that. Lucy looked doubtful, but Kane looked … relieved, maybe. He definitely seemed like a practical guy. Of course, the things that were going on around town and down at the lodge seemed pretty far from practical, and closer to supernatural.

"I don't know," Lucy replied. "Whatever it is, I think we still need to act on it."

"What if I told you that we have evidence that Bird had something to do with the kidnappings?" Bigsby said.

They didn't look surprised about that.

"We forgot to tell you. We saw Bird today."

"What?"

"Turning south on 385. He was in one hell of a hurry, too. Cut us right off. I'm not even sure he saw us."

Bigsby smelled something bitter and acrid and ugly. Like he had just stepped in a steaming pile of reality. That connection between Bird and Red. Even if there wasn't anything supernatural, maybe all roads would still lead to Rome ... and the recovery of those kids.

"Guys..."

The phone cut him off.

"Hold on a sec," he said, then answered his phone. "Sheriff Bigsby."

"Hi Sheriff, it's Stephanie Slidell."

"Steph? Have you heard from Tom?" he asked.

"No, not yet, but I turned on our computer just now and I saw his messages. I forgot I could see his messages on there."

"What do you mean? You received a message from Tom?"

"No," she told him. "Tom's phone is linked to our home computer. They have the same messaging app. I never remember because I'm not into these gadgets and all that."

He sat up straighter. Kane and Lucy had forgotten to pretend that they weren't listening, and watched with rapt attention.

"Are you telling me that you can see the texts on his phone?" Maybe Steph didn't understand the technology, but he had never even *heard* of it.

"Yes! And there was one from his friend Buster at three this morning."

"Okay, Steph. Tell me exactly what it says."

She read the message to him: *"Tom. Come out to Rising Sun Lodge as soon as you can. Cabin three. Hurry."*

Bigsby mulled that over.

"Sheriff, Tom replied to the text from Buster. He wrote, *'Be there in an hour. Don't make a move without me.'*"

"Okay, Steph. I'll check on Tom." He looked from Lucy to Kane, and added, "I think I know what's going on. No worries, okay?"

He thought Steph Slidell sounded relieved when they hung up. With more care than usual, he put the phone in its cradle.

Earlier the sheriff had two problems: finding his deputy and arresting Bird Taylor. Three problems if he added the kidnappings. As he pushed and pulled at his mustache, he reckoned it was possible maybe they were just three different ends of the same knot.

Bigsby gazed carefully at the two people across his desk. Silently, he asked God to forgive him if he was making a mistake. Then he reached inside his desk and pulled something out.

"Kane, what do you think about being a deputy?"

The sheriff reached over with his right hand and carefully set a shiny silver badge down in front of Kane. Law work was about evidence and logic, but there was also a heavy dose of intuition involved. Their story was crazy, but there was something about it that rang true. Which meant he was going to need help.

"Hey, what is this?" Lucy complained. "Look, Sheriff Bigsby, I may be..."

"Lucy Baker, let me finish," he cut her off. His other hand came out from behind his desk and he set another shiny badge in front of her. "I need your help, too."

*****

"Do you want to go over it again?" Sheriff Bigsby asked. "Our *master* plan?"

Lucy scowled. "You mean the one where we drive to Rising Sun Lodge and rescue those kids? That plan?"

"That's the one," Bigsby replied.

"There's a lot to be said for simplicity," Kane said with a small smile. "Besides, if this is how we think it is, I don't know that we can really plan for it."

"He's right, Lucy," Bigsby agreed.

"And we're not going to tell the other officers?"

It was an interesting question. Bigsby had been serious when he'd told Special Agent Martin that he was wrong, and he'd honestly had no intention of deceiving them again. At least not when he said it.

Then Lucy and the guitar player had come in. There was absolutely no way that Agent Martin and his cohort were going to go along with Bigsby without a bunch of questions. And questions would lead to a wild tale of fancy that no one in their right mind would believe, not even close. Bigsby supposed he could lie to them. But Martin was never going to approve a rush job without good reason. If he were going to weave lies, he may as well just leave the FBI out of it. He'd never been a good liar anyway.

"We're not going to tell the FBI guys." He tapped his hands together thoughtfully. "But the Alpine boys are okay. I'll talk to 'em."

"Great."

"Good."

The sheriff pursed his lips, and nodded slowly. "I'll swing by and meet you at your place in half an hour, then we can head out. We'll take your truck—mine is out of commission at the moment."

"She likes to drive," Kane remarked, and Lucy punched him in the arm. "Kind of bossy, too, Sheriff. We might need to toss her in the big house."

CHAPTER 39

The Lady in Red hummed an old and nameless melody to herself.

No one from modern times would have recognized it, but she recalled it vividly. In her mind, she watched the shirtless natives clapping their hands in unison. The thrum of heavy and repeated bass drums interspersed with the intermittent staccato of a smaller drum, much like the snare drum, filled the air.

Oh, and the priests were so good!

Sometimes she had to persuade one of the new priests of the value of participation. Just a little friendly cajoling to support the cause. An overnight visit to their home with a crew of prisoners, and the threat of violence, usually worked wonders. Something about that violation of personal space, and the loss of the feeling of security, usually changed their mind.

When that didn't help, they paid the priest another visit, but this time they didn't threaten anyone. Someone would hold down the troubled little priestling and force him to watch his younger sister—or brother, or mother— being raped, repeatedly.

That nearly always did the trick, except for the one or two who went insane, pushed over the precipice and down into a bottomless black void.

A pity, but the show must go on.

During ceremonies, the priests would line up and take turns carrying people to the sacred altar. Residue from the poppy plant left most victims woozy and compliant. Clubs stunned the rest. Words were spoken to the gods, ritual music played, and then the one true blade was swiped across the abdomen. Every priest got his turn to thrust his hand inside and pull out a living heart.

A living heart! The organ was still throbbing in their palms as the last vestiges of blood drained away.

That may have been her magnum opus. Hanging, beheading, burning them alive ... it all paled in comparison. To transform a decent man into a blood-thirsty demon. *Can you imagine?* The Mexicas ripped out hearts, *como niños comiendo dulce.* With wild abandon and glee.

She sighed contentedly. Really, it was true. There was nothing like the good old days.

CHAPTER 40

Kane wondered how much firepower they were going to need.

He had three magazines for his Smith & Wesson, including the one that was loaded, and he pushed his gun and mags into his pack. A mostly full fifty-round box followed them. If he needed more than that, it was probably time for them to call for reinforcements, or maybe a black ops team.

The three Texas lawmen were bound to have as much, or more, than he did. Another fifty rounds per person, maybe, or a hundred.

Lucy produced a revolver from her closet. It was her dad's—a blued out Taurus Model 65 with a rubber grip. A .357 Magnum. When she showed it to Kane, she said that her dad took her out to shoot it multiple times when she was a teenager, but that was more than ten years earlier.

"Do you remember how to use it?" he asked.

She tilted her head and looked at him like she'd discovered he had a handicap.

"Okay, but humor me, will you? Pop open the cylinder."

She pushed the release and opened it up.

"And you know which way the bullets go in?" he asked.

"You are *so* going to get it later, smartass." She hip-checked him. "I know how to load it. I've taken it out a few times and messed around with it even though I didn't shoot it. There's ammunition in the closet, but it's

297

ten years old. Maybe older. Do you think it's okay to use it?"

"Yeah. Your kids could probably teach their kids to shoot with it as long as there hasn't been a lot of exposure to moisture, or mishandling. What about the kick? Do you remember what it was like when you fired it? It's a three-fifty-seven, so it's got some muscle."

"I can handle it. I handle you, don't I?"

Kane didn't argue with that.

Even so, he preferred not to find out whether she could handle it. The simplicity of revolver mechanics was comforting. Load, aim, and pull the trigger. There wasn't a safety on most revolvers. Nothing to stop Lucy from putting a hole in someone—or some*thing*—if she had to.

He added her .357 rounds to his backpack.

Lucy had changed into comfortable-looking jeans, a T-shirt, and running shoes. He'd thrown on some cargo pants for the pocket space, a loose short-sleeve button-up, and some hiking boots for extra stability. Choosing the right gear for a mission was something Kane knew about; he'd reviewed their clothes for function and comfort in a variety of situations.

All the boys he knew growing up carried knives, and he'd had one in a pocket or on his belt for most of his life. Kane had run through seven or eight in the last ten years, but only three had survived.

The Benchmade flipped open from the side with the push of a button. He never parted with it. Slipped it into a pouch on his belt.

The Ka-Bar was bigger than he liked, but a Marine buddy had given it to him. It was more a good luck charm than anything else, but it was a scary looking bastard, and he slid it into his pack, too.

"Why don't you carry this." It was a small Gerber that flipped open, with a rubberized handle. He passed it to her. "Your hands are smaller … it'll fit well."

She opened it and closed it a few times, then thumbed it down into her pocket.

A somber mood descended on the pair. While they were eager to help the kids, there was anxiety, too. Kane had felt it many times. The feeling was an old acquaintance, but not one you're excited to see; it was the friend that came around and woke you up in the middle of the night or always needed to borrow money.

Kane looked at Lucy sitting quietly on the couch, aka the bed. The pallor of her skin was more pronounced. She rubbed her hands together now and then, and tapped absently on her leg. A distant, ominous rumble of thunder sounded the coming of night.

"We're going to be fine tonight, Luce. I won't let anything happen to you."

She looked at him intently, and more seconds ticked along, like caterpillars inching along on a journey. Lucy slid close to him and put her head on his shoulder. Canting her head to the side, she looked at him. Reached up and ran her fingers along his scruff—he hadn't shaved in a couple of days. If there was one thing besides privacy that made him nuts about the Army, it was shaving every day.

She was watching him, green eyes alive with different emotions, but he could feel how much she cared for him. Something about the mood and the way she was looking at him sounded the alarm bells inside his head.

Oh, man, she's going to tell me she loves me, he thought. His calm was destroyed as he anticipated it. Didn't know what to do. Or what he would say. Her eyes locked on his. Sweet smile…

And the doorbell rang.

Their cages were rattled and they pulled apart. He stole glances at her face, but didn't see what he'd seen only moments before. Maybe he had imagined it. Situations like this could mess with a person pretty good.

"I could use a shot," Lucy told him, going to the door.

He nodded in agreement and followed her. When she swung the door open, Bigsby was outside with two police-style duffel bags. Kane could hear the pleasant and throaty sound of an engine in the street and assumed it was the Alpine deputies.

"You kids ready to kick some ass?" he asked. His furry mustache went up on each end in what Kane believe was an unseen smile. "I sure am."

Lucy let out a nervous laugh. "Me too," she replied. They looked at each other, and Kane knew that, somehow, they were more than just three people thrown together by fate. Something deeper than friendship, even, connected them. Like small tributaries running into one another to form a swift river. Kane's body tingled from it, and unless he was mistaken, the other two felt it, as well.

"Let's load the truck," he said.

*****

"Looks like the weather is going south," Kane said. He'd been eyeballing the clouds since they left Marathon. Everything was tougher in bad weather. His drill sergeant had eaten that shit up. He swore the man had prayed for rain and wasn't happy unless they were slopping around in the mud. When they were good and filthy, he would smile broadly, cheeks stretched taut, and belt out, "Ladies, if it ain't raining, it ain't training!"

"Sheriff, you okay back there?" He tried to get in the back seat, but Bigsby had insisted. It just felt strange to Kane to have the older man in the back.

"Doing good," he said. "I was just thinking that you're right about the weather. The sky is getting dark, fast. Storms are getting closer. Be dark soon. Blake and Tim still with us?"

Kane looked in the mirror. The other car was hanging with them, the Alpine deputies invisible behind their darkly tinted windows. "Still there, Sheriff."

"Good."

"They seemed pretty eager to come along," Kane noted. The alacrity with which they had jumped into the old witch hunt had surprised him.

"Well, I told 'em I had a good line on the kidnappers. Couple of good old boys like that'll leap on the chance to rescue the kids and take down the bad guy."

Kane nodded.

"Course, I didn't tell them *every*thing," Bigsby added.

Through the passenger window Kane watched a sharp bolt of lightning hit the ground, and he started counting. Twenty-five seconds later he heard the thunder and knew it was about five miles away. An Air Force weather guy named Wes had taught him that on an exercise at Fort Polk, in Louisiana. It was called the flash-to-bang method of evaluating distance to thunderstorms.

The rain transitioned to a decidedly heavy flow halfway to the lodge. The beat of droplets on the window grew louder and Lucy kicked the speed of the windshield wipers up a notch to keep pace with the deluge. Water crept up his window in a ripple pattern like wet sand at the beach. Lucy dropped below the speed limit to compensate for the reduced visibility.

They didn't speak for several minutes, each person lost in their own thoughts. Outside the wind picked up, howling, and buffeted the truck, causing it to swerve a few times. Lucy fought the steering to keep control. The rain fell so hard she could barely identify the road, and she had no choice but to drop her speed again.

"Almost there, I think." Lucy was leaning forward, almost against the steering wheel, focused. "I can barely see the road, but the turnoff is right around here somewhere."

Kane leaned forward and stared into the mirror. He rotated in his seat, and stared out of the rear window for a long hard minute.

"What's the matter?" Lucy asked.

"I don't see the deputies."

Bigsby turned awkwardly in his seat. "I can't see the road," he said, a hint of awe in his voice. "As a matter of fact, I can only see as far as the bed of the truck, and I'd say there's four inches of water in there, and getting deeper. This is unbelievable."

"I think this is it," Lucy said. Kane concentrated, hoping for a glimpse of something—anything—but Lucy turned and Kane realized they were still on paved road, so it must have been the right place. Pressing his forehead to the passenger window, he could just make out the road along the side of the truck.

About two feet from his window he saw the hazy outline of the Rising Sun Lodge sign.

They moved forward another twenty or thirty yards.

"It's so dark ... Lucy, let's wait for the others," Bigsby said.

"Okay, Sheriff."

*****

"You know ... I don't think I've ever seen it rain this hard," Blake said. He was a stocky guy with a ruddy complexion. His features rode the fence between red and brown, favoring the red slightly. The boys at the shop called him a *ginger*.

He was driving, and Tim was riding shotgun, their standard configuration.

"Me either. It's coming down so hard I can't tell if the engine is on. All I hear, feel, or see is rain."

"Shit." Blake jerked on the wheel. He'd driven off the road, and fishtailed in the muddy shoulder before he jumped back onto the blacktop. "Close one."

"Yeah," Tim agreed. "Hey, where is Sheriff Bigsby?"

Blake realized he could no longer see taillights in front of them.

"Shit," Blake said again. "I think we lost them. Or they lost us."

"Right."

Both men stared intently ahead, scanning for signs of Lucy Baker's Tacoma. Blake glanced down and saw he was barely doing fifteen miles per hour, and it felt too fast. He dropped to ten.

"It'll slow down. We'll catch up any second," Tim said.

"Yeah," Blake agreed, but he wasn't so sure. It wouldn't have surprised him if Noah floated by on his ark. He thought briefly of the garden that he and his wife had invested so much time in this summer. There were sweet peppers, tomatoes, okra, and cucumbers, and it would break Debbie's heart if they were all ruined. A little rain was good for a garden, but this torrent could destroy it.

On their right, they came upon the turnoff and sign for the Rising Sun Lodge, but neither man saw it. The downpour was so heavy they were practically underwater.

"Why don't you try the sheriff on his phone," Blake suggested.

"You got it."

Tim pulled out his phone, opened his contacts, and tapped on Sheriff Bigsby. Nothing happened.

"Crap, man, I'm not getting any signal out here," he told Blake. He reached over to the dashboard GPS and punched in their destination, but got an error message. "Even the GPS isn't working … no satellites found … must be the weather."

"This is turning into a real shit sandwich," Blake said.

The road dipped suddenly and the Dodge bucked as it hit nearly a foot of pooled water. There was a moment when the car slid sideways and Blake thought they were done. Then the treads caught and they inclined out of the small river crossing 385.

"Holy hell, where did that come from?" Tim said. The faint light that had been present was fading fast, and he glanced at his watch and added, "I think we're about to lose daylight."

Blake barely had his foot on the pedal. When he saw the dashboard clock he couldn't believe it. They'd been on the road for nearly two hours.

"Brother, I'm pretty sure we missed our turn."

CHAPTER 41

The Lady in Red returned to the ceremonial chamber.

There was activity at the altar as four robed assistants moved surefootedly around it. Lodge guests would have recognized them as the quiet maids that cleaned their rooms.

The four women moved two large candles into place at either end of the ancient stone pedestal, two people per candle. Mixed with the same ingredients for millennia, the candles were the deepest shade of red, a hue nothing manmade had ever matched, not even with the fancy technological advances she'd seen over time.

While she watched, her helpers used exquisite caution to ensure the candles did not break. They knew that would lead to swift, harsh punishment so severe that death would be preferable. The candles themselves would not be lit until the moon was swollen and full. Red looked on approvingly, then strode to the smaller chambers to check on her cherished possessions.

She opened the door and flicked the light switch with a long red fingernail.

The dark man blinked rapidly and tears rolled down his cheeks, while the officer groaned and covered his face. Laughter bubbled up and erupted from her as she watched them squirm.

"Does the light bother you? Oh, I'm sorry. Don't you fret—I'll turn it off again soon. The last thing I want to do is cause you pain." She strode across the room and stopped in front of Buster. "You believe me, don't you, black man?"

Buster studied her for a minute as his eyes adjusted to the sudden and harsh light.

"Lady," he said. "I suppose that I trust you as far as I can throw you, or actually, less than that."

She narrowed her eyes and her face shimmered, replaced by a horned demon that hissed. Then it returned to normal and she laughed.

"Maybe you're the stranger. And maybe you are not. Either way, I'm going to make you suffer immeasurable pain. We can start by pulling off your fingernails. I always enjoyed that one. So simple, yet the reactions are so exciting! Then we can break a few fingers. Or all of them. Then we can twist your skinny little legs completely around until they snap. Your boyfriend over there can watch while I do it."

Buster sighed and lowered his head while she stood above him smugly, smiling down.

Then, slowly, he lifted his head and he smiled back. Chuckled. "You may be able to hurt me. Hurt me real bad. But you can never change the fact that you are one evil and ugly bitch."

The lights flickered several times. The Lady in Red continued smiling, but there was no longer humor there.

"Soon," she told him, "you're going to learn about real pain."

She slapped the light switch off and left the room.

Outside she stopped for a moment. Her body quivered with rage. The idea of some simple human getting to her like that made no sense, and yet he had.

She would make him suffer.

The door to the other chamber opened and her two men emerged pushing wheeled carts. They'd doffed their black jeans and shirts and donned black robes, like the women. The children were on top of the carts in their cages. Immediately, she was happy again, if happy was the correct word to describe her exultation in evil.

"Ah, good! My little men, so very brave; are you ready to sacrifice yourselves for yours truly?"

The kids whimpered and moaned.

She was smiling again when she sensed something, and looked inward. There were little mental tripwires around the perimeter of Rising Sun. A portion of her energy was reserved for protecting Rising Sun from unwanted guests, like a psychic set of security cameras.

"We have guests," she announced.

The two men looked at one another then back at her.

"Shall we take care of them?" one asked.

She shook her head.

"No," she replied. "Not yet. I'll send something to keep them company instead."

With that, she closed her eyes, and reached out for assistance.

CHAPTER 42

"You okay?" Tom asked.

"Yeah." Buster's voice was shaky. "I've never truly seen evil like I did just now. We're dealing with a monster."

Tom shivered. "Thanks, Buster."

"It's okay," Buster replied. "Get to work, Law Hammer."

They had agreed earlier that, if anyone came in, Buster would create a diversion, and Tom would move against the wall to block his handiwork.

He had been working steadily on unscrewing the bolts with his quarter, but it was tough. Unlike other bolts, they didn't seem to loosen with each turn of his cramped and sweaty hands. Every turn was as difficult as the first. The first one was sticking out nearly six inches when they heard Red coming, and Tom scrambled into place to hide it. He thought he might shit himself, he was so nervous they would be busted. It was actually a stroke of good luck she'd turned the light on. His eyes hurt so bad from it that he forgot about his nerves.

Tom started in on the bolt again. He used one hand to keep the object and his hand aligned, and he twisted with the other. Every two to three twists with his thumb and forefinger got the bolt around a single complete turn. As he twisted, he did the math, figuring fifteen complete turns per inch. Maybe more. That meant he had already twisted that quarter roughly two hundred and forty times.

He paused for a second and shook his hand to work out a cramp. The quarter fell out of his hand and he scraped around the floor looking for it.

"Tom?"

"Yeah, Buster?"

"Doing all right?"

"Yeah. Got a cramp and I dropped the quarter." He was still scraping around. "Got it."

He twisted only a few more times, and the bolt clattered to the floor. Tom exhaled and breathed easier.

"Is that what I think it was?" Buster asked.

"Yep. You sure you don't want me to toss you the other quarter?"

Buster gave an excited grunt. "No. I don't want to risk losing it. When you get free, you can find me, and we'll both work on mine. Just keep going ... I get the feeling we don't have much time."

"Me too," Tom replied, pushing aside thoughts of the other quarter in his pocket, and twisting at the second bolt with renewed vigor. He had a second quarter, but it was in his pocket. His fingers were aching, and he prayed silently.

God, please give me the strength to get us out of this...

CHAPTER 43

"Nothing," Bigsby said, slapping his cell phone down on the seat. "Still no signal. I'm sure Blake and Tim just missed the turn. Even if they went off the road or something, they're probably stuck until the rain lets up."

"And they knew where we were going, right?" Kane asked.

"Of course. They've been out here before, and not just for work. Nobody lives in this area without visiting Big Bend now and then. It's like Southwest Texas's amusement park, the place where we go to have fun on the weekends and holidays."

Lucy snorted with nervous laughter, and Bigsby smiled. Lucy was a strong girl, and if she was nervous, the situation was probably something you should be worried about.

"Getting awfully dark out there, Sheriff." Kane looked like he was itching to go. "What do you say we move on?"

"Yeah," he looked around. "I agree. Take us on to the lodge."

Lucy put the truck in drive. They reached the fork in the road and she chose the right path.

"It's like the lodge just disappeared," Kane remarked. "Good thing the road is here or we'd never be able to get there in this."

Lucy inched along so slowly the speedometer appeared to have died on the zero.

Thump!

"What was that?" Lucy exclaimed. Looking back and forth through the windshield. "Something hit the truck!"

Thump! Thump! Thump!

They strained to see through the torrent of windblown rain that seemed to be going in all directions at once. Bigsby couldn't guess what might be smashing into the front of the vehicle.

And then he saw the beasts.

"Coyotes … big ones," he told the two in the front seat. While he watched, gray shapes slammed into them, and his mind flashed to the wreckage that he and Tom had inspected. He recalled what Tom said that day…

It's like Mother Nature is conspiring to kill these people. Kill their cars, and then send in the animals.

"Can you move a little faster, darlin'?" he asked.

Lucy pushed on the gas and Bigsby watched as the needle went up to ten miles per hour, practically speeding. There was another thump, and the truck shuddered violently. The speedometer fell back to zero, and Bigsby realized what happened at the same time that Lucy spoke.

"I think they busted my tire," she said.

She pressed down on the accelerator, but the vehicle barely moved. It was as if the rain and mud and flat tire held them in a vise grip.

"Keep trying," Bigsby urged.

Another thump and one of the headlights went out. The day's light fell away as if a starless, dark blue curtain were being drawn across the sky.

"It's not going," Lucy needlessly announced. She pressed on the gas, the engine roared, and they slid sideways. "I think we're off the road on the right side."

"We are," Kane confirmed. Just then the rain eased just enough for them to see the lodge. It was only a hundred yards away. Kane looked at both of them and shrugged. "Let's hoof it."

"Let's do it," Bigsby agreed, reaching into one of his duffel bags. "Put these on."

He handed them Kevlar vests. They took off their jackets, put the vests on, then donned their gear again. Kane put on a headlamp and clicked it on. The animals outside were shaking the entire vehicle with their battering onslaught. The other headlight shattered.

"Ready?" Bigsby hollered. He looked grim.

The other two nodded.

"Sheriff, I'll lead if you don't mind," Kane told him. "This is pretty much what I did in the Army."

"Sure, son."

Kane stepped outside first. His pants were soaked quickly from the knee down. He scanned each direction with his weapon in front of him. Out of nowhere, a snarling coyote charged him and leapt.

Crack! Crack!

It dropped from the air with a spine-tingling howl.

He walked forward with the other two close behind him, Lucy in the middle. Another coyote charged, teeth bared, and he triggered a round right into the gaping jaws and blew its face off. The body quivered where it fell.

Crack!

A pair of matching striped snakes swam by, heads both turned watching them, dangerously close, and Kane ended their beady staring, forever.

Crack! Crack! Crack!

Bigsby leveled his shotgun and blasted another.

Boom!

The rain eased up a little more, and they began moving forward. Kane laid waste to two more snakes, and Bigsby mused to himself that he'd never seen anyone that could shoot like that.

Suddenly, there was a roar, and Bigsby was hit hard in the hip and lifted off his feet. The shotgun slipped from his grasp and clattered to the ground as he soared through the air and landed ten feet away. When he hit the ground his leg twisted under him and cracked.

Bigsby cried out in agony. It felt as if he was a rubber band that had been stretched too tight and snapped. His thigh was on fire, and any movement generated bolts of pain that extended from spine to foot.

Where Bigsby had been just seconds before, a giant bear stood on its hind legs and roared again. The sheriff's eyes flicked around desperately searching for his gun, but it was out of his reach, and he couldn't move anyway. He wasn't going to make it. Then, suddenly, two shots fired, and the bear staggered backwards and dropped to all fours. Another shot rang out, and the bear let loose an unearthly wail. It sat still for a moment staring at the three humans, and Bigsby could swear it had a look on its face like it was just waking up, and totally disoriented. Another second went by, then it turned and ran off, a blackish ball of wet fur, moving fast and hard.

When Bigsby looked sideways, he could see Kane's arm still extended with his pistol. Lucy came to his side, and a moment later, Kane joined them.

"How you doing?" Kane asked.

"Been better," he replied.

Kane moved his hands up and down the sheriff's leg, causing him to cry out in pain several times.

"Closed fracture," Kane proclaimed. "Probably two breaks. Can you support your own weight?"

Bigsby tried to stand, but couldn't. He desperately wanted to walk, but sometimes, a man can't think himself through his own limitations. Mind over matter could only get you so far; then it was matter over mind, for damn sure. He spit.

"Maybe we can support you between us," Lucy said, but Bigsby just shook his head.

"I can't walk, and you'll never make it if you try to carry me."

"He's right," Kane said. "But I'm going to get you back into the truck. I won't hear any argument. Inside the truck you can protect yourself. You're too exposed out here."

Bigsby nodded.

"All right. I'm going to squat down over you. Just loop your arms around my neck, and hold on tight. I'm going to drag you to the truck. It's going to hurt."

At one point, Bigsby thought he might black out, but he held on like a bloodsucking leech and Kane got him back to the truck, then up and inside. Lucy was there beside Kane with his shotgun. It should have been Tom with him there using it—he loved that gun.

"I'm good guys. Go … go find Tom and those kids."

Lucy fretted over him another few seconds, making sure he had a bottle of water and his cell phone. Kane left his spare rounds where Bigsby could grab them quickly. Kane gave him a little salute, then they shut the door and started off toward the lodge at a fast jog. It was nearly dark—he only hoped they weren't too late.

CHAPTER 44

When Red entered the ceremonial chamber this time, she was decked out in a red gown that went from her neck to the ground. A silky red hood left her face in shadows. Around the room nearly two dozen *lodge employees*, her minions, chanted, using words and phrases that few on the planet had ever learned or known through all of time. They were the ritualistic incantations her priests had used at Tenochtitlan, repeated over and over to prepare the children for sacrifice. The chanting readied her to receive their life force once they were slain.

The children watched silently from the corner, their senses blunted with an ancient herbal concoction. Their eyes reflected the light like unseeing, shiny little buttons. Unaware of the magnificent contribution—the *sacrifice*—they would be making soon.

Incense burned around the room. A casual visitor might have mistaken it for a cathedral or monastery. The sounds and the scents were very similar. Perhaps those similarities weren't accidental. After all, her ceremony celebrated the giving of many lives for one, while the Christian ceremonies celebrated the giving of one life for many.

Yin and yang.

The Lady in Red circulated throughout the room, moving to the rhythm of the chants, like a one-person waltz. The sound consumed her, and she danced with a zealous fervor, spinning around and around. The others remained still, heads cloaked in the darkness of their hooded robes.

When her appetite for the music was finally sated she twirled her way to the front of the room and took her place behind the altar. Torches were lit on the wall behind her. The sacred knife waited, gleaming, changing colors between red and silver and orange, as the flames flickered. She leaned forward until she saw her own reflection in it, then smiled at herself.

She nodded to her two men, and the one without the bandaged hand walked toward the cages. He moved solemnly, hands clasped together, each step deliberate, like a bride making her way to the front of the church.

The cages were fastened simply. Even if the inhabitants had escaped, they couldn't reach a doorknob, much less get beyond their room. The man unlatched the farthest cage and reached inside. The small boy sat silently, rocking from side to side. He scooped him up and pulled him out. The boy stared at him, drooling slightly. The man carried the child to the altar in the same fashion as he'd approached the cage, then he placed him in the center, for all to see.

The other man approached and they took up their positions behind and to either side of the Lady in Red. She lifted the baby above her head and whispered the words she had whispered so many times before. Nobody could hear them then, and nobody ever would. They were part of the mystery of her continued life.

Red set the child down and then picked up the knife.

She raised it high above her head and sang softly to the knife, as she had with the boy. Then she lowered the shimmering blade and held it in front of her face, where she puckered up and kissed it softly, like a lover.

It was time.

*****

Kane and Lucy were at the rear of the lodge. They'd taken out a few snakes along the way that were five or six feet long, and appeared to be swimming aimlessly in the shallows, but Kane wasn't taking any chances. The only good venomous snake was a dead one.

They encountered nothing with four legs, or two, for that matter. No creature stirred as they skirted the building, eventually stopping when they came across the black SUV and red Audi. The vehicles were like a giant green neon arrow: "Bad guys this way."

After a few minutes they located the door.

"Looks pretty solid," Lucy said.

"Yeah, it does." Kane ran his fingers around the borders, but there were no hinges on the outside. In his experience, however, the area where the lock was mounted usually presented a demonstrable weakness in the structure of a door.

He looked around and noticed the landscaping was bordered with four-by-four pieces of lumber. After handing Lucy his pistol, he hefted a piece about three feet in length and brought it back to the door.

"Here goes," he said.

Kane rammed it under the doorknob several times, just like he would have done with the battering ram when he was in the Army. The door was metal.

However, the frame was wooden, and he could hear it splintering. It was completely dark outside now, and he was relying on the light from his headlamp, and the Maglite he'd given to Lucy.

She refreshed his magazine, and handed the Smithy back to him. After having her step out of the way, he aimed at the spot he thought would be most vulnerable and fired three quick shots. Smoke rose. He backed up to gain momentum, ran hard, and raised his foot at the last second to give it a thunderous kick.

The door busted inward.

"Come on," he told her. "Stay behind me with your pistol ready, but pointed past me. Keep an eye on our rear, too."

"Gotcha."

They walked rapidly down the hallway, Kane turning corners in small, choppy steps as he cleared them. There was nobody standing guard, and no one stopped them as they worked their way deeper into the bowels of the Rising Sun Lodge.

Finally, they found themselves outside of an older, wooden door, that reminded Kane of something someone might see in a castle. There was a strange noise coming from the other side.

"Do you hear that?" he asked.

"Yeah." Lucy pressed her ear to the door and listened for a moment, then her eyes got wide. "It sounds like praying or chanting."

Either way, it probably wasn't normal for the basement of a lodge.

"Same as before," he told her. "Follow me in and aim past me at anything you think is a threat."

She nodded.

"One … two … three."

Kane swung the door open and pushed inside, with Lucy close behind. He was momentarily stunned by the scene in front of him.

At the front of the room was an altar with a baby stretched out on it. Behind it, the Lady in Red kissed the glittering knife in her hands, then she raised it high above her head, just like the pictures had depicted, in order to sacrifice the child.

Kane was already in motion and down on one knee. He squeezed off two back-to-back shots and the knife bucked out of Red's hands.

Behind the altar, the evil woman's eyes glowed brightly, and her fanged mouth opened. She howled in rage and pointed at them. All around Kane and Lucy, the robed figures turned toward them, the crazed humans, or beasts, or whatever they were, lunging at them.

"Kill everything," Kane said loudly to Lucy as he made his gun talk to their new friends.

Crack! Crack! Crack! Crack! Crack!

Kane fired as they attacked, hitting every time. Next to him, Lucy squeezed off a few rounds, too, the bullets flying easier once she got warmed up. He was about to put a slug into another thing coming at him when his slide locked to the rear—out of ammo.

He reached down into his pocket for a new magazine, but it was going to be too late. He braced for impact, but just as he expected to feel the person-thing collide with him, a chain went around its neck and yanked it off its feet. When Kane looked up, Deputy Slidell and Buster were in the fray with them, and he was able to slap the new mag into his piece.

"Watch out!" Lucy screamed, and Kane ducked, but not fast enough. One of his buddies from the other night—he saw the bandaged hand—caught him on the side of his head with a crowbar, and things went black for a second. He heard Lucy's rage and the roar of her gun as he tried to hold onto consciousness and dropped to his knees.

As he wobbled and fell to his elbow, his view of the room changed; it was as if he were observing the scene from inside a Tilt-A-Whirl at the county fair. Another robed figure approached, but was brutally kicked to the ground by ... Bird Taylor?

Kane groaned and tried to get up, but lost his balance. Lucy fired again, on the other side of him; at what, he couldn't see, but he heard her cry out in pain. Behind the altar, that bitch in red was bringing the knife up again, and he tried to lift his gun-hand but something disconnected between his brain and the signals going out to the rest of his body.

Everything was out of control.

Bird Taylor appeared then, a gigantic running blur flying at the Lady in Red. He collided with her just as she brought the dagger down, putting himself in front of the arcing blade. It sank deep into his body, and she screamed in rage. They fell to the floor and struggled. Kane blinked in shock. Bird had saved the child ... for now.

Bodies were strewn across the floor, and all over the room, between Kane and the two fighting beside the altar. He watched Red pull the knife free from Bird's body, and jab it into his neck. As if once wasn't enough, she jabbed it into his neck a second time, Bird's body already limp and quivering in the throes of death.

In his blurred peripheral vision, Kane saw his friends. The deputy was down, not moving. Buster was on his knees. Lucy was hitting someone with her gun. He was on the verge of blacking out again. Red was converging on the altar once more, dagger in hand.

Kane focused and summoned his remaining strength. He lifted the pistol and brought everything he had to bear on the dim tunnel of vision that remained of his eyesight, squinted down the sights, to Red, and pulled the trigger once, twice, three times, before he fell to the floor and blacked out.

CHAPTER 45

Kane could hear beeping.

It was the kind of steady beep-beep-beep that you heard on television shows when someone was in the hospital. Which was weird. Because his eyes were closed. And the sound was coming from somewhere near his head. There were other voices. Lucy? He tried to speak, but couldn't. Tried to open his eyes, but it was an impossible task.

Then he blacked out again.

When Kane came to, the next time, he was able to open his eyes. The first thing he saw was Lucy smiling at him from a chair. He tried to return the smile and pain spiked through his forehead.

"Ouch," he placed his left hand, the one without an IV plugged into it, against his head.

"Want some water?" she asked.

"Please."

He took the glass she brought and drank several satisfying gulps. Water had never tasted so good. May as well have been laced with cocaine, because he wanted the whole pitcher next. While he was refilling and drinking, he realized he was in a hospital room.

"How long have I been out?"

"A few days," she said.

"Wow."

It was only then that Kane noticed there were balloons and flowers all over his room.

"Who is all that for?"

"Duh," she rolled her eyes and smiled. *"You!"*

"Me? From who?"

Lucy read the cards to him and every name surprised him. Stephanie Slidell, The Wilson Family, Dot Beckman … even old Bob had gotten him a balloon. If Lucy hadn't been sitting there, he might have suffered from a sudden allergy that made his eyes water, but he fought it off.

*****

A few days later, Kane was released, and he and Lucy went back to her place. Several people had come by the hospital to see him, but they all avoided talking about Rising Sun Lodge, or what happened there. One of the people he expected to see, never did come by, and that was the sheriff, though he understood he had his own medical healing taking place.

Kane and Lucy stayed holed up at her place for several days. She was back at work already, but he didn't go—just asked Lucy to give his regards to Bob, and tell him he wasn't feeling up to it.

One night when she came back from work, he waited until she was settled next to him on the couch, Netflix turned to some movie, then asked her, "What happened to her, Luce?"

She paused with a bottle of beer at her lips, looked at him, and then took a slow swallow. "You don't remember?"

"No."

She set down her drink.

"This is going to sound crazy." She was speaking low, like they were at the library. "After that woman killed Bird, she went for the kid again, and you shot her. Three times."

He waited for her to continue.

"Well, she dropped to the floor, and her body started convulsing. Changing. Transforming. Her mouth opened and this terrible sound came out ... it makes my skin crawl thinking about it. Then there was a noise like an explosion, and smoke, and when it cleared ... she was gone. We were all still there, you, me, Tom, Buster, and the others.

"The building started shaking, and then Blake and Tim came rushing in and they carried you out. And Tom. Buster was able to walk, and we all went down those hallways and out of the building. When we got to the parking lot we kept going. Then Rising Sun Lodge collapsed to the ground."

Neither of them spoke, while Kane considered that.

"Good," he said finally.

*****

It was the Friday before Labor Day when Kane finally made it over to see the sheriff. The bell over the door jangled, announcing his entry, and Sheriff Bigsby hobbled out from his office on crutches.

"Hey!" Bigsby said, and he did that almost smile thing where his mustache seemed to change positions, like maybe it was just rolling over in its sleep. Kane could tell he was genuinely pleased to see him.

"Hey, Sheriff." The two greeted each other warmly and did a modified man-hug around the crutches. Kane poured them two coffees from a pot that, obviously, Harriet had made, and they settled into some chit-chat in Bigsby's office.

"Did you know the Villareals were okay?"

"No, but that's great news," Kane replied.

"Yeah. An anonymous caller phoned in, said that they were locked up at this abandoned warehouse in town. The Villareals weren't too pretty to look at, but they were doing okay. Had water and all that."

"Wow."

"Yep. I heard the tape. Caller was Bird Taylor. Of course, the person who took 'em was also Bird Taylor."

Kane laughed, and Sheriff Bigsby almost smiled.

"And I'm sure you heard all the kids were safe." Bigsby leaned across the table and looked into Kane's eyes. "Thanks to you."

Kane nodded, finally, and they both sipped their coffees quietly. Neither man spoke about what happened out at the Rising Sun Lodge. As far as Kane knew, Sheriff Bigsby never saw anything definitively … out of the realm of possibility. Kane thought about it and figured that someone like Bigsby preferred to be grounded in reason. He was going to ask if they'd ever found Red's remains, or a body, but he knew the answer would be no. He studied Bigsby, the question on his lips, but then decided to let it go.

"You going to stick around a while?" Bigsby asked.

That is the question, isn't it? Bigsby is a damn mind reader.

"Don't know," Kane answered honestly.

"Plans for Labor Day weekend?"

"Lucy's going to take me over to the Marfa Lights Festival."

"Good. That's a good time."

The two men passed another hour together, and Kane realized just how much he liked the man sitting across from him. One of the good ones, as his dad might have said.

"Sheriff, I'm gonna head out," Kane said finally.

"Okay, Kane."

CHAPTER 46

Kane's interest in the parade was mild salsa: tasty not spicy. He surrendered to nostalgia … he'd watched similar homespun gatherings many times in his life.

Charming buildings with maroon awnings and green canopies flanked the street. Parking spaces jutted into the road at a forty-five-degree angle to match the flow of traffic. People hugged the curbs of downtown Marfa, armed with portable chairs and coolers. Friendly patrolmen, eyes hidden behind sunglasses, did their best to keep the crowd on the sidewalks

The spectators were clad in every type of garment imaginable. Jeans. Khakis. One or two suits even though it was a Saturday. A healthy peppering of men in madras shirts, mostly in blues, reds, or greens. And, always at least one guy without a shirt wandering around.

Lucy was dressed in jeans with her T-shirt tucked in. She wore a delicate gold chain around her neck, so thin it was more like a thick strand of hair than jewelry. It brought attention to the beautiful line of her neck, which was maybe the point.

The high school band marched by in purple and white T-shirts. There was heavy emphasis on the drums, and a strong brass section. The tuba players were saucy, holding their instruments like intense lovers doing some sexy pressed-up-against-one-another dance.

It was nice—a genuinely American sound—and Kane immediately felt like he should be in the stands of a hometown stadium somewhere, watching a halftime show.

Cheerleaders and football players were next. The boys tried to look tough and imposing. Warriors. The girls were all smiles. Purple and white pom-poms moved around. They chanted about the Shorthorns being number one. Kane assumed the shorthorn must be a relation to the longhorn.

With less horn, of course.

There were classic cars, tractors, former beauty queens, current beauty queens, local teen beauty queens, local tween beauty queens, and local beauty tikes. There were guys on Harleys, guys in little go-carts with tall hats, dance teams, and finally a bunch of kids in superhero outfits. It was a parade of culture more than it was a parade of floats and flash. See and be seen.

"Tacos carne asada!"

Good food. They couldn't get better tacos without going into Mexico, which was right next door. Lucy and Kane decimated some tacos from a vendor that was turning out tacos as fast as the steaming beef could be slapped into tortillas. Lucy nodded silently and closed her eyes while she ate. It was what she looked like during...

"Like the tacos?" he asked.

"Mmm-hmm." Eyebrows jogged when she answered. She looked like she had a secret. Like the *I'll have what she's having* scene from *When Harry Met Sally*.

There were bands and music. Heads nodded along to a guy called FullyMaxed. Long blond hair spilled out from beneath his ball cap, and when he played the keyboard around his neck, it sounded to Kane like some strange blend of funk, electronic sounds, and sound bites.

It reminded him of music from the TV show *Shaft*—maybe a bar scene where he meets a groovy *thang* with big hair-- *Can you dig it?*

Lucy had a good time. She was always satisfied, it seemed. Never overly demanding. Peaceful. He watched her profile and the shape of her lips and the little artist in his head etched them delicately across the surface of his mind.

*****

Later, they were laying on the foldout couch. Kane's head was propped up on a pillow, his arm wrapped loosely around Lucy. Her head was on his chest, but he couldn't see her face. It was dark, and she was angled away from him.

"You're going to leave, aren't you?"

It was a question, but it wasn't a question, and even though it wasn't a question, he couldn't leave it unanswered. It was a slow dance of words and ideas. The time passed until he couldn't let the silence continue without crossing some line into something unkind.

He slid down next to her and swam in her eyes.

"Yeah," he said quietly.

She brought a hand up and pushed it delicately across his hairline. `

"Yeah," she whispered back.

The next morning, he packed, and pushed his things into the bed of his old trusty steed. He'd arrived in Marathon nearly a month earlier with no real plans other than to play his guitar and get lost in the music. Instead, he'd discovered an almost ethereal beauty in the most unlikely of places.

Kane went back inside. The refrigerator hummed and clicked and he just stood there unable to move again.

I can't leave, he thought. *I might love her.*

Open your eyes. If you open your eyes, I'll stay. I'll never leave.

Kane waited, but Lucy didn't open her eyes. Slowly, slowly … he nodded. From his pocket he removed an envelope and left it next to her. Kissed her head with the lightest of touches.

His eyes grew damp.

*****

Lucy was awake. Sleep was sparse and unfulfilling.

She listened to Kane moving around, gathering his things quietly. He was like a ninja in the morning, while she banged around uncontrollably. It was one of those little differences that she thought made them perfect for each other.

There was no running today. She wasn't going to see him tiptoeing into the bathroom when he came back covered in sweat.

When he carried his bags outside, she opened her eyes for a second and the debate raged in her head. She wasn't going to make him stay if he didn't want to. He toiled with his demons, and he wasn't ready.

Except, she didn't want him to go.

She heard the door open and closed her eyes. Could feel him standing over her, unmoving.

Please don't leave, she thought. *Stay with me.*

She almost opened her eyes. Wanted to look at him so badly. Screamed silently at herself to jump up and grab him and not let go.

But she didn't move.

Lucy felt the delicate brush of his lips on her head...

Then he was gone.

*****

Kane got in his truck and backed out of the driveway. He waited until he was a few blocks away before he wiped the tears from his eyes. There was nothing to be sorry about, not for two people who simply loved when the time wasn't right.

He reflected that the town of Marathon seemed happier as he pulled out onto the highway. Restored. In the Army, they were always telling people to leave things better than they found them. He felt he had done that.

As Marathon grew smaller and smaller in his rearview mirror, then disappeared, he smiled to himself.

Who knew ... maybe one day he would be back.

ACKNOWLEDGMENTS

It takes special people to help breathe life into a novel.

My heartfelt gratitude to Michael Ross, Wes Cornett, Mia Sutton, and Mari Davis. Your incredibly keen eyes, sage advice, and encouragement made me better. Thank you.

Next, I owe a very special thanks to my dad. We discussed this book almost daily, for months, and I couldn't have done it without him. Thanks, old timer.

As with all other events in my life, the best of my efforts is a reflection of the support of my awesome wife and kids.

Finally, there are the readers. You are the key ingredient in this recipe—a book that isn't read may as well not be a book. I am forever in your debt.

ABOUT THE AUTHOR

Bart Hopkins is originally from Galveston, Texas, but lived all over the world during his twenty-two years in the U.S. Air Force.

He was born in the middle of the 1970s, owned an Atari 2600, and can use the card catalog like nobody's business. He once sold a Mickey Mantle baseball card to buy a wetsuit.

Bart enjoys pretending he's a photographer and watching movies. He relishes any opportunity for laziness. Three awesome kids, a beautiful wife, and a scraggly dog live with him.

The Bends is Bart's fourth novel.

Connect with Bart

Email
bart@barthopkins.com

Web Site & Blog
www.barthopkins.com
www.barthopkins.com/blog

Facebook
www.facebook.com/barthopkinsauthor

Twitter
@bart_dead_ends

Made in the USA
Lexington, KY
10 February 2018